THE
TIARA
ON THE
TERRACE

Also by Kristen Kittscher

The Wig in the Window

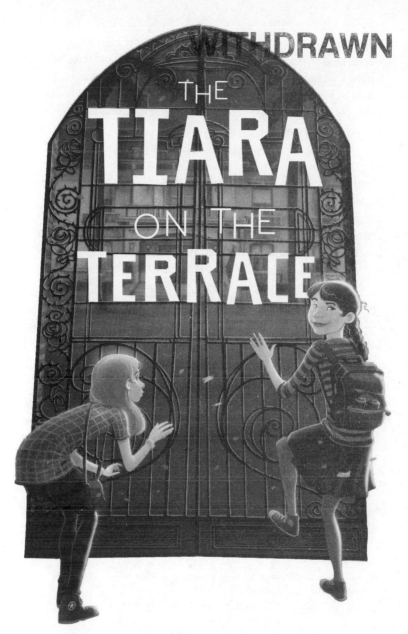

THE TIARA ON THE TERRACE

KRISTEN KITTSCHER

HARPER
An Imprint of HarperCollinsPublishers

The Tiara on the Terrace
Copyright © 2016 by Kristen Kittscher
All rights reserved. Printed in the United States of America.
No part of this book may be used or reproduced in any manner whatsoever without written permission except in the case of brief quotations embodied in critical articles and reviews. For information address HarperCollins Children's Books, a division of HarperCollins Publishers, 195 Broadway, New York, NY 10007.
www.harpercollinschildrens.com

Library of Congress Cataloging-in-Publication Data
Kittscher, Kristen.
    The tiara on the terrace / Kristen Kittscher. — First edition.
      pages cm
    Sequel to: The wig in the window.
    Summary: Best friends and amateur pre-teen sleuths Sophie Young and Grace Yang go undercover at their town's annual festival and parade to catch a murderer before he or she strikes again.
      ISBN 978-0-06-222798-0 (hardback)
      [1. Mystery and detective stories. 2. Murder—Fiction. 3. Festivals—Fiction. 4. Friendship—Fiction.] I. Title.
    PZ7.K67173Ti 2016   2015015555
    [Fic]—dc23   CIP
                                                             AC

Typography by Lissi Erwin
15 16 17 18 19   CG/RRDH   10 9 8 7 6 5 4 3 2 1
❖
First Edition

❀

For the kids in my life, big and little—
especially Sofia and McCormick

Contents

Chapter One

Operation Winter Sun

I grasped the cold metal rung of the scaffolding and pulled myself up, the steel frame clanking and swaying beneath my feet like a wobbly ladder. The warehouse floor far below spun dizzily toward me and away again. I shut my eyes and took a deep breath. My mouth was dry. My heart hammered. But I couldn't stop now. Not with our target in reach.

Grace and I should never have accepted the mission. What had we been thinking? It was too dangerous, even for expert spies like us. It was too late. We were in too deep.

And up too high.

"T-minus one minute and counting!" Grace panted as she scrambled up behind me. "Keep going, Sophie!"

"Roger," I called back, my voice hoarse. In my free hand I held our mission supply box—a long, shallow, open cardboard container. I reached for the top rung of the scaffolding, struggling to keep the carton level. If I spilled it, the mission would be doomed.

I heaved myself onto a narrow wooden plank stretched over the warehouse floor like a balance beam. The target was only twenty steps away, tops. Twenty steps across a splintery, wobbly board tied in place by a fraying rope—but still, only twenty steps.

"Approaching target. Prepare to take position," I said.

"Affirmative," Grace said. "T-minus thirty seconds!" Grace's watch beeped frantically. "Go ahead without me!"

My stomach churned. A drop of sweat trickled down the back of my neck. The mission was scary enough without having to face it alone.

"Roger," I said, trying to hide the quaver in my voice. "I'm going in."

I gritted my teeth and inched out onto the shaky plank, holding the cardboard flat in one hand. I took one small step, and another. Then I bent my knees and side-shuffled faster, hoping the momentum would make it easier to balance. It did—for a few steps. Then my ankle buckled. My weight tipped. I swayed and rocked on the board like a beginning surfer. But it was too late.

Wind whistled past my ears as I sailed into the emptiness.

"Sophie! No!" Grace's shriek echoed in the rafters.

Time really does slow down when you're about to die. Years fold up inside of seconds and your brain has time to replay every memory—twice, if they're awful. Laughing too hard and peeing on Stacy's down comforter at her sleepover birthday party. Getting caught giving my American Girl doll a buzz cut with my dad's shaver. Gagging down a cold heaping spoonful of liver-flavored Whiskas. (Tip: *Truth*, not *dare*. Never *dare*.)

I was starting to imagine Grace's teary tribute at my funeral when it hit me that, if time had slowed down that much, I should probably try saving myself.

I thrust up my hands and managed to catch the wooden plank one level below, my body jerking like a piñata as my arms nearly yanked out of their sockets. Our supply box cartwheeled overhead, sending thousands of red flower petals shimmering into the air. I tilted my head back, closed my eyes, and let them shower over me like confetti.

It was a Winter Sun Festival miracle.

Who knew that decorating parade floats could be so dangerous? My muscles burned as I tried to hold my grip. Splinters pierced my fingers. I opened my eyes again and stared at the giant fake ice cream scoop on Luna Vista's Root Beer float looming over me. I deserved a better final sight. Something more noble. More meaningful. Something that wasn't an oversized imitation dairy product. I wondered if I should shout for Rod Zimball so I could finally profess my undying love. It wouldn't matter if he didn't say anything back.

I'd already be hurtling to my death.

"Hang tight!" Grace hollered. I cringed as my fingers started to slip. Over my head, a banner sagged from the rafters, counting down the happy moments I might never live to see: 6 MORE DAYS TILL PARADE DAY! it mocked.

"I'm trying!" I called back to Grace. The scaffolding rocked as she climbed faster to reach me. Below me volunteers dashed around, too distracted by their own float decorating to notice me dangling. Kids shouted for cranberry seed refills and lugged buckets of strawflower and silverleaf through the "float barn," as everyone called it. Once upon a time there had been an actual barn on the Ridley Mansion grounds where the Festival was headquartered. Now the "barn" was a big drafty white warehouse that housed the parade floats. Most of them still looked like oversized papier-mâché projects speckled with paint-by-number patches of color. Eventually, we'd decorate them all with fresh flowers, but for the time being we were gluing a color base of seeds and finely chopped petals onto them.

"Let yourself fall, if you have to!" Grace shouted. *Let myself fall?* Ten seconds was all it took for my best friend in the world to give up and let me die? Then I remembered. The nets! Relief rushed through my aching limbs. The town of Luna Vista would never let a bunch of seventh-grade volunteers prance around on rickety scaffolding decorating parade floats without at least *trying* to make sure we didn't kill ourselves. Marissa and Kendra Pritchard's dad would have already filed, like, ten trillion lawsuits.

As I loosened my grip and braced myself for the fall, Grace's footsteps pounded against the plywood scaffolding one level below. A second later, her arms reached up and wrapped themselves tightly around my hips. "I gotcha. Go ahead, let go," she said as she gently eased me down. I sighed as my feet met the solid, wide boards.

"All clear, Agent Yang," I said, trying to keep up our pretend spy lingo. My voice shook.

"Over and out." Grace smiled, but she kept a steadying hand clamped on my shoulder. "You're getting good at that."

"Dangling from ledges?" I grinned back. "Practice makes perfect." Two months earlier I'd nearly tumbled out of my second-story window while creeping out on one of our missions. Things had changed a lot since then. That was before our spy games turned real and we'd nearly gotten ourselves killed trying to capture a dangerous fugitive who'd been hiding out right in Luna Vista. We were town heroes now.

Town heroes who were laughingstocks, apparently. A chorus of giggles had broken out behind us. I turned to see Marissa Pritchard covering her mouth and twirling a lock of honey hair around a finger as she huddled on the Root Beer float with the identical twins from my homeroom, Danica and Denise Delgado. Big puffs of cotton spilled from the box next to them as they worked on creating the "foam" on top of the giant root beer mug. For a while I'd thought Marissa and I had finally made our peace. We'd even been lab partners in earth science. But she'd figured out that I liked Rod Zimball, and since then she took every opportunity to embarrass me whenever Rod was within a five-mile radius.

Marissa wrinkled her nose. "Are you playing spy? What, are you, like, in preschool?" she asked loudly.

If Rod still had ears, he'd heard her for sure. He was standing on the float not far behind us, gluing flaxseed to the giant root beer mug. Marissa smiled slyly at Danica and Denise. "I thought Festival volunteers had to be at least twelve years old. Am I wrong?"

I felt my cheeks turn red as the twins erupted into giggles again. Ordinarily, I would have shrugged it off, but that morning we were on their home turf–Winter Sun Festival territory. In a few years they'd probably even be princesses in the Festival's Royal Court. I could already see them sporting sparkly tiaras as they waved from their parade float. In fact, Marissa's older sister, Kendra, was probably going to be chosen as a Royal Court princess that very afternoon. She'd already beaten out hundreds of girls in the interview rounds to be a finalist. And Marissa and her friends were shoo-ins for royal pages, the mini-princesses whose job it was to buff and powder and spray tan their royal highnesses. But just because they thought they were royalty didn't mean that *I* had to.

"Yeah, we're playing spy games. So?" I asked, puffing up my chest to look taller. "Maybe you remember when those little 'spy games' helped catch a killer?"

Marissa rolled her eyes. "Not that again. Please. How long are you going to ride that? 'Ooh, remember when I caught the Tilmore Eight fugitive?' Whatever. It was forever ago."

She shifted her eyes to Rod Zimball. His brown curls hung over his eyes as he painted a new layer of glue on the mug. My stomach sank. When I'd captured a killer, I'd thought I would capture his heart, too, but it hadn't worked out that way. Yet.

"Yeah, forever ago," I repeated, trying to stay calm. "Like when you threw up raspberry slushy all over the ice rink last weekend?"

Danica and Denise gasped, and Marissa flushed redder than, well, a raspberry slushy. Target acquired. Direct hit.

Marissa hooked arms with the twins and glared at me. She flashed a smile at Grace before they turned away. "Those jeans are supercute, Grace," she said sweetly. "*You* always look supercute."

"Thanks." Grace straightened in surprise. "You, too."

You, too? I was about to ask Grace what the heck she was thinking when a voice thundered from the warehouse floor below. "Young! Yang!"

Grace groaned. The Floatator—aka Ms. Barbara "Barb" Lund—had spotted us. I swear that woman had cameras sewn into every inch of her denim overalls, and possibly into the eyes of the Winnie the Pooh patch plastered on the front of them. There was a reason we all called her the Floatator. A direct descendant of Festival founder and former root-beer magnate Willard Ridley, she ruled Winter Sun Festival float decorating with an iron fist—and a totally unnecessary megaphone.

Her staticky voice blared through it now. "Sundae inspection in five!" she called.

Ms. Lund wasn't all bad, really. Her round, plump face peeked out below a goofy mushroom cloud of short dark-blond hair, and she looked almost friendly on the rare occasions she smiled. She even chuckled at her "Floatator" nickname and proudly made up new ones for herself like "Chairman Barb," "Barbarossa," and—Grace's favorite—"the Grand Pooh-Bah." She also thought it was fun to toss around what she thought were popular slang terms, but which we suspected were either from 1994 or made up entirely. Still, she flipped out if she thought someone wasn't living up to her crazy high standards for the Festival. That morning her face had actually turned purple when she saw that my petals on the ice cream sundae had clumped messily over the glue.

Barb lifted her megaphone again. "Quit yer chit-chattin' or I'm going viral on you two!"

Grace shot me a puzzled look.

"I really don't want her to go viral," I said.

"No kidding." Grace stifled a laugh. "I think I'd rather land on her Watch List." There were a lot of rumors about what being Barb's Watch List involved, and death sounded like a nicer option.

Barb narrowed her eyes at us, pointed her megaphone into the air, and whooped its built-in siren three times.

"Okay, Agent Yang," I called out, nudging Grace. "Sounds like it's time to wrap up this mission and head back to headquarters."

"Uh-huh," she said, distractedly. Her eyes flicked to Marissa and the twins gluing cotton root-beer "foam."

"What's wrong?" I asked, but as soon as the words had left my lips, I noticed her cheeks had turned a shade darker. I knew exactly what was wrong. She was embarrassed. Of me.

"Nothing," Grace said. Her eyes stayed locked on the girls as if she were memorizing the details of their too-short jean cutoffs to incorporate into one of her own outfits.

"Jeez, you think those cutoffs can be any shorter?" I asked. "They're like, loincloths or something."

Grace shrugged. "I think they're supercute."

I flinched. Heaviness settled over my chest as I wondered what else was on the list of things she and Marissa agreed were *supercute.*

"I can't believe I forgot to tell you," I said, trying to shove the feeling away and distract her. "I found out about the coolest code. Have you ever heard of a Polybius cipher?"

Grace sighed and picked up another empty cardboard flat. "I'm getting bored with the spy games, Soph. Aren't we beyond all that now?"

A couple of months didn't seem like long enough to be "beyond" anything, let alone something that'd made us heroes. Judging from the face she'd made, though, you'd have thought I'd suggested we drag out our old Barbie collections to play with in front of everyone.

I ignored her. "Anyway, it's this cool knocking code that prisoners used to communicate with. It's kind of like Morse, but everyone knows Morse, so with this one—"

Grace's eyes flashed. "Soph, seriously! Let's take a break on the spy stuff, okay?"

I snapped my mouth shut. A sick, sad feeling poured through me as Grace pressed the cardboard flat into my hands. "We'd better hurry on that petal refill. I heard that last year Barbarossa made kids on the Watch List scrub down the parade port-a-potties." She arched an eyebrow. "With *toothbrushes*."

I grabbed the box, trying to tell myself that Grace was acting strange because she was homeschooled and wasn't used to being around so many kids. Or that capturing a real fugitive had scared her off spying for good. Something told me there was a different reason she'd tossed out her FBI "Most Wanted" posters and had given away her walkie-talkies to the fourth grader down the street from us, though. She'd gotten really into browsing fashion websites and reorganizing her room—which was weird, because before, she was basically on track to be on one of those reality TV shows about people who can't leave the house because they're trapped behind all the old magazines and empty ramen packages and cat pee-soaked blankets they've hoarded.

Sometimes I wondered if she was changing faster than I could ever keep up.

Grace started for the scaffolding. "Come on, Sophie," she said, sighing. "I can't wait for you forever."

I stared at her, a sinking feeling in my gut, and for the first time it struck me.

Maybe she really couldn't.

Chapter Two

Festival Fever

E ach year "Festival Fever" struck as early as November, when crews started setting up bleachers along the main boulevard. The Winter Sun Festival was like Luna Vista's Fourth of July and New Year's rolled up into one. Even though the parade was on the winter solstice, just days before Christmas, the only signs of our holiday spirit were a few door wreaths and a scrawny tree outside the shopping plaza.

Festival Fever felt doubly intense that year. Not only was it the parade's 125th anniversary, but Luna Vista had become a national joke when it turned out we'd been harboring a fugitive as a school counselor for *two years*. Everyone was determined to show off our town and make this Winter Sun Festival the best yet.

The truth was, I didn't know who Luna Vista was showing off for anymore. Until the 1990s the Festival was actually a nationally televised event. People all over the country would tune in to check out sunny Southern California and its bright, flowery parade floats in the dead of winter. It was just what the parade's founder, Willard Ridley, would have wanted. After all, showcasing California's warm December days was exactly why he and his hunting club had started the parade in the 1890s. That, and to advertise famous Ridley root beer, of course.

In the meantime America had become way more into Internet cats than parades, but Luna Vista still prepped for the Festival as if the whole world were watching. Marching bands from all over Southern California auditioned to appear in it. Hundreds of local high school senior girls competed to be selected as a princess or queen on the Royal Court. Designers worked months in advance on new fancy float plans. And kid volunteers like us swooped into the float barn to decorate them as soon as school let out for our winter break.

Grace and I had been dying for Prep Week to kick off—even more than most seventh graders. Not only was it the first time we were old enough to volunteer, but it was also the first time she and I and our friend Trista Bottoms would get to hang out together all day, as if we went to the same school. We even made our own special Winter Sun Festival calendar to count down the days. But as I stood there in the float barn trying to shake off the strange twisty feeling I had about Grace shutting me down on the spy stuff, I found myself wondering if the Festival was really going to be as much fun as I'd thought.

"Sundae inspection in FOUR minutes!" Barb Lund blared through her megaphone again as Grace and I hopped off the last scaffolding rung and scooted past her to get more chopped strawflower petals. "And Zimball!" she shouted up to Rod on the Root Beer float. "Where's your dad? I need him to help adjust the starboard confetti cannons, pronto!"

Poor Mr. Zimball. Rod's dad was very high up in the Festival ranks, but he was so nice that Chairman Barb was constantly roping him in to help with something or other. We'd only been volunteering three days, and he'd already fixed the flat tire on her golf cart, oiled her squeaky office chair, and sanded down a splintery scaffolding board. And those were just the things I happened to witness.

Grace linked her arm with mine and we headed to the flower refill station at the back of the warehouse, passing dozens of colorful floats that featured everything from giant cartoon figures to replicas of Ferris wheels and palm trees. Festival rules said that every inch of the float had to be covered with organic material of some kind, so buckets of bark, seeds, flowers, seaweed, and every type of plant you can imagine lined the aisles. Petals drifted in the air like snowflakes, and Barb Lund's favorite eighties oldies echoed through the warehouse.

"Have you asked Rod if he wants to sit with you at the Royal Court announcements yet?" Grace asked as Mr. Zimball hustled past us in his trademark Festival root-beer-brown business suit with another "Brown Suiter," as we called all the Festival officials.

I guess she thought I couldn't embarrass her with spy-game talk if we focused on my love life instead. "Not yet," I mumbled. "I think I should ask him to go to something else with me, don't you? It's too weird."

Grace didn't have any crushes, not unless you counted my older brother, Jake, who was a high school junior—and that crush was obviously the result of early brain injury and/or serious vision impairment. Being homeschooled meant limited romantic options.

"I mean, it's not like it's a dance or something," I explained. "He probably has to sit with his family. They'll be sitting on the terrace with all the VIPs, I bet."

Grace sighed. "He likes you. It's so obvious. He's just shy! If you ask him, he'll know you like him, too."

"And if he says no?"

"He's not going to say no. And if he did? He doesn't understand what he's missing." She hugged my arm closer to her side. Just then another Brown Suiter zipped past us on one of the motorized white Festival scooters, a clipboard tucked under her arm.

"Royal page sign-ups!" someone squealed from the Girl Scouts of America's Beary Happy Family–themed float. It was like someone had blown a whistle. Before the Brown Suiter had even slowed to a stop, a mass of khaki-uniformed girls streamed away from their decorating stations, their badge sashes flapping as they raced past a surprised Goldilocks and the Three Bears huddled around a fake Girl Scout campfire. *Just Right*, read the loopy cursive script at the front of the float underneath them. Nothing felt "just right" about it.

Our good friend Trista Bottoms got caught in the crush of the crowd. Wearing her own version of a scout uniform—a khaki cargo vest that she'd sewn all her Girl Scout badges onto—she stood in front of the Beary Happy Family float like a boulder in a rushing rapids. The big mop of dark curls that sprang from her head made her seem bigger than she was. As a second wave of middle-school girls from other floats jostled by her, she turned toward us with a helpless shrug. Grace and I shot her a sympathetic look.

"Exc*uuuu*se me!" an annoyed voice whined behind us. Grace had accidentally bumped into Marissa's sister, Kendra Pritchard, who was carrying a basket of sunflower seeds. Kendra brushed off her uniform and flashed us a death stare, which hardly seemed right coming from a Girl Scout.

Grace apologized, but Kendra was flouncing back to her station on the Beary Happy Family float, stopping to give Marissa an encouraging pat on the back as she waited to sign up for the auditions.

"I think she put some kind of a hex on us," Grace muttered to me.

"She's just afraid we'll audition for royal pages and beat out Marissa," I joked.

Grace clapped her hands together. "Oh my gosh, how perfect would that be?" she asked, a glint in her eye. The flyaway hairs that had broken free from her ponytail gave her a wild look.

"I was kidding!" I backed away. I couldn't tell if the drifting petals made the air feel hazy or if Grace's suggestion made me feel woozy. It was probably both.

"We can all audition together," she said, breathless. "Think of how much fun it'd be if we made it!" She turned to Trista, who'd finally waded upstream and made her way to us. "Right?"

Trista bumped her fist against ours in greeting. "How much fun?" she asked in her booming voice. "Let's see. Living in a mansion for a weekend waiting hand and foot on high schoolers who believe they are actual royalty." She pretended to do some mental calculations. "I estimate roughly *negative* 3.5 tons of fun. Possibly less."

I laughed. "What, you don't want to buff Lily Lund's toenails every night?"

"You guys," Grace scowled. "It wouldn't be like that! A whole long weekend together, twenty-four/seven. Festival parties. Cool traditions. Riding on the Royal Court float!" She practiced her pageant wave and blew a kiss to an imaginary crowd.

Trista and I traded a look. I think we both would've rather grated cheese all over ourselves and spent the night in a rat-infested sewer.

"I'm not sure we're royal page material," I said. The Festival claimed the Royal Court wasn't a beauty contest—that they were just looking for the "ABCs." That is, girls who were "Articulate, Bright, and Charming." Still, I'd never seen a middle-school page as short as me or as wide as Trista. Not even once.

"Don't be silly." Grace rubbed red mum petal dust into her fingers, then swiped each of my cheeks. "All you need is a liiiiittle bit of blush."

"What're you talking about?" I smiled mischievously as I repeated the Royal Court judges' famous advice to contestants. "We just need to be ourselves."

"Ha!" Trista snorted, ducking out of the way as I grabbed a huge handful of petals and launched myself forward. I tugged on the collar of Grace's T-shirt and tossed the petals down her back. Grace squealed, then filled both her hands and returned the favor.

"Hey, there," a voice called out behind us. My heart skipped a beat as I turned to see Rod Zimball. He put down his flower bucket and gave a little wave. White petals were caught in the crests of his dark curls like whitecaps, and his hazel eyes shone. The only way he could've possibly looked any cuter was if he were cradling a baby panda.

He cocked his head and squinted at me. Thanks to Grace's "blush," I was pretty sure I looked like Ronald McDonald.

I followed his gaze to the trail of petals spilling from the bottom of my shirt and collecting on the warehouse floor in a puddle.

I felt the rest of my face blaze as red as my cheeks.

"Did I hear you guys say you're trying out for pages?" he asked. "You have to go for it," he said.

I scanned his face for signs that he was teasing. But

he blinked back, his expression as sweet and serious as could be. A warm tingle spread through me, and I stood up straighter. It wasn't until I tried to catch Grace's eye that it hit me. Tall and thin, with hair as long and glossy as all the Royal Court front-runners, she'd snag a spot as a page in a millisecond. The tingle faded, and my insides hollowed. Rod wasn't talking about *us*, he was just talking about *Grace*.

"No time this year," Trista replied abruptly. She hooked her thumb in one of the pockets of her cargo jacket. "Float engineers need some backup."

"Too bad." Rod shrugged, not at all thrown by how seriously Trista had taken his question. "I doubt you'd even have to try out."

I must've looked confused because he looked right at me and raised his eyebrows. "Town heroes as Royal Court pages? People would love it!" He wiped his hands on his jeans and picked up his bucket again. "There's no way you wouldn't get a spot."

If my face was red before, it was on fire now. What was I thinking? Of course that's what he'd meant.

I smiled back. I tried to brush petals from my own head, but my hands were so sticky with glue that I yanked out some of my hair. Then—because hands shouldn't sprout long brown hair and flowers—I clasped them together in front of me. Maybe, someday, I would be able to *un*clasp them.

"You call that a line, ladies?" Barb Lund's thundering question made us jump. She was waving her hands at a group of seventh-grade girls, trying to steer them past the Girl Scout float to the sign-up clipboard. "Now let's see those patooties in single file, PDQ!" she barked at them.

"Patooties?" Rod's forehead wrinkled. "I feel like I need a translator," he said.

"That would be bomb diggity," I said, imitating Barb's awful slang. Rod laughed.

"You think the Floatator would be in a better mood," Grace said. "Just three hours till Lily's crowning, after all."

"Unless Lily doesn't make the cut," I said.

The three of them chuckled as if I'd cracked another joke. Barb Lund had been preparing her daughter, Lily, to be on the Winter Sun Festival's Royal Court since shortly after her birth—even before, if you count the parade anthems Barb probably blasted to her in the womb. If the judges rejected her, Luna Vista could likely expect to be visited with seven years of plagues, starting with swarms of locusts personally imported from the Sahara Desert by one very, very angry Ms. Barbara Ridley-Lund.

"Passing over a Ridley in an anniversary year? Not gonna happen," Rod said.

I followed his gaze to the dried-flower-cutting tables where Lily Lund was working next to a group of gorgeous senior girls who were obvious Royal Court front-runners. Like me, Lily never would have ordinarily been royal material, no matter how hard Barb worked at it. Lily was taller than I was, but not a whole lot, and she had dull brown hair, thick glasses, and unfortunate bangs that she tried to curl to control a cowlick. I assumed her glasses were absolutely necessary—otherwise, Barb would have forced contact lenses on her long ago. Clustered near her, with their identically cut silky blown-out blond hair, glossy lips, and crazy long legs, her Royal Court–hopeful friends looked like a single strange but beautiful alien life-form. One of them flipped her hair over her shoulder and whispered something to the girl next to her. I felt like I could smell her shampoo from where I was standing until I realized it was just the overpowering scent of mums and roses.

I sneaked a glance at Rod as he watched them and wondered if he thought they were pretty. Then I wondered if I'd ever look like them when I was in high school. It was hard to imagine. Something about them seemed faded and weirdly stretched out, like a Photoshopped magazine picture.

"C'mon," Grace said. "We only have two more minutes until Lund—"

A bone-chilling shriek rang out next to us. We whipped around to look.

"What the heck . . . ?" Trista's mouth fell open in surprise.

There, beside the campfire feature of the Beary Happy Family float stood Kendra Pritchard, her face twisted in horror.

A wisp of smoke hovered over her head.

Chapter Three

Fire in the Hole

Kendra Pritchard unleashed another bloodcurdling scream as she slowly backed away from the float. Behind her, a group of Beary Happy Girl Scouts froze in confusion before two rushed to her side, nearly tripping over the float's s'more replica on the way. A smell that reminded me of an early experiment with my mom's curling iron hung in the air.

"Looks like her hex rebounded," Grace joked, but her worried expression didn't match it.

Barb Lund whipped her megaphone out so fast it felt like she was in a duel in some old Western. "Fire in the hole! Fire in the hole!" she cried out.

"Pyrotechnics test misfire," Trista clarified when she saw my ashen face. "We'd better clear out." The tools on her leather utility belt clanked together as she broke into a jog past the Royal Court float near the warehouse door. "Sparks must've singed her hair. She got off easy. One of these days the Festival's going to learn the hard way that flames and ten thousand pounds of palm fronds don't mix."

"She's screaming like that over her hair?" Grace asked, looking back to Kendra Pritchard and the Girl Scouts. They weren't the only ones treating her hair accident like a national state of emergency. Kids at the nearby flower-cutting tables poured forward to help, but a Brown Suiter held up his hand and murmured urgently into a tiny radio microphone clipped to his lapel. Seconds later several officials on scooters buzzed into the warehouse and came to a screeching halt in front of the Girl Scout float.

Barb Lund didn't need any convincing to raise her megaphone. "Keep the area clear!" she shouted so urgently you'd have thought armed troops were invading. "I repeat, keep the area clear!" She shooed us toward the large, open warehouse door.

My legs felt shaky as we streamed onto the Ridley Mansion grounds. I tried to convince myself it was from balancing on the scaffolding so long, but the nervous fluttering in my stomach wouldn't let me. Grace hung back, craning her neck for a better view. I looked over her shoulder. Kendra Pritchard hiccuped sobs as a Brown Suiter gently led her away. The two Girl Scouts who'd rushed to Kendra's side wobbled behind them, their faces a sickly gray green.

Murmurs rushed through the crowd as we headed up the stone path under the rose arbor toward the mansion. "She burned off her hand," a girl next to Grace said, eyes so wide I worried they might launch themselves right out of her head.

"No, she found a hand," another voice chimed in. "I saw it. I swear."

"Just a hand, like, sitting there?"

"C'mon, people," a slouchy eighth grader ahead of us scoffed. "They found a bomb. This parade is totally the perfect terrorist target."

Maybe he sounded so convincing because his voice had already changed, but suddenly I was sure the warehouse was about to explode, turning tiny bits of plastic bear replica into speeding projectiles. I fought the urge to run. Better to die by fireball than be the girl who ran for her life because Kendra Pritchard singed an eyelash.

I tried to calm down by reminding myself that Festival officials were the leading experts in overkill. The year before they'd practically called in the National Guard when bugs infested the rose crop. I wouldn't have been at all surprised if they'd ordered up a SWAT team to clear out some dead field mouse barbecued in a float pyrotechnics test.

Grace strode ahead of me, her watch glinting in the sun as she undid her ponytail and let her long hair flop over her shoulders. From behind, she could have been part of the Royal Court front-runners' shiny-haired crew. A couple of months ago, she would have been begging me to hang back and investigate. Now that seemed to be my job.

"Grace, wait up." I jogged to catch up. "Don't you think we should check it out?" I nodded toward the float barn.

"Nah, it's probably nothing. You know how Kendra is." Grace tossed her hair over one shoulder. Her eyes flicked to Marissa and the twins.

"Sure doesn't look like nothing," I said as three police cars came blazing down the mansion's side driveway toward the float barn, lights flashing.

We watched as the officers spilled out of their cars and jogged inside. A gleam came in her eye. She was curious. She had to be.

"C'mon, Agent Yang." I nudged her. "One last mission. For old time's sake? Then we retire for good. Promise."

"I don't know, Sophie." Grace looked back as Barb Lund marched the troops toward the mansion, her sturdy arms swinging. "It's not worth landing on the Watch List for."

"Lund'll never even notice," I lied. The truth was, I'd have scrubbed down ten port-a-potties with toothbrushes if it meant Grace would go back to being her old spy self.

"Officer Grady's on the scene," I said, pointing.

"Uh-oh. They're doomed." Grace smiled. Officer Grady had nearly botched Deborah Bain's capture a couple of months ago, but we'd set him straight. Grace bit her lip and looked back to the group heading up the path.

"Don't tell me you're worried what they'll think," I said, jerking my head toward Marissa and the twins.

"Of course not," Grace said, but she didn't sound convincing. "Okay. Five minutes," she said, holding up five fingers.

I broke into a grin and slapped her hand as if she'd been angling for a high five. Then we launched ourselves toward the warehouse. As we raced ahead, half crouching, a burst of happiness surged through me and I could practically hear the *Mission: Impossible* soundtrack swelling up in the background.

"Now, that's more like it," I said, as we flattened our backs against the warehouse metal siding, spy style.

Grace laughed. "Roger that."

She jerked her head toward the open door, counted down silently on her fingers, then flashed me a signal before springing around the corner. I followed, trying to keep my sneakers from squeaking on the polished warehouse floor as we crept up to the ocean-themed Royal Court float, its rippling blue "waves" rolling toward a huge figure of a grassy-bearded Neptune at the front of the float. We climbed aboard, slipped past the giant half clamshell where the Court would wave from on parade day, then tucked ourselves into hiding behind two leaping dolphins along the side of the float.

Slowly, we peered over their sunflower seed–decorated backs. Grace leaned forward and—cupping both hands behind her ears—opened her mouth wide. She looked as if she were imitating a surprised fish. "Spy trick," she whispered to me when she saw the look on my face. "Helps you hear better."

I imitated her, trying not to laugh. She was back in the game. But my giddy, happy feeling fizzled away as soon as I saw the expression on Officer Grady's face. He stood with his hands on his hips next to the Girl Scouts of America Beary Happy Family float, frowning. Goldilocks and the Three Bears posed stiffly in their Girl Scout uniforms, flashing toothy daisy-petal grins as other officers swarmed around, taking pictures of the float from every possible angle. Meanwhile, a gangly, pink-faced officer who couldn't have been all that much older than my brother Jake roped off the area with yellow crime-scene tape. A deputy kneeled by the fake campfire, muttering and jotting down notes.

Grace let her hands fall to her sides again and shot me a dark look. My stomach fluttered.

The Festival vice president, Harrison Lee, paced back and forth in front of the float, jangling the change in the pockets of his brown suit pants. Head of the Asian American Business Association and a local car dealer in town, he was known for his big grin and goofy commercials where he ran around "cutting" prices with an assortment of chainsaws and other sharp instruments. He sure wasn't smiling now.

Officer Grady pointed to a giant hard-plastic marshmallow on the float's s'more feature and muttered something in his gravelly voice that I couldn't catch.

"He'd make his rounds every night around ten or eleven," Harrison Lee replied to more of Grady's mumbling. He patted his jet-black hair nervously. It was so stiff with product I almost expected it to shatter on contact.

Officer Grady pursed his lips and gazed down at the campfire pit on the float. "Looks like blunt-force trauma to the head." He sighed and walked over to inspect the s'more.

Meanwhile the young pink-faced officer had finished

roping off the scene. He rested his hands on his hips like Grady, then turned to Mr. Lee and shook his head. "We can't rule out homicide."

Grace grabbed my arm so tightly that I had to clench my teeth to keep from crying out.

"Homicide?" Harrison Lee repeated, his voice flying up an octave. His normally light-brown skin looked closer to gray.

"It's a possibility we have to consider," the officer said, hitching up his belt.

Homicide. As in, someone had been killed. Murdered. Grace turned to me, eyes wide. My pulse throbbed in my ears, and my hands started to sweat.

Harrison Lee sipped nervously at the purple thermos he held in one hand. His gaze flitted over the campfire, the officers at work, and the worried Brown Suiters huddled nearby. Then he closed his eyes and pinched the bridge of his nose. "Sure is shaping up to be one heck of a Festival anniversary," he said.

Grace, hands cupped around her ears again, leaned over the dolphin's back to hear better. Her long legs barely touched the ground anymore. I cringed, hoping no one could see her.

"We'll need to interview the witnesses," the officer

continued. "It'll take a bit before the coroner's report is ready. LA's got a backlog. But things should be clearer in a couple of weeks."

"A couple of weeks?" Harrison Lee sputtered in disbelief. He rubbed the back of his neck. Other officers huddled with Grady to inspect the giant marshmallow. They rolled out measuring tapes at different angles, calling out numbers and scribbling them down. Lee swiveled back to the young officer. "Please tell me you won't have to announce it as a murder investigation—"

"Take some more pictures of the scene, Carter," Officer Grady interrupted, striding back.

"Yes, sir!" The young cop straightened. "S'more pictures of the s'more, on the double," he added with a smile as he scooted off. Grady rolled his eyes. "Second day on the job," he explained to Harrison Lee. "Rookies, I tell you."

Lee ignored him. "The press is going to go nuts over this, Paul, you know that. It could go national. First all that business with the fugitive? Now, this?" He tugged at his collar uncomfortably. "We have to get to the bottom of this. Fast. We've got six days till parade day. The Royal Court will be announced this *afternoon*. What am I supposed to tell—?"

"Mmph!" Grace's stifled cry interrupted him. I turned to

see a flash of jeans and red Converse sneakers flip skyward, followed shortly by a thump as she planted herself face-first in a tangle of fake seaweed.

Every head in the warehouse turned toward us. There was no time to think. I ducked out of hiding, pulled Grace to her feet, and we tore off—vaulting over the lip of an ocean wave and out the open warehouse door.

Chapter Four

S'more Struck

We raced up the steep hill to the mansion, stumbling over sprinkler heads and zigzagging past flower-beds. By the time we'd reached the terrace, my lungs were on fire. Grace leaned on the white stone railing. "Oh my god, Soph," she said, gulping for air. "I never thought it'd be something *real*."

It was real all right. My head buzzed, and my heart pounded against my chest like a frantic bird was trapped inside it. Dazed, I followed Grace through the French doors into the mansion.

"*Murder*. In Luna Vista," she whispered, still catching her breath as we tiptoed unsteadily down the dark hall-way toward Barb Lund's voice blaring from the front living room. Ridley family ancestors stared out at us from gold-framed oil portraits, cold blue eyes following each of our steps. The hair rose on my forearms.

"Let's keep this beehive bling-a-blinging," Ms. Lund's voice rang out from behind a partly open wood-paneled sliding door off the front foyer. If we hadn't been so shaky, Grace and I would have laughed about her newest crazy slang. Instead we approached the door warily and peered inside. Barb had planted herself in front of a flickering fireplace, not at all fazed that her float-prep assembly line was taking place in a living room decorated with hunter-green fabric wallpaper and antique brass lamps.

The volunteers were still rattled, though. They sat cross-legged in clusters around the room, trading worried looks as they snipped dried petals and jumped at Ms. Lund's commands. A few kids glanced uneasily at the flames licking the fake logs in the gas fireplace. I looked around for Rod but didn't see him anywhere.

When Barb fumbled for something in a neon fanny pack slung around her overalls, we slipped in and plunked ourselves down by a potted plant against the back wall. Grace borrowed a pair of scissors from the ninth graders next to us, I grabbed two dried strawflowers, and we huddled together as if we'd been hard at work for years—though I'm pretty sure no volunteers had ever worked so hard cutting petals that they had to pant to catch their breath. Trista shot us an odd look from across the room.

"Young and Yang, report to me immediately at the lunch break," Barb grunted. She hadn't even raised her head. How did she *do* that?

I was about to mumble an apology when there was a gentle knock at the oak-paneled door. It slid open to reveal Lauren Sparrow. A hush fell over the room.

The special adviser to the Royal Court and one of the official Festival spokespeople, Ms. Sparrow was always perfectly put together, from the sleek copper waves of her hair to the rose-patterned skirt and tailored silk blouse she was wearing that day. Her features were so delicate and birdlike that sometimes I wondered if she'd invented her last name just so it would match her. If there's one thing Ms. Sparrow seemed to love, it was matching.

"Forgive me," she said quietly, her face pale and pinched. When she stepped into the light, my stomach dropped. Her mascara was smudged. Lauren Sparrow's mascara was never smudged. Worse yet, her eyes were puffy and red-rimmed as if she'd been crying. There was no doubt about it. She'd known the person who'd been found on that parade float. And if she knew them, chances were we did too. I squirmed. Grace pressed her knee into mine. I pressed back so hard I think I bruised us both.

"If I could make a brief announcement . . . ?" Ms. Sparrow asked.

Barb Lund tossed up her hands as if Ms. Sparrow had cut her off in traffic. "Be my guest! It's not like we're doing anything *important* here!"

"Thank you, Barb." Lauren Sparrow smiled frostily and crossed to the center of the room. Ms. Lund flashed her a look that suggested she'd be releasing a thousand angry scorpions into her bed later.

Once Ms. Sparrow had taken the power position at the fireplace, she stared down at her shoes, then cleared her throat. It was strange to see her so unsure of herself. Though she'd been part of the Festival for years, she'd recently also become a bit of a local celebrity, thanks to the line of skin-care products she'd developed called Pretty Perfect. Testimonials from some big Hollywood stars in nearby LA had made the brand really popular. So, on top of being "pretty perfect," Lauren Sparrow was also pretty rich.

Ms. Sparrow drew in a deep breath before she finally spoke. "As you're aware, we've had an emergency here at the Festival. I'd like to thank the Festival leadership"—she tilted her head stiffly in Ms. Lund's direction—"for ensuring such a smooth evacuation. It seems there was a problem testing the campfire feature at the Girl Scouts of America float, but I'm relieved to tell you the misfire caused no damage or injury."

A ripple of relief ran through the room. Grace and I traded puzzled looks. We were both pretty sure that murder counted as injury.

Ms. Lund stood up from her plush armchair as if it were a throne, ready to send us back to work. Lauren Sparrow held up a hand. "I'm afraid, though, we've made a terrible discovery as a result." She bowed her head and smoothed down her skirt before looking up at us again. "I am heartbroken to share that our Festival president, Jim Steptoe, has passed away."

What little air was left in the room rushed out of it all at once. The bright-pink roses on Lauren Sparrow's skirt spun before me like a kaleidoscope pattern as I tried to take in her words. *Passed away.* She made it sound like Mr. Steptoe's death had nothing at all to do with Kendra's shrieks or the police crawling all over the Girl Scout float—and certainly nothing to do with murder. He had simply tiptoed off when no one was looking, never to be seen again.

"The float barn will be closed while the police conduct a very thorough investigation." Ms. Sparrow raised her voice above the murmurs. "It goes without saying that this is a deep blow to all of us in the Festival family." She paused to collect herself. "Harrison Lee will be sworn in as Festival president. He will be taking over Jimmy's—I mean, Mr. Steptoe's—duties immediately." She stared, glassy-eyed, at some invisible point over our heads. I could tell she was fighting to keep her emotions under control, but her lower lip trembled.

Grace turned to me, looking as sick as I felt. It didn't seem possible. Jim Steptoe—jolly, lively Mr. Steptoe, king of corny puns and knock-knock jokes—had been wandering around Luna Vista's Root Beer float just the day before, laughing his deep belly laugh as he joked around with Grace and me. "Ah, Young and Yang," he'd called out. "The too-wise two Ys!" He'd winked and slipped us each a piece of gum, even though he probably knew that, under the Floatatorship, gum chewing by anyone other than the Grand Pooh-Bear herself was an offense punishable by roughly eighty-two years of hard labor. Then he'd gone back to remembering the "good old days" that he'd spent with Rod's dad as middle-school float volunteers. They were still good friends. Or *had been*. A lump swelled in my throat.

It wasn't hard to see why the Festival hired Lauren Sparrow to train the Royal Court each year—or why Harrison Lee had chosen her to deliver the bad news that day. As a CEO of a company, she was used to giving speeches. Her voice cracked occasionally, but she gave matter-of-fact replies to each question—no matter how ridiculous they sounded. Kendra had discovered Mr. Steptoe lying hidden from view behind the fake logs stacked around the Girl Scout float's campfire feature. The morning's pyrotechnics misfire was unrelated and "did not affect the victim at any time." From what they could tell, he had been struck in the head by the fake marshmallow in a giant animatronic, dancing s'more that had swung down unexpectedly. A full police report would be made available when it was ready. Counselors were on-site if we needed to talk to anyone. We should contact our parents right away.

When Trent Spinner asked whether someone was more likely to be killed by a ginormous fake marshmallow or a velociraptor, Lauren Sparrow wisely wrapped up the Q&A and announced that all Festival activities—including the Royal Court announcements—would be on hold until further notice.

"I'm so sorry." Ms. Sparrow blinked at us, her voice catching. "If we do return to normal operations, I ask that you all be very careful. The floats are complicated, heavy machines with a lot of moving parts." She looked pointedly at Ms. Lund and cleared her throat. "It's important that you be properly supervised at all times. You never know when an accident might occur."

The gas flames flickered against the ceramic logs in the fireplace behind her. I shuddered and looked away. Maybe supervision could protect us from accidents, but what could protect us from a killer? Something told me the Winter Sun Festival was going to be more dangerous than anyone could have ever imagined.

Chapter Five

Suspicious Minds

The mansion living room burst into a nervous buzz as soon as Ms. Sparrow left. Kids sprang for their cell phones. A few grabbed their uneaten bag lunches and headed for the door. Others huddled in corners with friends, as if they might be able to erase the terrible news by sticking together and hiding from it.

"This is messed up," Trista said once she'd finally pushed her way through the maze of fancy antique furniture and upset volunteers. "Majorly messed up." She fumbled in her cargo jacket pockets for her asthma inhaler and drew in a quick puff, then squinted at us. "You two found out something, didn't you?"

"Shh. Not here." Grace's eyes swept the crowd. Through the French doors I could see kids lining up along the circular driveway already, waiting for rides home. "We need a plan."

"Rose garden?" I offered.

"Perfect." Grace nodded. Trista was already striding ahead. We scooted after, and were about to slip through the door when a gruff voice stopped us.

"Young! Yang!"

We turned around to find ourselves staring directly into Barb Lund's narrowed eyes. She stood so close I could see a hair quivering on her cheek mole. She snapped her gum. Grace and I flinched.

"What part of 'see me' didn't you two understand?" she asked.

A cluster of eighth graders behind her fell silent and stared. Grace looked toward the door. For one terrifying second, I thought she might actually be crazy enough to make a run for it and leave me there.

Barb sighed heavily, sending a sickening, warm cloud of spearmint-tinged tuna-fish breath wafting over us. I tried not to make a face. Grace pressed the back of her hand against her nose and pretended to fight back a sneeze.

"First, you two jibber-jabber the morning away. Then you mosey over here via the slow boat to Timbuktu!" Barb flung up her hands. "Welcome to the top of Barbarossa's

Watch List, ladies. Report to me at oh seven hundred tomorrow. Got it?"

"But . . . ," Grace blurted, "will we even be here tomorrow? I mean, considering what—"

"I asked a simple question, Ms. Yang." The muscles jumped in Barb Lund's jaw as she snapped her gum again. "Two words. Got. It?"

I swallowed hard and stepped forward. "Yes, ma'am. We got it."

Grace hesitated, then raised one hand in an awkward salute that I prayed Ms. Lund wouldn't think was sarcastic. "Loud and clear," she sang out.

"Awesome possum," Ms. Lund said, looking as close to pleased as I'd ever seen her.

❀ ❀ ❀

"It's like she didn't even hear Ms. Sparrow," I hissed as we crunched down the gravel path to the rose garden near the float barn. Trista had already parked herself at the stone table next to a trickling white fountain. She'd laid out her lunch and was bent over her phone, fingers flying. Probably playing TrigForce Five. She'd been glued to that game for weeks. Trista usually beat games in a day or two, so this one must have had 180 levels or something.

"Highly unlikely," Trista said without looking up. "Barb

was sitting right next to her."

"Maybe she's deaf from her megaphone," I suggested, rubbing my ear. "I might be."

"Oh, Lund heard her, all right. She just doesn't care!" Grace slapped her lunch bag on the table and sat down. "Now, get this . . . ," she began.

Trista tucked her phone away and listened carefully, zipping and unzipping one of the zillion pockets on her jacket as we updated her. It felt so strange to talk about murder while a fountain burbled next to us and palm trees swayed in the perfect blue sky. I found myself wishing Grace would hurry up and finish so Trista could wave away all the crazy talk of murder and shake some sense into us. She always did.

But when Grace finished, Trista stayed silent for a long time.

"It can't really be murder, right?" I said, pulling my sandwich out of my lunch bag. "I mean, no one can, like, time a dancing s'more to malfunction and hit someone's head."

"There are more direct ways of taking someone out, yes," Trista said.

The tension ran out of my shoulders. Finally, she was going to set us straight. No one was more logical than she was—or as smart. Her mom was a head rocket scientist at AmStar, the company that made technology for the military, where just about everyone in town worked, including my parents. Everyone thought Trista would be head rocket scientist there one day, too. There was a reason AmStar engineers had already recruited her to assist the Festival's float-tech team.

"I thought so. I mean, they said they were looking into it as a *possible* homicide," I said.

"But it is technically possible," Trista added abruptly. I tensed up again. "For one, the s'more animatronics are controlled by computer. It'd be easy to mess with the code." She rattled off a bunch of technical details I didn't understand.

"And it sure would be a stealthy way to kill, wouldn't it? I mean, who'd think of that?" Grace arched an eyebrow and reached for her Diet Coke.

Trista looked lost in thought. "Usually, I'd say it's crazy. Seriously, murder by marshmallow?" She snorted. "But here's the thing. A hydraulic jack operates that s'more. I find it hard to believe that it could swing down accidentally. The odds of it malfunctioning out of the blue like that? They're thin. *Really* thin."

She pulled a pen from one of her jacket pockets, smoothed out her lunch bag, and drew a diagram of the levers involved in making the s'more move. "There's a manual override lever over here"—she tapped her lunch bag—"but there's no way Steptoe could've triggered it *and* been hit all the way over here." The bag rattled as she slid her finger to her sketch of the campfire. "Someone else had to have been involved."

A chill ran through me. Ordinarily, Trista could have *witnessed* Steptoe's murder and still had doubts.

"And if someone else was involved, why didn't they get him help before Kendra was screaming bloody murder over a Girl Scout campfire?" Grace asked, taking a bite out of her apple.

"Precisely." Trista nodded. "I'm not surprised they're looking at this as potential homicide. Not one bit."

A lump knotted in my throat as I pictured Mr. Steptoe. Only two days ago he'd had lunch with us at the very same table. Steptoe was an animal lover and a vegan, which meant he didn't eat or use any animal products. He was always eating weird stuff like sprouted barley and "cheese" made from almonds, so we used to stop by and play a funny little "guess what food this is" game with him. Even though we were teasing, we thought it was cool he loved animals enough to ban himself from pepperoni pizza and ice cream for life.

I shrank into my hoodie. "Who would ever murder someone that nice? I mean, the guy literally has never hurt a fly."

"As far as we know." Trista said, cocking an eyebrow. "People have secrets."

My stomach twisted as I forced down a bite of my ham sandwich.

"And Mr. Steptoe was the Festival President. Lots of people might have wanted him out of the way," Grace added, flipping the tab of her soda can nervously back and forth.

"Doesn't that seem a little much?" I asked, but as soon I heard my own words I realized it was possible. Barb wasn't the only adult who took the Festival way too seriously. People volunteered for years—decades, even—hoping to get a top Festival position. Committee spots opened up only when people moved or died. Landing one was like getting appointed to the Supreme Court or something.

"Not at all. Take Mr. Katz. Think how bitter he must be," Grace said.

Mr. Katz used to be the principal at Luna Vista Middle School. After at least twenty years of working his way up in the Festival, he was finally supposed to be sworn in as president. Two weeks earlier it had finally occurred to the Festival officials that maybe the guy who'd hired a dangerous fugitive as a school counselor without a background check wasn't the best public face of the anniversary parade. They'd demoted him to Head of Parade Route Integrity, aka the Pooper Scooper Brigade of kid volunteers who shoveled horse droppings so the floats didn't roll over them. It had to have been rough trying to wear the trademark brown suit with pride while you're literally shoveling poo.

"Poor guy. He'd already hung all his inspirational posters in the mansion office," I said.

"He's going to need a new one." Grace smiled slyly. "NO LOAD IS TOO GREAT TO BEAR."

"Ha! Showing a guy shoveling horse turds," I added.

Grace giggled. Trista cracked a smile.

"DOWN IN THE DUMPS? TIME FOR A PICK-ME-UP!" Grace sang out.

"How about"—I swept my hands out like a star imagining her name in lights—"HORSE POO: THE PATH TO A NEW YOU!"

Grace snorted Diet Coke out through her nose, which made us laugh even harder. It was a nervous, out-of-control laugh that let out my tension—but only for a second. We trailed off and looked around guiltily. We weren't exactly dealing with a laughing matter.

"OK, let's think about this." Grace pulled a black sketchbook from her messenger bag and set it on the table next to her uneaten lunch. She had been into drawing lately—mostly designs for clothes that no one could ever possibly wear because they involved large, funky head wraps and skirts made of venetian blind slats. She flipped to an open page and wrote SUSPECTS in large letters, listing Katz first.

"Like it or not, if the Festival goes ahead, we're going to have to try out for pages." She eyed me firmly. "We're going to need access. Royal access. Up close and personal."

"Whoa! Wait a minute, now." I pictured the glint in Grace's eyes that morning as she tried to convince Trista and me that being royal pages could be fun. Not to mention the way she straightened when Marissa complimented her jeans. Suddenly it hit me that she might be way more interested in hanging out with cool, older girls than in actual spying. The police were investigating, after all. They didn't need us.

"I don't think an entire weekend running around making smoothies for Kendra Pritchard is really going to help here."

"You're kidding, right?" Grace looked puzzled. "The best thing we can do is get into that mansion. We'd have after-hours access to the offices of all the major players. Think what we could do with three days there together. Night ops, constant surveillance, no sneaking around our parents."

Trista and I traded looks.

Grace's eyes danced mischievously. "I even heard that the Festival lectures the parents on how they're supposed to let the Court 'bond with their Festival family' and not call unless they absolutely have to. 'Tradition,'" she added with air quotes.

A pit opened in my stomach. Grace's parents were really protective of her, so she liked the idea of getting some freedom. Meanwhile, I'd never spent a full weekend away from home, let alone one without talking to my family at all.

"I'm with Sophie on this," Trista said. "If a murderer is on the loose—and it sure looks like it—we can't just start running night ops. It's way too dangerous. The police are working." She reached for her plastic fork. "Better to wait and see."

"But the police said it could take weeks! We can't wait around for that. It's safer to get on the Court now." Grace darted a glance up the hill. "We'll investigate Lund first," she barreled on as if we'd already moved into the mansion. "Mr. Steptoe dies and she's all obsessed with putting us on her Watch List? I swear she smiled when Ms. Sparrow broke the news."

"That's just what happens when her mole itches," I said.

Trista nodded as she tucked her paper napkin into her

T-shirt like a bib and opened her Tupperware container of salad. "Agreed. Probably had a small seizure. At best a facial spasm," she added. "Happens under stress."

"Stress from having taken out Mr. Steptoe?" Grace offered.

"Could be," Trista said, squeezing a packet of vinaigrette dressing over her salad. "But that doesn't mean we have to audition for royal pages."

"Exactly," I said. "Besides, Lund doesn't want the Festival canceled. It's her life! Rod told me she even has the Royal Court tiara logo on a toilet seat lid in her house."

Grace wrinkled her nose. "Probably one of those cushioned ones."

"Totally." I chuckled.

"If there's no parade, Lily Lund can't be queen," Trista piped up. "Her life dream. Up in Girl Scout campfire smoke." She wriggled her fingers for effect.

Grace didn't crack a smile. She tapped her pen against her notebook. "But we also know how Lund felt about Steptoe. Think about it. If Barb's not the police's number one suspect, she should be."

We had all seen Lund and Steptoe's standoffs over float decorating that week. Unlike past presidents, Jim Steptoe liked to check progress each night and list problems for

Barb to look into. It didn't matter how helpful Mr. Steptoe was trying to be; Barb wasn't having it. The afternoon before, she'd called him a nincompoop right in front of us. Mr. Steptoe had turned as red as a carnation petal. "You're right, Barbara," he'd shot back. "I am a nincompoop—for not replacing you when I had the chance!" Then he'd stormed off. Later we all wondered how much it would affect Lily Lund's chances of making the Royal Court, considering he was the head judge.

"What are you saying?" I frowned. "That Barb took out Steptoe so he wouldn't sway the Royal Court committee vote?"

"I'm saying it's possible." Grace pursed her lips. "I mean, I doubt Mr. Steptoe would ever try to shut out a Ridley in an anniversary year. On the other hand, can you see him really getting behind Lily? For one thing, she *hunts*."

It was true. Lily's sport was archery—and she didn't just aim at paper bull's-eyes. I had a flash to two days earlier when Mr. Steptoe made Lund take down photos in her office of Lily and her with their extended family on some weekend rabbit-hunting trip. Lund had flipped out—considering Ridley and his hunting club started the whole Festival. She'd accused him of ignoring tradition, which is bout the worst thing you can accuse *any* Festival volunteer of, let alone the president.

"And that's not even taking into account how much he couldn't stand Lund," Grace added.

"Maybe," Trista said, her napkin bib crumpling as she folded her arms. "But I can't see Barb Lund pulling off something technical like this. Pretty sure she hasn't even found the brakes on that golf cart of hers yet."

I almost laughed. It was true. Everyone knew that Barb had plowed said golf cart right into the bow of a replica pirate ship the morning of the parade last year. It had been Luna Vista's official float, so pictures of the poor dented thing were all over the local paper.

"She could have lugged the body to the float after," Grace said quietly. "Especially if she had help."

I raised an eyebrow. "From Lily?"

"Hey, those two are close," Grace said. "And they do hunt together. . . ."

"Grace, that's awful."

She shrugged. "It's true!"

Trista ignored us, stroking her chin as she squinted down the hill toward the float barn. The yellow police-tape on the path flapped loudly in the breeze. "Tell me about Harrison Lee again," she said. "He didn't seem upset?"

I thought back to the way Lee had jangled the change in

his pockets and paced. "Not even a bit," I said. "He was just nervous about the media and the police."

Grace sat up straight. "Now you two are thinking. You'd think he'd be at least a little sad. I mean, how long had he worked with the guy? Ten years?"

"He's got motive, too." Trista said.

I put down my soggy ham sandwich and studied her. She looked distant, and her eyes darted back and forth as though she were reading an invisible page. The back of my neck prickled. "Yeah? What are you thinking?" I asked.

"Think about it. Mr. Maxwell got rich after his term as President. Moved into that ridiculous spread on the bluffs with the tennis courts," Trista continued. "All that press from the parade? It's no accident he opened up two more Preppy Plus stores. Maxwell's sales went through the roof, but no one even remembers who the Festival VP was that year."

Grace's hair fell across her face as she leaned forward. "So true. Harrison Lee could rake in a ton of cash. He could put away those giant cardboard chainsaws for good. Who needs cheesy late-night ads when you have months of free publicity? And his body language this morning? Super-sketchy. The liar's trifecta. Nose touch, neck scratch, and the collar pull!"

"That so?" Trista's eyebrows shot up.

I had no idea what a trifecta was, but I didn't feel like asking. My lunch bag crackled as I shoved my half-eaten sandwich back inside it. I was starting to wish I'd left Grace to hang out with Marissa and discuss more *supercute* short-shorts together.

"I thought Ms. Sparrow was acting odd, too," Grace said. "Did you notice she called Mr. Steptoe 'Jimmy' during her announcement?"

I chuckled. "Are you saying Steptoe was her *loverrr*?" I asked, drawing out the word. I was desperate to lighten the mood.

Grace laughed. "Maybe. Though I cannot picture them together at all!"

"They say opposites attract." I shrugged. Ms. Sparrow was smooth and elegant and liked everything to be perfectly in place. "Jimmy" was goofy and kind of clumsy, and his gray hair was always messy.

"She'd be, like, trying to slick down his hair every day," Grace said. "You know, yesterday I actually saw her rearrange some books in the mansion foyer bookshelf so they were in order of height. And she's not even in her own house." She paused. "What if he dumped her, and she couldn't bear it?"

"Possible, I guess," Trista said. "She sure didn't kill for money. She's loaded now that all those celebrities are flipping out over Pretty Perfect stuff."

Grace lowered her voice and looked toward the mansion. "Everyone's a suspect," she said. "It's just a question of motive and opportunity."

An uneasy feeling rolled through me as Trista and I followed Grace's gaze to the mansion. The afternoon sun reflecting in its windows almost looked like flames.

Trista pulled off her napkin bib and folded it neatly next to her. "Maybe you're right about this royal page business, Grace. Awful lot of suspects for a nice dude," she said.

"Sure are," Grace said, eyes flashing. She clapped her notebook shut with a smack that made me jump. "It's a good thing the police are not alone."

Chapter Six

The Tiara on the Terrace

N
ews of Mr. Steptoe's death spread so fast that by the time I was back home, Grandpa Young had already gotten the full rundown at the Veterans of Foreign Wars club where he spent most of his time. "Fine man, that Steptoe," Grandpa had said, strands of thin gray hair wriggling up with static as he clutched his baseball cap to his heart. "Died in the line of fire. Wearing his brown suit, I heard."

Even though Grandpa had never been a Festival big-wig, the parade was really important to him. He'd prodded the VFW to prep their parade marching routine even before some of the floats had been built. It was no wonder Steptoe's death was hitting him especially hard. I'd given him a hug that afternoon. He wasn't usually into hugs, but he'd squeezed me extra tight.

My parents had rushed home from work early and sat glued to their cell phones in the kitchen, their faces lined with worry. Like most Luna Vistans, Mr. Steptoe had worked with them at AmStar. I think my parents had really liked him. At more than one dinner they'd repeated his silly puns to make us laugh (and groan), and they never complained about him, which is saying a lot. They complained about other people in their office, especially the guy who always used the microwave to heat up stinky fish leftovers.

As they muttered into their cells, sometimes their voices would echo the same word or phrase—"terrible accident" or "unbelievable"—and they'd whirl around to each other, startled, before turning back to their conversations.

They never mentioned murder.

Neither did the email that the Festival sent out that evening. It stated that the Winter Sun Festival would be held on schedule despite the tragedy, and the postponed Royal Court coronation would take place the next afternoon to be sure the local media could cover the event as planned. The float-decorating barn wouldn't reopen until the following day. To anyone who didn't know about Mr. Steptoe, the last lines would have seemed unimportant:

We regret that the Girl Scouts of America Beary Happy Family float will no longer be in this year's parade. We hope that all Girl Scout volunteers will continue their valuable community service by reporting to Ms. Barbara Ridley-Lund at 8:00 a.m. Thursday to contribute their talents to the Luna Vista Root Beer float instead.

❧ ❧ ❧

I didn't think I'd see Kendra at any more Festival events, but she was at the rescheduled Royal Court announcements the next afternoon, floating around the mansion lawn in her blue sundress and a string of pearls. Turns out that when you're a Royal Court finalist, you can recover pretty quickly from finding a body on a parade float.

Kendra handed off her purse to Marissa. It wasn't until it barked that I realized tan furry purses weren't some new fashion statement: Kendra was toting an actual dog around in a bag. The poor puffy thing yipped and snapped every time its blue bow drooped into its eyes, and it nearly took off Kendra's nose as she bent down to kiss it before heading up to the Ridley Mansion's wide front terrace to take her seat with the other contestants. Her smile glistened like everybody else's, showing no sign that a day earlier she'd practically snapped her vocal cords screaming bloody murder.

At first glance the mood was cheery. The sun had burned away the morning fog and reflected in the French doors of the bright white mansion—a sprawling, three-story building that Ridley had built to look like some famous old villa in Italy. Brown bunting hung from its balconies, announcing that the Festival was "CELEBRATING 125 YEARS." Anyone watching the live feed from the news cameras panning the crowd would have had to look closely to see the sad expressions on many of the faces.

From a distance Grace might have looked relaxed in her loose cardigan and sundress too. But she was on high alert. The muscles in her neck jumped as we made our way to the neat rows of white chairs set up on the front lawn. Her eyes flicked across the crowd. When Harrison Lee brushed by us on the way to the podium on the terrace, she squeezed my forearm so hard her nails dug into me. "Sure seems like he's enjoying his first big appearance as president," she said with a knowing look.

"No kidding," I replied, even though Lee was acting like any of the other Brown Suiters—focused yet stressed. I had to admit, though, the happy mood felt creepy. Caterers flitted about under the white tents set up alongside the mansion, fanning out cookies on platters and stacking tea-cups. Laughter echoed from clusters of well-dressed people mingling on a lawn so green and perfect it looked like a lush new carpet that had been rolled out for the occasion.

"Divide and conquer," Grace whispered as we headed for spots in separate rows so we could observe the suspects better. Our parents had been more than happy to let us sit wherever we wanted, probably because they wanted to be far, far away if there was any repeat of last year, when we'd been struck by an epic snorty-laugh attack for no good reason. Unfortunately, Trista had been roped into working the soundboard, but she'd promised to keep a lookout for anything strange. She already stood at her station set up in the center of the audience, her wiry, dark curls trying to spring free from the stiff, new LA Dodgers cap she wore to keep the sun out of her eyes.

I was about to slip into a back row when Rod walked down the center aisle toward me, looking a little lost. His curls were plastered damply against his head, and his tie was knotted very tightly, as if he hadn't had much practice dressing up. He gave a half-wave.

"I like your blazer," I said lamely, making a mental note to work on my greetings.

"Thanks." Rod rubbed the back of his neck and shifted

uncomfortably. "My mom and dad made me wear it."

I made a face and pointed to my flowery skirt. "Same."

"We look nice, though, right?" Rod forced a grin, and I wasn't sure if he was trying to compliment me. I blushed anyway. He glanced back at his little brother, then jerked his thumb over his shoulder. "I guess I have to—"

"I'm really sorry about Mr. Steptoe," I blurted.

"Yeah." His Adam's apple bobbed as he kicked his shoe against the grass. "I am, too," he added quietly. He gestured awkwardly to the rest of his family, who sat—pale and unsmiling—a few rows behind me. When I saw them there all together, I kind of wished I'd sat with my parents after all. Maybe the day wouldn't have felt so weird.

I shielded my eyes from the sun and squinted at the Royal Court contenders sitting on the terrace, their hands folded in their laps. As the Festival's official brass quintet warmed up next to them, the girls stared straight ahead, smiles frozen as if a tuba blaring inches from their ears was actually quite pleasant.

I wouldn't last a second as a royal page.

Harrison Lee stepped up to the podium. Two men in white suits stepped forward on either side of him and raised silver trumpets. But instead of the brassy bursts that usually started the Royal Court announcements, sad, wilted notes oozed from them. Harrison Lee bowed his head as if he were praying. As the cameras zoomed in on him, the forest of his thick, gelled hair filled the two large TV screens mounted on either side of the terrace.

"Today is a difficult day," he began, lifting his head again at last. He plucked a light-brown handkerchief from his front blazer pocket and dabbed at the sweat glistening on his brow. It was a warm day for December, but not that warm. I suppose it could have been nerves. He hadn't had much time to prepare.

My cell phone buzzed in my lap. It was a text from Grace:

Look at Lee sweat! Guilty much?

Lee took a nervous sip from his thermos on the podium and continued. "Many people thought we should cancel the Royal Court coronation altogether. But anyone who knew Jim Steptoe also knows he believed the show must always go on. As he liked to say: 'The winter sun always shines.'" Lee brought his fist to his mouth and closed his eyes. I felt bad because even though he was probably struggling not to cry, it looked like he was holding back a burp.

I looked across the aisle. Grace was scanning the crowd. I followed her gaze to the very back of the lawn, where Mr. Katz stood in his brown suit, shoulders stooped, waiting to usher latecomers to seats. His eyes darted across the crowd shiftily.

"I hope all of you will join me in remembering his life in a special service at St. Luke's on the Sunday after the Festival, when we can give him the farewell a great man like him deserves," Lee added. Splotches of moisture darkened his tan shirt. I wasn't used to seeing him in such drab colors. Usually he wore bright pastel golf shirts—and sometimes even screaming loud plaid pants.

"In presidential tradition, Jim chose this year's parade theme," Lee continued. "He was inspired by the lyrics of his favorite song—a song that sums up the Festival spirit." He cleared his throat so hard I thought he was going to cough up a hairball right there on the stage, which was better than belching, I supposed. Some of the adults in the crowd nudged each other uncomfortably, and I was relieved I wasn't the only one horrified by the weird funeral-parade kick-off combo. Poor Rod. It was bad enough that a giant marshmallow had taken out his family's friend. Now he had to sit through a strange, sweaty, hairball-coughing tribute to him, too. It all felt like the kind of crazy bad dream I have when I'm running a fever.

"We. Are. Family," Harrison Lee said, pausing dramatically after each word. "And we've lost a dear member of our family." A few sniffles rose up from the crowd. I caught a glimpse of Trista at the soundboard. Head cocked and mouth open, she looked as if she were watching a family of cockroaches scurry across the floor.

"However, we're here to announce the newest representatives of our Festival family. Please join me in congratulating our Royal Court finalists!" Lee swept his hand toward the contestants seated on the terrace. As applause rang out, their strained smiles grew even wider. Kendra Pritchard actually showed gum line, she was trying so hard. One of Jake's friends, Sienna Connors, was the only girl who looked comfortable up there. Her sandy brown hair looked windswept, like she'd come to the announcements after a morning of surfing.

The man next to me fidgeted and sighed as my cell phone vibrated with another text from Grace.

Check out Barb. Purple muumuu. 10 o'clock.

I was bad at following clock directions—but it wasn't hard to spot Barb in the crowd. Women wearing bright purple have a way of standing out. She definitely did not look like a mother who'd waited eighteen years for that moment. Arms tightly folded, she looked, in fact, like someone who'd recently caught a hefty whiff of raw sewage. She fanned herself with a half-crumpled program. No way that was landing in Lily's Royal Court scrapbook. Not without some serious magic from an industrial-strength steam iron.

I caught Grace's eye and gave a single nod. I wondered if, with every moment I went along with her, I was nudging us closer to being royal pages.

The audience straightened in their seats as two Brown Suiters removed a fancy cloth covering the famous royal tiara pedestal and the velvet-lined glass case on top of it where the tiara itself would soon rise into view.

"But first, it's time to unveil the Sun Queen's tiara," Harrison Lee said. "And the flower that Jim Steptoe chose to grace it." A hush fell over the crowd. Each year just before the Festival started, it was tradition for the Festival President to choose a symbolic plant or flower for the parade, which was first revealed with the Sun Queen's tiara. Only the jeweler who made the crown featuring the flower, and the president himself, knew the secret choice. We all realized that locking that tiara inside the secure hollow pedestal had to have been one of last things Mr. Steptoe ever did.

"From nineteen-ninety's memorable choice of the Venus flytrap to last year's bird-of-paradise that Scott Maxwell chose to represent our own sliver of paradise here in Luna Vista, we've seen some amazing selections over the years.

And now we have it. Jim's final gift to us all," Lee said as the queen's tiara spiraled from the depths of the pedestal compartment and appeared on the velvet lining. "The official symbol of the 125th Winter Sun Festival!"

The crowd clapped soberly as the tiara filled the outdoor screens with its glittering fake diamonds. The camera panned across the fancy metalwork and zoomed in on the flower insignia at the front of the crown. "A Coral Beauty rose," Harrison Lee announced as the unmistakable folds of petals came into view. For someone who didn't seem all that broken up yesterday, he sure was milking the moment. The applause grew louder.

I leaned forward to catch Grace's eye, but Lauren Sparrow blocked my sight line. Her face was drawn, but she looked much more together than she had the day before. Her outfit—an Asian silk jacket and dark pants—somehow managed to be both festive and serious.

"How fitting that Jim Steptoe left us with a symbol of love and friendship." Lee's voice echoed across the lawn. "Now which of Luna Vista's own lovely roses will wear it? We take many characteristics into consideration when we select our Court," he said, sounding an awful lot like one of his late-night ads as he mugged directly into the local news cameras lined up near the white tents. I found myself wishing Trista would spill her iced tea and short-circuit the soundboard.

"But, most of all, we look for effortlessness. The Festival is no beauty contest. The Royal Court is made up of smart, talented young women who are shining ambassadors for our community just by being themselves," he said.

If Grace had been sitting next to me, my ribs would be cracked from her elbowing. I shot off a quick text to her with a smiley face.

"Before we honor those ladies, let's take a moment to pay tribute to the people who made it possible for us to gather here today. In my book, they're Luna Vista royalty too."

Trista pulled her cap lower as Harrison Lee looked toward the volunteers at the soundboard. For someone whose regular speaking voice was a shout, it was surprising how much Trista hated being in the spotlight—even to be thanked.

Harrison Lee's blinding white smile filled the outdoor TV screens. "Officer Grady? Can you please stand?"

I frowned. Why did we need pay tribute to a police officer? Trista looked back at me in shock as Officer Grady stood up from his seat in the row in front of her and pretended to humbly wave away the crowd's cheers.

Lee bumped the microphone as he clapped over-enthusiastically. "We couldn't be more grateful to Paul

Grady and his fine team at the LVPD for quickly determining the cause of Jim Steptoe's accident. It isn't easy kicking off our Winter Sun Festival under the shadow of tragedy, but thanks to their thorough investigation, we have closure. We can move forward—with full peace of mind. We salute you, officers."

My chest tightened. Closure? A little more than twenty-four hours had passed since we'd eavesdropped on the police in the float barn. Pink-faced Officer Carter's voice echoed in my mind. *Homicide,* he'd said. We'd heard him right. He'd said it would take weeks to investigate. How could they have tied everything up so fast? My heart started to race.

Grady sat back down again. I turned to Grace. Staring straight ahead, she looked at Harrison Lee as if he'd grown a second head. Next to her, Lauren Sparrow wore an almost identical look. Her Royal Court program dropped to the ground and abruptly fluttered shut.

Chapter Seven

Royal Upset

Grace locked her panicked eyes on mine. My head felt light, and Harrison Lee's voice sounded warped and far away, as if he were talking underwater. The Court finalists—their ankles crossed, their smiles like grimaces—looked like a row of plastic puppets.

There was nothing to worry about, I told myself, even as my heart pounded and a trickle of sweat slid down the back of my neck. The police had discovered some missing piece of the puzzle. That's all. They knew how Mr. Steptoe had died, and it wasn't at the hands of some deranged killer. Or poor Mr. Katz in his horse-turdy suit. Or even Barb Lund, whose arms were so tightly crossed that she looked as if she were trying to keep herself from throttling someone that very second. It had been an accident. Pure and simple. So what if the police had said the force would need weeks to investigate? They might've made a mistake. It's not like bodies showed up in parade floats every day on their watch. Besides, we'd heard one snatch of conversation only minutes after they'd arrived. Things had changed.

Obviously.

"The envelope, please!" Harrison Lee bellowed, chuckling at his own corny imitation of an Academy Awards host as he took the list of Royal Court winners from the Brown Suiter next to him. The contestants sat up as if tugged by an invisible string.

Lauren Sparrow straightened in her chair, too. Her program was neatly tucked halfway into her leather handbag and she wore a relaxed smile. Suddenly I wasn't sure I'd ever seen that flash of surprise on her face at all.

As the cranes on the news vans hinged outward, elbowing their way in for close-ups, I felt queasy as I remembered how worried Lee had been about the press. He'd practically begged Officer Grady to wrap everything up faster because of the Festival. But the police would never rush to give us "closure" if a murderer was on the loose, would they? My head started to throb.

Lee prepared to announce the Royal Court's first new princess. "Siennnn-na Connnnn-nors!" he boomed.

Trista had to rip off her headphones and fumble for the

soundboard levels as a chorus of ear-splitting shrieks rose up. Shocked, Sienna tottered on her heels toward the podium. One of the previous year's princesses who was wrapped in a tight gauzy dress that reminded me of a mummy—or a patient recovering from full-body surgery—pressed a bouquet into her arms. Sienna might have been surprised, but the rest of us weren't. She was everything the Festival could want in a princess and still managed to be ridiculously nice. The genuine, fun kind of nice. Not the boring kind people pull off because they have no opinions.

As Lee turned back to the crowd, Kendra was already smoothing down the folds of her dress, ready to stand. She blew a kiss to someone in the crowd—possibly to her sister, Marissa. Possibly—and even more likely—to her dog.

Harrison Lee drew in a noticeably longer breath before he announced the next Court member. "Allow me to introduce . . . Princess Lily Lund!"

A stunned hush fell over the crowd as they put it together. If Lily was princess, she couldn't be queen. If Lily wasn't queen, then—

The crowd broke into an awkward cheer while craning their necks to look for Barb. I whirled around to see her expression for myself.

She sat like a statue, her feathered bangs ruffling in the

breeze. She wore a look that . . . well . . .

A look that could kill.

Meanwhile, Lily stood stiffly on the terrace clutching her bouquet of flowers so tightly to her chest I wondered if the rose thorns were drawing blood yet. She struggled to keep her smile, but when the camera swept across her face, I saw her glasses were misting up with tears. My lap buzzed with a stream of exclamation-point-filled texts from Grace. As I leaned to catch her eye across the aisle, I saw Lauren Sparrow cheering, her quick claps reminding me of beating birds' wings.

The sun glinting on the bell of a trumpet blinded me as the heralds sounded out another blast. "Hear ye, hear ye, Faithful!" Harrison Lee cried out the coronation announcement. It sounded so silly, but it was part of the tradition. "All rise to welcome the new reigning Sun Queen of our Anniversary Festival Royal Court."

Kendra's gummy dental-office smile could not have been brighter or wider. She'd practically stood up from her chair already.

"Jardine Thomas!" Lee finished.

Kendra's smile froze and her eyes went wide as Jardine Thomas hopped up and rode the roar of the crowd over to the podium, chin leading the way. "Jar-*di*!" someone hooted as some of the older Luna Vistans stiffened and shifted in their seats. Even with the camera's close-up magnifying Jardine's every feature, her flat-ironed hair and dark-brown skin looked perfect. Behind her, Kendra and the losing finalists beamed and clapped so hard their hands must've stung.

Lund tossed her balled-up program to the grass as last year's Sun Queen balanced the royal tiara on Jardine's head. The band burst into a slowed down version of "We Are Family," that 1970s song Grandpa Young hummed as a joke at the dinner table sometimes. Silver and gold confetti filled the air, shimmering in the sun as people poured into the center aisle.

As I filed out of my row, Grace pushed her way through the crowd, her gaze dark and urgent. My mouth went dry.

She threw her arm around me and leaned in. "We're looking at a cover-up," she whispered. "A royal one. And you know what that calls for, don't you?"

My stomach lurched as she answered for me.

"That's right, Soph." Grace squeezed my shoulder, eyes gleaming. "Undercover royals."

Chapter Eight

The Beach Ball

"There's no way the police are going to risk leaving a killer at large," I told Grace when she repeated her police cover-up theory to me that evening in the mansion kitchen. Weeks ago we'd signed up to be servers at the "Beach Ball," the gala dinner celebrating the new Court. Behind us cooks bustled around the sizzling stove. Clattering dishes mixed with the faint sounds of piano drifting in from the ballroom.

"This is the Festival, Soph. You heard what Lee said about the press," she whispered, her eyes darting nervously to the other middle-school Beach Ball servers hustling in to change into their white waiter jackets. "If this got out, it'd be a disaster for Luna Vista's reputation. First we harbor a fugitive, now a murderer?" She shook her head. "The Winter Sun Festival was supposed to make everyone *forget* about the Tilmore Eight fugitive. What if they—"

"Listen," I interrupted, tugging her closer. "The police investigated. It was an accident. Case closed." I wasn't sure I believed it, but I was desperate to shut down her royal page plan. "C'mon. Tonight's supposed to be fun!"

A week earlier when Grace and I had found out that we'd snagged one of the Beach Ball's few volunteer waiter slots, we'd been so excited we'd pretty much thrown our own ball. Well, a spontaneous dance party, actually—even if it had come crashing to a halt when Jake had walked in to borrow my three-hole punch. Grace had been so embarrassed that Jake had caught her shaking her butt in the air, she hid in my bathroom for a full ten minutes before I managed to coax her back onto the "dance floor." I wished it were as easy to get her to lighten up for the actual Ball.

"Besides . . ." I pulled a waiter jacket from a hook and slipped it on. "Everyone is on high alert. I heard some parents are freaking out so much about safety they're going to make their kids wear helmets in the float barn. Somebody else is all over this, I promise."

Grace's brow creased. "Helmets?"

I nodded. "Rod told me Peter Murguia's mom is making him wear a neon one. You know, for extra visibility."

"Whoa."

Grace let the thought sink in. If other kids' parents were making them wear safety helmets, the Yangs were probably one step away from fitting her for a padded float-decorating suit. They didn't mess around.

"Yup." I crossed my arms. "Also, for all we know, the police are still on it and just announced it was an accident. It's not like you tell a murderer, 'Ready or not! Here we come!'"

Grace pursed her lips. "I sure hope so, Sophie. Because if they're not—people could be in serious danger. Steptoe wasn't the only one on that judging committee. What if there are more targets?"

My shoulders tensed as I thought of Barb Lund's expression at the announcements. I had to admit it wasn't entirely crazy to think she could've snapped. If someone spent years dreaming of something only to have it taken away at the last second, couldn't they lose it? I mean, I had a total meltdown when my parents went back on their promise to get us a Golden Retriever puppy—and I'd only begged for, like, a year.

"It's not like they shut Lily out of the Court altogether, Grace," I said.

"Tell me one time Trista was wrong about something," Grace said. "Ever. Because that's the only way I'm going to buy that the s'more swung down by accident." She glanced through the archway into the ballroom where guests in sequined dresses and tuxedos were pouring in.

It was hard to argue with her. "I can't." I let my arms slap to my sides. "But please, Grace, we don't have to be pages. We can still investigate. Here. Tonight! When else are all our suspects going to be in one place?" I waved my hand toward the ballroom.

"Okay, it's a plan. Let's find out everything we can now," Grace replied as she rolled up the cuffs of my oversized white waiter jacket and brushed the lint off of it. She smiled slyly. "And if we don't solve the case . . . we audition for pages."

"Grace, seriously. I'd rather die."

"Oh, I hear the judges *love* zombies." She thrust out her arms at me stiffly and imitated the Court contestants' empty grins.

I laughed. "But will they love my moves?" I did one of our more ridiculous dance party steps, which was something like a cross between a jumping jack and a can-can kick. I was midjump, holding a dinner roll, when Marissa Pritchard waltzed in with Danica and Denise Delgado.

"What are you doing?" Marissa asked, her lip curling. The twins stared, openmouthed.

"Sophie's teaching me a new form of sign language," Grace explained. She turned to me and scratched one armpit while hopping up and down on one foot, then we both totally lost it, clutching our stomachs as we cracked up. It made me really happy that she didn't care what Marissa thought. Maybe I'd been wrong about her wanting to hang out with them. Danica and Denise turned to each other and laughed too—though more *at* us than with us.

Just then Rod Zimball came in with his friends, Peter and Matt. My laughter faded as Marissa smiled sweetly at them. "Sophie's teaching us sign language," she announced. "Want to learn?"

I felt my face turn an even deeper shade of magenta than the napkins Danica and Denise had started laying inside empty breadbaskets.

Rod ran his hand through his hair and rested it on the back of his neck. "Uh, kinda busy right now?" He looked at me apologetically. "Maybe later?"

I was trying to think of something to say when Harrison Lee ducked in through the ballroom archway and saved me. "Good evening, ladies. How's the finest waitstaff this side of the Mississippi?" he asked, smiling as widely as he did on his car commercials. Principal Katz was hovering behind him with a strange look on his face. Lee turned to him irritatedly before we could even answer. "Listen, Josh, I told you," he uttered in a low, firm voice. "It's not up to me! It was a committee decision, it was the right one, and we're not revisiting it." He made a show of wiping his hands. "This discussion is over."

Grace widened her eyes at me. Meanwhile Katz pressed his lips together so tightly they turned white, then he shuffled to the back of the kitchen to say hi to one of the cooks. Harrison Lee plastered on his smile and turned back to us. "Don't those look good!" he looked longingly at some bacon-wrapped figs on a silver tray. "Now, what do you say you serve some of those up, kiddos?"

As soon as we grabbed our trays and stepped through the archway to the ballroom, Grace drew in a sharp breath. "Wow," she said. "Gorgeous."

Candlelight flickered over the faces of guests as they milled around, bobbing their heads along with a jazzy tune floating up from the baby grand in the corner. Big bouquets of pink roses decorated each table, and old-time photos of past Winter Sun Festivals lined the wood-paneled walls. Giant arched French doors reflected it all back, making the room seem twice as big.

My parents stood across the room with the Yangs and some other neighbors from Via Fortuna. Grace's dad must have been telling a hilarious story, because everyone erupted into guffaws and clinked their champagne glasses with his. Grace's mom dabbed away tears of laughter with her cocktail napkin. She seemed especially happy to be in a sleek tailored evening suit instead of her usual white doctor coat.

"It really does look beautiful," I said.

"No. I meant your brother." Grace grinned. "He looks gorgeous."

"Ew!" I swatted her with my napkin. "You did not just say that."

Jake had sat down at a table with a bunch of his high school friends. The bow tie of his rented tuxedo was crooked, and his light-brown hair was slathered with so much gel I swear he must have paid a visit to Harrison Lee's hair dresser. If that was Grace's idea of cute, she needed a full mental-health assessment. Not to mention an eye exam.

Jake caught my eye and waved his index finger in the air. "Garçon! Garçon! Help!" he called out, elbowing one of his friends. "I think there's a fly in my soup!" He laughed and winked.

"He's all yours," I said to Grace.

"I do like a man with a sense of humor." She smiled, then turned and surveyed the room. "Okay, Agent Young, you take the right flank. Tables two through ten. I'll cover the left and the Royal Court banquet table."

"Ten-four, Agent Yang." I looked up at her glumly. "I wish we still had the walkie-talkies."

"Aw, we're beyond all that now, remember?" Grace's eyes danced. "But that code you were talking about? The Poly-bee-something? *That*, we need to check out, my friend."

I laughed. "We really do," I said, as a bubble of happiness rose in my chest. If I weren't carrying a tray, I would've high-fived her. But the bubble deflated when Grace's face fell suddenly. She grabbed my elbow and nodded toward the Royal Court banquet table. "Who's missing from this picture?" she hissed.

I turned to follow her gaze. Dressed in evening gowns and sporting their glittering tiaras, Sienna and Jardine were beaming with excitement as they circulated among their parents and some Festival officials. Or tried to, at least. They wobbled around in their slinky dresses like mermaids recently washed ashore. Next to them, in a matching Court tiara that looked dull in comparison to her sparkling braces, was none other than Kendra Pritchard. She looked so happy she practically glowed.

"Lily Lund . . . ," I said, too loudly, right as Marissa and several of her friends were sweeping by with breadbaskets.

"Oh, didn't you guys hear?" she asked. "Lily dropped out. Or her mom pulled her out. She said she couldn't support the Court's values." She flipped her hair over her shoulder. "I'll say!" She smiled smugly. "They chose my sister instead."

"That's great, Marissa." I said unenthusiastically. "Congrats."

"Now things are the way they were meant to be." Marissa tilted her chin higher. "And when I'm a royal page, they'll be even better."

"*If* she's a royal page," Grace muttered to me as Marissa flounced off. "I have a bad feeling, Soph. Very bad. And if the police are still on it, well . . ." She arched an eyebrow and jerked a thumb toward a table in the far corner by the piano, where Officer Grady was swigging back his drink. The back of his neck rolled over his tuxedo collar as he laughed at a joke. "They might want to work a little harder."

"Officer Grady doesn't have to be on it *personally*, Grace." I was doomed. With every passing moment, I was one step closer to being wrapped up in some sort of poufy taffeta dress, cowering in the shadow of the giant half clamshell, trying—and failing—to wave in sync with the rest of the Royal Court. "Okay, right flank, you said? Mission commences in three, two, one. . . ." I adjusted my grip on my tray and strode forward. "Maybe you can eavesdrop on—"

Grace's eyes widened in warning, but it was too late. "Young and Yang," a deep voice bellowed behind me. Harrison Lee smiled and pointed to the long banquet table at the center of the room. "Our Royal Court could use some of those appetizers."

"We're on it, Mr. Lee," Grace sang out, balancing her tray in one hand like a pro waiter. "Ready, Sophie?" She leaned in and lowered her voice to a whisper. "Think of it as practice."

I sucked in a deep breath. I sure needed practice.

"Maybe they can use some appetizers," I muttered to Grace as we started to wind our way through the crowd to the Court's banquet table. "But their dresses are too tight for them to actually *eat* them."

I hadn't taken two steps before guests descended upon me like a flock of birds, plucking hors d'oeuvres from my platter. One lady set her lipstick-stained wine glass right on my tray without a word. Another dumped her coat over my free arm. "Oh, sweetie, could you take care of this for me?" she asked, already turning away. Grace cruised effortlessly ahead, snaking through the crowd, tray balanced high as I ran interference as a human coatrack and litter collector. By the time I reached the Court, I had three measly hors d'oeuvres left and enough used toothpicks piled up to play an extended game of pick-up sticks.

"Deviled egg?" I held out the tray to Kendra and Jardine. They turned up their noses as if I'd offered them boiled monkey brains.

"Um, no thanks?" Jardine said. As I struggled to juggle the coats in my one hand I must've tilted the tray a little too much. Or one of the deviled eggs had simply decided it was time to show off. Like a tiny circus acrobat, it somersaulted through the air toward Jardine, and landed *splat* on the front of her evening gown, smearing its foamy yolky yellow across her chest.

Jardine's face twisted in shock. I let the coats fall to the floor as I scrambled for a napkin and leaped forward, spewing apologies. Grace shoved my arm clear of Jardine's chest like a goalie making a save. "We'll be back with more in a sec!" she sang out, widening her eyes at me. She scooped up the coats and her own tray, and we dove back into the crowd. I caught sight of Rod, water pitcher in hand and mouth open, staring at the major scene I'd caused, and my cheeks itched with heat.

"See? I'm not cut out for this, Grace. I told you," I groaned as we hung up the guest coats and prepped the soup course that—lucky for me—adult waiters were serving. The last thing I needed was to splatter boiling hot puke-green split pea soup in someone's lap.

"Practice makes perfect," she said with a smile.

"Or even pretty perfect?" I nodded toward Lauren Sparrow who was gliding over the dark polished wood floors in her high heels, visiting clusters of guests like a hummingbird floating from flower to flower. Her cheeks glowed—probably thanks to a little Pretty Perfect magic—and her hair cascaded to her shoulders in relaxed waves. Grace gazed at her as if in a trance.

As Ms. Sparrow nudged Mr. Lee and Mr. Zimball away from the group they'd been talking to, I shot Grace a look. I'd told her about Sparrow's reaction at the Court announcements—and neither of us was sure what to make of it. Was she trying to tell Zimball and Lee something? "Eavesdrop opportunity at ten o'clock," I whispered. "Or is it two o'clock?"

"Target acquired," she said, grabbing another tray of deviled eggs. "Going in."

As Grace held out her tray to the cluster of people next to Mr. Lee and Ms. Sparrow, I lingered at the table behind them, filling water glasses and wishing I could use Grace's mouth-open, hands-cupping-ears spy trick to hear better.

"I'm just saying we need to do some damage control here, that's all," Ms. Sparrow said, sounding like she was at a board meeting. "Typical of Barbara, isn't it? I mean, she knew two days ago that's what we'd all decided. And she doesn't pull Lily then? She waits until we *crown* her? It's an embarrassment. And cruel to her daughter, by any stretch. What kind of person does that?" She shook her head. "As if the Festival doesn't have enough of an image problem right now."

Grace slipped off with her tray toward the kitchen. I rushed behind. "Did you hear that?" I whispered. "*Two days* ago. Barb knew Lily wasn't going to be queen."

Grace nodded solemnly. "Motive: established."

A tinkling like a bell interrupted us. Harrison Lee stood at the head of the long Royal Court banquet table at the center of the room, tapping the rim of his champagne glass with a spoon. "A toast," he called out. His cheeks were flushed. Rod's dad sat next to him, smiling; he was the Festival's second-in-command now, after all. I caught myself wondering if Rod would look the same when he was older. Mr. Zimball had brown curls, too, only gray and wispy at his temples.

"To our beautiful Roses," Lee raised his glass to the Royal Court, obviously still relishing his new role as Festival President. As Sienna beamed and held up her water glass, Jardine turned to the ballroom crowd as if expecting something more, like a ritual foot washing—or mass kneeling in worship. Kendra Pritchard smiled, her braces gleaming. I had to blink away a vision of myself polishing her headgear at bedtime.

Grace leaned closer to me while everyone clinked glasses. "Listen, I'm trying out for pages—alone, if I have to."

Her words stung like a slap. Just like that, she'd do this without me? I looked over to the Royal Court. They'd recovered from the hors d'oeuvres crisis and were squeezing in for a picture, their arms slung around each other like they'd been friends since daycare.

"That's a terrible idea," I said quietly.

Grace shrugged. It was like she thought deciding to go undercover alone was no bigger deal than picking an ice cream flavor. "Sophie, someone killed Steptoe, I'm absolutely sure of it, and if we don't—"

"Ladies?"

My heart shot up to the mansion's top floor and back. I turned to find Lauren Sparrow smiling back warmly, completely unaware she'd nearly thrown me into cardiac arrest. "Table Six needs a bread refill when you get a chance," she said. "Got to get ready for the soup course."

Grace and I both practically flew to the kitchen to get more bread.

"She heard me, didn't she?" Grace said breathlessly,

pulling a loose strand of her hair to her mouth. "Oh, man. She totally heard me."

I seized my opening. "This is what I mean, Grace! If a murderer is on the loose—that's a huge 'if'—and they find out what we're up to? They might try to kill us."

Grace blinked as she gazed through the archway at the guests. The piano had stopped, and the roar of conversation had overtaken the room. She let the strand of hair drop back to her shoulder and turned back to me. "You know, maybe you're right, Sophie—"

A crash and thud rang out from the ballroom. We whirled around.

Rod's dad stood at the banquet table, waving both hands like a shipwrecked castaway. His chair lay knocked over on its side. "Someone call nine-one-one!" he shouted, cords straining in his neck.

Next to him a man was slumped over his soup bowl.

The gelled black hair was unmistakable.

It was Festival President Harrison Lee.

Chapter Nine

Now or Never

Two Festival Presidents down within forty-eight hours. My knees went weak. The ballroom air suddenly felt stifling, and the yellowed photos of past Winter Sun Festivals along the wall blurred together. The Doctors Yang sprang from their seats, pushing through the crowd that had closed in around the Royal banquet table. Sirens wailed as Janice Yang felt for Mr. Lee's pulse. Moments later paramedics tromped across the ballroom floor, their first aid kits and oxygen masks rattling. The lights from the ambulance flashed through the ballroom's arched windows. Grace and I stood in shock as their red glow swept over us dizzily.

We didn't speak. No one did. I gripped Grace's sweaty hand as the paramedics hauled Harrison Lee past us on a stretcher, my heartbeat crowding out the other sounds in the room. Lee's eyes were half closed, and his hair was slicked to his forehead in greenish pea soup–drenched clumps. He let out a long moan. Thank goodness—otherwise I wouldn't have even been sure he was breathing. It was a relief, too, that he looked only a little bit worse than Kendra Pritchard, who had also required medical attention for her fit of hyperventilating—and for the nasty gash on her forehead where Jardine Thomas's tiara had hit her when it tumbled off her head. One more inch and Kendra would have been waving from the Royal Court float wearing a bedazzled eye patch.

I caught sight of Rod across the room, clutching his mom's arm. He locked his wide eyes on mine. And that's when I realized it. His dad could be next.

⚜ ⚜ ⚜

By the next morning my mind was a whirling mess. All night I'd tossed and turned, nightmares of Mr. Zimball being drowned in vats of pea soup and Coral Beauty rosebuds playing on a feverish loop. Grace had probably sent me a zillion texts, but once I'd come clean about getting in trouble with Barb Lund, my parents had confiscated my cell.

Grace and I had expected Officer Grady to leap into action after Lee's collapse—to rope off the banquet table with crime tape, to gather witnesses to interview, to hustle soup bowls off for evidence. But, apart from some help with crowd control, Grady didn't call other officers to the scene. The adults were really worried, of course, but if they thought it was strange that a *second* Festival President was down, they sure didn't show it. The most I heard were a few people muttering about a cursed Festival. "The ghost of Willard Ridley is getting his revenge," the lady who'd handed me her lipstick-stained glass had joked. The Yangs explained to everyone that Lee had most likely collapsed from stress, dehydration, and low blood sugar. "He sure has been dealing with a lot," Mr. Zimball had said, sighing, but I thought I saw a nervous flicker in his eyes.

When I came out to breakfast, Grandpa and Dad were sitting at the table sipping their coffee and silently trading sections of the newspaper as the dishwasher hummed behind them. "Oh good, you're up," my father said as I came in. He tried to look stern. "Last thing you need is to be late reporting to Ms. Lund."

"Huh!" Grandpa squinted at his section of the newspaper. It showed a really complicated diagram of what I assumed was the Girl Scout float. He rapped his knuckle on the picture and gave a low whistle. "What a way to go."

I stared down at the 3D cross-section diagram with all its swooping arrows. It looked so official, as if the police had flown in a team of physicists specializing solely in fake marshmallow deaths to figure it all out.

"Have you heard any updates on Mr. Lee?" I asked my dad.

"The Yangs say he's still resting in the hospital, as far as I know."

I cleared my throat. "Do you think it's weird that, you know, first Mr. Steptoe has an accident"—I stumbled over the word—"and then Mr. Lee collapses?"

"Why would that be weird?" My dad frowned as he smoothed the tufts of hair around his ears—the only hair he still had—then looped his AmStar lanyard around his neck and straightened his tie. "Poor Harrison. It's no wonder. His good buddy dies, he's thrust into the spotlight, in charge of everything. He has to manage the press, take over the Festival, give improvised televised speeches—all while putting on a brave face? I doubt he's slept at all since they discovered Jim. I'd have fallen apart even earlier with all that stress."

"I don't know," I said. "I thought it could look like—like maybe someone was after the Festival Presidents on purpose." I mumbled that last part as quickly as I could.

Grandpa scratched his head, as if seriously considering my theory. He turned his newspaper sideways and peered so closely at it that his nose practically grazed it.

"The thing is, after Kendra found Mr. Steptoe, Grace and

I . . ." I wasn't sure how to put it without getting myself in more trouble. "We went back into the float barn and overheard the police saying that it would take at least two weeks to investigate—"

"You sneaked back into the float barn after they evacuated you?" My dad interrupted before I finished, his blue eyes widening. "Soph! Do you realize how dangerous that could've been?"

He shook his head at me and leaned forward in his chair. "Listen, you and Grace went through a lot with all that Tilmore Eight fugitive business." He softened his tone and ruffled my hair. Usually, I liked it when he did that, but right then it made me feel about six years old. He might as well have counted the freckles on my nose, like he used to do when he tucked me in at night. "You were excellent investigators. I know that. We all know that. If it weren't for you girls, Deborah Bain would still be on the loose in this town."

"Darned straight!" Grandpa interrupted, winking at me. "Ow." He frowned and rubbed his knee under the table where my dad must've nudged him too hard.

My dad ignored him. "But you're getting carried away." He sighed. "And I think your pal Trista is getting carried away too. Last night Jason from AmStar told me that she thinks she knows the float couldn't malfunction. She asked the float engineers to explain it to the police."

"Did she?" I asked, relieved to hear it.

"She's a firecracker, that one," Grandpa Young interrupted. "We could have used someone like her in the 187th Airborne."

My dad ignored him. "This was a terrible, one-in-a-million accident, but trust me, Sophie. The police have covered their bases." He waved to the newspaper. "Ensuring a safe Festival is everyone's number one concern." He grabbed his car keys and gently squeezed my shoulder on his way to the door. "Now why don't you worry about staying off Barb Lund's radar instead, huh?"

I stared at my half-eaten toast and nodded. Little did he realize that staying off Barb Lund's radar was exactly what I was worried about.

❊❊ ❊❊ ❊❊

"Lee is still in the hospital, Sophie," Grace said, shaking her head as we walked into the float barn to report to Barb that morning as commanded. The floats' half-built ice cream sundaes and Ferris wheels and cartoon figures looked creepy without volunteers scrambling all over them. I shivered a little. The fog had made the morning especially chilly, but I would have been freezing no matter what. I felt cold from the inside.

"The doctors say it's stress, but off the record, they told my parents they don't know what's up. They're keeping him there. Dehydration? Stress? Or attempted poisoning? I think this was an attack. Pure and simple." She shot me a firm look and then held out her pen.

"It's now or never, Sophie."

I knew she was right, but I kept my arms glued to my side. "You know, Lee *has* been under an awful lot of stress," I said, repeating my dad's words at breakfast.

She thrust the pen toward me again. "You really want to wait around to see who the killer hits next? Rod Zimball's dad is Festival president now, you know."

I looked at the white teardrop-shaped half of our yin/yang friendship pendant hanging around her neck. She used to claim the necklace didn't go with any of her outfits, but we'd both worn our pendants every single day since we'd captured Deborah Bain. I felt a little pang as I remembered that night on the beach below the bluffs two months earlier, when it looked like we might not even make it out alive—gunshots echoing above, waves crashing around us.

Grace sighed impatiently. "You captured a killer and now you're afraid of a little royal-page primping?"

I opened my mouth to argue, but Barb Lund's screechy voice saved me.

"That you, Young and Yang?" she shouted from her office.

Grace and I cringed and bolted down the float barn aisle like Olympic track runners, stopping to catch our breath for only a second before shuffling into Lund's office. It was a stuffy little room in the far corner of the warehouse.

It took me a moment to even notice Barb Lund amid all the clutter. She might have run a tight ship when it came to float decorating, but her office looked like the entire archives of Festival history had exploded inside of it. Photo collages of past Winter Sun Festival floats hung crookedly on the wall next to autographed headshots of former members of the Royal Court. "Love and Hugs, Princess Stephanie," read one photo of a big-haired teenager wearing a pink dress that looked like a birthday cake. Then there were the stuffed animals. I mean, I like Winnie the Pooh as much as the next person, but do you really need a shelf of twenty of them in various sizes?

Barb hunched over a dusty computer monitor reading email. Judging from her deep frown, she wasn't anywhere near over Lily's royal snub. If anything, she looked even angrier. "Late with the onion seed delivery again," she exclaimed. "I could wring their necks!" Her chair squealed as she turned to us. "Speaking of late." She thrust a finger at a dusty digital clock. The clock's red numbers stared back: 7:00 exactly.

Grace opened her mouth to say something, but Lund cut her off. "Don't tell me you don't know about Festival Time," she said, then singsonged a little rhyme: "On time? You're late! Gotta hurry up and wait!"

Grace and I stood in silence, not daring to look at each other. "We're really sorry," I offered, at last.

Ms. Lund didn't seem to hear me. "You don't even want to know what happened when Queen Marianne only showed up *on time* for float boarding on parade day in 1998," she said, shaking her head. Ms. Lund took Festival tradition so seriously, she talked about past Royal Court queens as if they were actual monarchs. If Lily were still on the Court, Barb would have been so busy bowing and curtseying to her she would have had trouble showing up at any time, let alone Festival time.

We flinched as Barb unclipped a Winnie the Pooh key chain from her belt loop, unlocked a desk drawer, and shoved two jars and two pairs of tweezers our way. "Start with the ice cream sundae. Any wrong-colored petal"—I gulped as she leaned forward—"make sure it's gone for good. Understood?"

"Yes, ma'am!" Grace cried out before we both turned

and ran away. We didn't stop until we were back at the Root Beer float. "Jeez, that was scary," she said, leaning against the side of an ice cream cone as I caught my breath. "How can a woman with that much love for Winnie the Pooh be such a pain?"

"Haven't you heard?" I looked at her sideways. "She's not a pain, Grace. She has high standards."

Grace laughed. "Guess I didn't get the memo."

"Maybe she's just misunderstood," Trista interrupted, poking her head out from the camouflaged front compartment where a driver would hide away to steer the float during the actual parade. I was surprised—and relieved—to see her there so early. She grunted as she shimmied herself free from the compartment. "Ugh, it's awful in there," she said, then sneezed into the crook of her arm loudly—twice. She held up a small device with several levers. "Remote control is going to revolutionize this festival. Worth showing up early to get the quiet time in."

"Hey, weren't you supposed to be volunteering with us last night?" I asked, realizing she probably didn't even know about Lee yet. I couldn't wait to hear what she'd think.

Trista shrugged. "My tuxedo T-shirt was at the dry cleaners."

"Oh," I said, as if that actually explained it.

Grace launched into a reenactment of the Beach Ball disaster, stopping short of actually imitating Lee's moan as they carried him off on the stretcher. When she'd finished, Trista set down her remote control and made a face. "Dehydration? Stress?"

"Ridiculous, right? You'd think he'd be stabilized by now." Grace folded her arms.

Trista sighed and ran her hand through her thick curls. "I'll tell you what's ridiculous. I went to the AmStar team and asked for help explaining why it can't be an accident to the LVPD. They wouldn't take me seriously." She looked at us sheepishly. "They think I'm letting you two mess with my head. Like, we think everything's a murder mystery now because of everything that went down."

"My parents think so too," I said quietly.

"Mine think I just *really* want to be a royal page." Grace looked at us. "What?" she asked. "No way I was telling them this crazy stuff. They'd flip!"

"The lead guy from the AmStar team did talk to the police for me, though. They said they'd take another look," Trista continued. "But I'm twelve, what do I know about physics?" She snorted sarcastically.

"I'm thinking it's slow-acting poison," Grace piped up. "Polonium. Thallium, maybe. With AmStar in town, people can get access to some pretty intense stuff."

She may have been into designing miniskirts made out of papyrus now or whatever, but her crime trivia was obviously still rattling around in her brain. Trista shook her head. "Thallium poisoning causes significant hair loss." Then she raised an eyebrow. "I think it's pretty clear *that's* out."

"With as much hair as Lee has, you'd never even notice," Grace said, and I couldn't help but laugh.

"Fair point." Trista looked thoughtful as she wiped her greasy hands on her jeans.

"Tryouts are today. If we want inside access, we have to act now." Grace countered. "I'm already signed up."

I felt a surge of dread. I still couldn't believe she was charging ahead into all this without me. Trista glanced back at the float-driver compartment, then to the sign-up clipboard.

"Now that's a recipe for disaster," Trista said. "The last time I left you two to your own devices, you got yourselves locked in a criminal's basement!" She looked down at her cargo jacket and brushed it off. "Auditions are at noon, you say?"

"Oh, no. I'm not going." I stepped back. "I am not smearing myself with Pretty Perfect make-up and bowing down to Princess Kendra. Ever."

"This isn't about bowing to Princess Kendra, Soph," Grace pleaded. "The whole town's depending on you." She tugged my arm gently. "On us."

"Depending on me to trip in my platform shoes and face-plant in a pile of Festival horse dung in front of the bleachers?" I crossed my arms. Grace shot Trista a helpless look.

Trista shrugged, a smile playing at her lips. "You know, I heard horse poo could be the path to a new you."

Grace's chuckle faded fast. As she looked at me pleadingly, a stream of images tumbled through my head: I imagined Trista botching a covert mission thanks to her inability to either tiptoe or whisper. Grace "accidentally" toppling over a third-story railing and landing in the marble entryway after thinking it was a great idea to confront the murderer with evidence. I saw a target hovering square at the center of Mr. Zimball's head.

I looked down at my nails and pictured them painted candy-apple red. I looked at my feet and tried to imagine wearing heels and not falling down. Then I looked at Grace and Trista. Their faces were hopeful, their eyes desperate. I sighed.

"Okay. Where's that sign-up sheet?"

Chapter Ten

Turning the Page

I wrote my name on the sheet right under the all-caps BOTTOMS Trista had scrawled, adding a heart over my *i* to fit in with all the other sparkly gel-inked names. The next thing I knew, Grace, Trista, and I were in the Ridley Mansion living room for royal-page auditions, drowning in a sea of rustling satin and swoopy updos.

I wouldn't have been surprised to find out every middle-school girl in Luna Vista had packed into that room. Even all the upholstered antique furniture and wood-paneling couldn't absorb the squeally chattering. Flowery hairspray hung so thick in the air you could taste it on your tongue. If someone had lit a match, the whole place would've exploded.

That would have been one way of backing out.

I'd been in the mansion at least a dozen times—for field trips and boring tours with my parents and their out-of-town guests. And I knew, or at least knew *of*, half the girls in the room. Still, I felt like I'd landed on an alien planet. As Grace led us past a group of seventh graders, their eyes flicked up and down my glue-stained jeans and hoodie before traveling over to Trista and the welding helmet she was holding at her side. My former friend Stacy Pedalski was one of them. She shook her head slowly as if we'd violated a sacred law. I couldn't believe she and I had once spent an entire weekend huddling inside a sofa cushion fort, sipping Coke through Red Vines while we watched all eight *Harry Potter* movies.

Grace had tried to snazz up our outfits by raiding the lost and found. Unfortunately, the same scarf that had transformed her into a *Teen Vogue* model had made me look like an accident victim in a neck brace. Trista had refused to even try it on, citing health risks. Something about lost-and-found fungus and the importance of proper airflow for people with allergies. "Besides," she said, flashing jazz hands over the Girl Scout badges sewn on her cargo jacket. "It distracts from my flair."

Meanwhile, Grace had pulled together leggings, a skirt, and cardigan to create a cool vintage style that made her look like she was in high school already. Leave it to her to look fashion-shoot ready in a moldy lost-and-found skirt.

I squared my shoulders and tried to make myself look

taller. "Too bad there weren't any heels in the lost and found," I mumbled.

"You got this, Soph." Grace plucked a stray flower petal from my shoulder and adjusted my pendant. "We're town heroes. We don't have to be perfect."

"We'd have to really mess up for them not to let us in," Trista agreed.

Grace elbowed Trista when she thought I wasn't looking.

"What?" Trista blinked. "Am I wrong?"

My throat went sandpaper dry. I remembered Rod's smile in the float barns when we were joking about trying out for pages. His words echoed in my head: *There's no way you wouldn't get a spot.* I glanced around the living room. Girls eyed us jealously and turned back to their friends, whispering. Every person in that room expected us to coast to victory. I looked up at Grace, hovering a head taller than me, her silky hair tumbling down her back. The judges would pick her in a second. But what about me? I pictured myself standing at the judges' table as they shook their heads at me slowly in perfect imitation of Stacy Pedalski. I could already hear the shocked whispers—could already feel my cheeks blazing red as I insisted that, really, it was no big deal. I hadn't even wanted to audition in the first place.

It turns out there was something worse than being a royal page.

Not being a royal page.

A giggle erupted next to us. It was the twins, Danica and Denise Delgado, who seemed to giggle each time their spaghetti straps slipped off their shoulders—which was roughly every two seconds. I was already practicing in my head how I'd break it to Rod that I was backing out, when I caught sight of Mr. Zimball wandering casually through the room. He smiled broadly as he shook hands, not even a hint of worry clouding his face.

I wiped my sweaty hands on my jeans and stayed put. The man was a sitting duck.

"Welcome, you three!" Mr. Zimball peered down at Trista's welding helmet. "May I, uh, hang that up for you?"

Trista hugged her helmet closer and eyed the crystal chandelier dangling above her head. "It's cool, thanks. Might come in handy."

Mr. Zimball hovered awkwardly for a moment. The way he shifted his weight from foot to foot reminded me of Rod. When a Festival official cruised past with a silver tray, he leaped at the chance to wriggle away. "Well, best of luck to you this afternoon," he said, grabbing a mini egg roll before he strolled off.

"See that? Even the judges are wishing us luck," Grace whispered.

"Well, he should," Trista said, way too loudly. "Considering his life might depend on it."

"Shh!" I hissed. "I'm pretty sure we get disqualified if it sounds like we're threatening to kill judges!" I glanced around to see who might've heard. My blood froze. Lily Lund was lurking outside the open sliding paneled door, eyes locked on us.

"Don't turn now, you two, but look who's in the hall," I whispered.

Trista turned immediately. "Oh, man," she said, as Grace slyly took her own peek. My legs felt shaky as I wondered whether Lily could be scoping out her next target.

"You think Barb's sent her to spy?" Grace whispered.

Before I could answer, Marissa Pritchard appeared in front of us, peering out from under the fringe of her ruler-straight blond bangs. "I think it's awesome you went with a natural look for the auditions, Sophie." Her understanding of *awesome* sounded like it involved mopping up cat vomit.

"Oh no, Marissa!" Lauren Sparrow stopped short on her way to greet a group of girls coming through the doorway. In her bright sundress, she almost could have passed for one of the Court. It was hard to believe that Barb, not she, had once been Queen. She frowned and tapped a spot near the corner of her mouth. "You've got a little something here. Lipstick smudge, maybe?"

Ms. Sparrow swiveled back to us as Marissa furiously rubbed at her cheek. "So glad you all decided to try out," she said with a wink. "We could use some celebrities in the mix!"

Marissa's poufy dress might have actually deflated a little. Grace had to duck her chin into her shoulder to hide her smile.

The Royal Court huddled by a podium set up by the fireplace, nervously adjusting each other's tiaras and smoothing down their dresses. Jardine Thomas sucked in a deep breath, then jingled a tiny brass bell. The buzzing crowd quieted.

"Okay, everyone. Let's get this party started," she said, sounding more like a business official than the newly crowned Sun Queen. Maybe she was trying to play it cool, but her eyes glistened with excitement and her hands were trembling. Sienna and Kendra stood next to her, shoulders thrown back, beaming proudly.

"Today is totally chill," Jardine continued. Sienna and Kendra nodded. "Remember, whether you're chosen as a royal page or not, we're all one big family here at the Festival."

"Totally," Sienna echoed, eyeing Jardine's tiara warily. It definitely looked like it could take another tumble.

"Just relax, mingle, and we'll come around to get to know you better. It's supercasual!" Kendra Pritchard sang out. She whipped out a small notepad and uncapped her pen like she was drawing a sword from a sheath.

Grace, Trista, and I traded looks.

"Supercasual," I whispered. Dread crept through me.

Trista shrugged, gave a small salute, and waded into the crowd. I wouldn't have been surprised if she'd put on her welding helmet and actually flipped down the plastic safety mask first.

Grace squeezed my hand before heading off herself.

The crowd whirled into action as if a stage curtain had risen. Mr. Zimball, Ms. Sparrow, and the Court fanned through the room to evaluate us. I turned to chart my course through the mob and nearly ran smack into Marissa Pritchard. Her lips pulled back in a broad smile.

No doubt about it. This was war.

Before I could slip away from Marissa, Sienna Connors floated over. "Hey, you're Jake's sister, right?" she asked, tossing her light-brown hair over one shoulder. "I have math with him." She let out a goofy laugh that relaxed me, even with Marissa Pritchard hovering at my elbow. Maybe this wouldn't be so bad, after all.

"So, you guys do any sports?"

"Tai chi," I said. "It's a martial art," I added hurriedly.

"Cool," Sienna said. "Your team make it to regionals?"

"It's not really a team sp–" I began. "Um, no," I corrected myself. "Not this year."

"Tai chi?" Marissa's forehead creased. "That's, like, superslow karate?"

I stiffened. "Actually, you can speed up the movements and–"

"That's so cute," Marissa prattled over me. "At the senior home where I volunteer they do tai chi too. And Aqua Zumba, which is like Zumba but, you know, in the pool?"

I stared straight at Sienna in hopes we could both pretend Marissa was a figment of our imaginations. "Soccer players train with tai chi sometimes," I lied. "Quickens the reflexes."

"Yeah?" Sienna repeated, but her eyes had already glazed over.

I grabbed a paper cup of pink lemonade from the tray and downed it in one gulp.

"So, ladies," Ms. Sparrow's voice rang out behind me.

She was talking to Danica and Denise, who I was seriously beginning to suspect were actually conjoined twins. They'd yet to stand more than an inch apart. "Toughest question yet." Her eyes twinkled as she held out a tray of cupcakes. "Vanilla? Or chocolate?"

Danica and Denise looked at each other and giggled. "One of each, please," said Danica.

"We'll share," said Denise as her spaghetti straps fell for the hundredth time.

I held in a sigh and scanned the room for Grace. I was done going it alone. It took me a moment to find her. She blended in almost too well. She was clustered in a group around Jardine Thomas. It looked like any one of them could make the perfect page, right down to their cute shoes. Trista stood a little off to the side. I slipped closer.

"The Festival looks for kids with a unique style. People who aren't afraid to stand out," Jardine said. From the way she was looking at Trista's cargo-jacket Girl Scout getup, I was guessing that wasn't exactly the unique style she had in mind. "But we need practical style, too. Form and function. When you're up on a parade float in front of thousands, beauty emergencies can strike, you know? We need to be ready."

The group murmured as if they'd had years of experience

with parade-float beauty emergencies.

"So. How would you help a Royal Court member accessorize on parade day?" Jardine finished.

Two hands shot up. Jardine called on gorgeous Anna Sayers, whose mom had been an actual model. She had to be one of the likeliest picks for royal page. But Anna flushed red and froze.

The group shifted uncomfortably. Jardine looked ready to end Anna's misery by calling on someone else.

"A backpack!" Anna blurted out at last. "I think it'd be awesome to celebrate Luna Vista as a beach town with maybe a sea-creature backpack? Like, you know, maybe a miniturtle with a hard shell? That flips open and inside has all the essentials?"

Even Trista wrinkled her nose.

"Cool, thanks," Jardine said. She looked around. "Anyone else?"

"With like, maybe really skinny straps, I guess . . . so it doesn't hide your dresses. Or maybe it should be a pelican with a beak that hinges open and it'd be sooo funny. . . ." Anna couldn't help herself. She'd be muttering about sea-creature accessories decades from now, when they wheeled her away to the old folks' home. No amount of words or ideas could save that disaster.

"Maybe something a little, uh, smaller might work?" Grace piped in delicately. She pulled a star-shaped tin of lip gloss from her pocket. "These come in all kinds of shapes. Maybe we can find one like a Coral Beauty rose, drill a hole in it, and put it on a chain. Then it's like a really cool necklace. We could even use root-beer-flavored gloss, for fun!"

Jardine looked seriously impressed. So impressed, in fact, that as the crowd broke up she and some of the others stayed huddled around Grace to chat more as Anna Sayers glowered at everyone. Jardine and her friends checked out the earrings Grace had made out of colored paper clips. Sienna, who'd just joined, snuck out her phone to snap a picture to upload to her feed. Grace tried to look casual as they oohed and ahhed, but she knew she'd rocked it. So did everyone else.

Meanwhile, Kendra Pritchard had cornered Trista—or tried to, anyway. Trista rested one arm on a wing chair casually as she fielded questions in her booming voice. Grace pulled herself away from the earring lovefest long enough to notice. She shot me a nervous look, muttered a quick excuse, and we both made a beeline to make a rescue.

"Okay, Scenario C," Kendra said solemnly, pencil

poised above her notepad. "It's fifteen minutes before the parade starts. The queen has a run in her stocking. What do you do?"

Trista pursed her lips. "Piece of cake. Nylon's a synthetic polymer. Fuse the plastic fibers with low heat. Maybe high-frequency electromagnetic welding, if you've got the equipment." She slapped the top of the helmet she still held at her side. "Then you're good to go."

Kendra squinted. "Welding?"

"Great idea!" Grace chimed in, throwing an arm around Trista. "Wish I were smart enough to think of that."

"Hard to top," I added.

Trista shrugged. "I know."

Kendra looked confused and tucked her notebook away without writing a word. Grace and I both sighed in relief as she moved on to the next cluster of girls. Trista pulled out her phone and sank into the armchair to settle in for another round of TrigForce Five.

"So, Ms. Yang, Ms. Bottoms," I said, holding out an invisible microphone to Grace and Trista as I put on my smoothest pretend middle-aged pageant-judge voice. "What do you think is the most essential quality for a royal page?"

"That's easy," Grace bit her lip mischievously. *"Grace!"*

"Yesss! Nice one." I slapped her five. Trista reached out

for a high five without taking her eyes off her video game.

"Oh shoot!" rang out a cry behind us. It was Jardine. She held up one hand helplessly. "I broke a nail!"

Marissa Pritchard sprang into action before it even dawned on the rest of us that Jardine was testing our royal page-skills. But as she sped to the rescue, her knee bumped the end table by the couch. Marissa turned, horrified, as an expensive-looking porcelain vase on top of it tipped and—after some uncertain wobbling—somersaulted over the edge. As it hurtled toward the hardwood floor, I lunged low into Needle at Sea Bottom, arm extended.

It landed square in my palm with a satisfying slap.

"Tai chi," I explained to an openmouthed Marissa as I set the vase back on the table. "Quickens the reflexes."

"Whoa." Sienna Connors' eyes went wide.

I spun back around and sauntered over to Grace and Trista, who stared at the floor and gulped in deep breaths to keep from laughing out loud.

"Wow, Sophie." Grace locked her eyes on Marissa Pritchard and, raising her voice, added a perfect imitation of Marissa's earlier sneer. "That was *awesome*."

I fought to hide my grin, but it spread across my face like a wave breaking.

As the judges disappeared to make their decision, I slipped to the first floor restroom to splash water on my face and try to calm down. I knew I'd done it. I was in—whether I'd wanted to be or not. The next day I'd be in one of the mansion bedrooms upstairs, unpacking my T-shirts and researching how to remove Royal Court underarm sweat stains from silk.

All while chasing down a murderer.

Piece of cake, as Trista would say.

I zipped up my hoodie, smoothed my hair and was about to head back to the living room when I noticed the row of minibottles of Pretty Perfect moisturizer lined along the counter like soldiers at the ready. I smiled to myself and snatched one up. *Give us ten weeks and we'll take off ten years*, the slogan on the front read. Since I looked about ten, unless it was possible to look zero years old, I'd probably be able to sue them for false advertising. Still, I squirted a little on my hand. It felt so velvety and smooth. *Royal*, I thought to myself as I rubbed it into my cheeks.

I slipped out the door and was sauntering down the hall, imagining my "pretty perfect" glow and smugly replaying Marissa's look of defeat, when I heard hushed voices in the alcove by the back stairway.

I inched closer to hear and peered around the corner.

I could only see who was talking from the knees down, but I immediately recognized the tiny brass buttons with the anchor imprints on the lady's blue shoes. It was Lauren Sparrow.

"Having town heroes as pages in an anniversary year could be really fun. It would be great publicity," Sparrow's cheerful chirp rang out. I knew she'd be pulling for us. That wink after she'd put Marissa in her place hadn't been an eye twitch. "But maybe it's best to have them ride in the lead car instead?" she finished.

I almost tripped over the Oriental rug.

"That's an interesting thought," a deep voice rumbled in reply. It had to be Mr. Zimball.

"Don't get me wrong," Ms. Sparrow continued. "I think they'd be fantastic. Grace Yang's a gem. She'd fit in perfectly. And Sophie and Trista are great kids. It's just . . . I'm worried for them."

Heat prickled across my body. I saw myself in her eyes. My rambling about tai chi. My dirty jeans. My stupid babyish freckles. The way my feet barely touched the floor when I sat in one of those pretty antique chairs with the pale pinstripes. I fixed my eyes on the anchors on Ms. Sparrow's shoe clasps and wished I could sail away someplace where no one could find me.

"I know what you mean, Lauren. Kids can be so cruel, can't they?" Mr. Zimball said, and it felt like I'd been stabbed through the heart. It might as well have been Rod himself agreeing. "I have to admit, I'd thought about it too. They aren't the most, uh, conventional picks."

"On the other hand, I'm positive I could help them along." Ms. Sparrow sounded genuinely concerned, which somehow made me feel doubly worse. "A touch of mascara, some wardrobe changes. Maybe some wedges for Sophie to give her some inches? They're diamonds in the rough, but they could really shine."

"I bet you could work wonders, Lauren. But I agree. We do have to take the other girls' reactions into account." Mr. Zimball sighed heavily.

I couldn't listen to another word. So I couldn't tie a scarf. And I looked terrible in big satiny dresses. But was I really that far from royal-page material? My legs felt like blocks of lead as I forced them down the hall and back to the living room. Heads turned as I slipped through the door, and I was suddenly certain everyone knew exactly why my cheeks were so red. In truth, they were all too busy scrambling for seats to wait for the judges' announcement. Grace was crammed onto the sofa in the center of the room, laughing with Danica and Denise. The brass lamp on the end table reflected a hundred of her smiles back to me. In a minute, all hundred of those smiles would crumble. I turned away.

As Mr. Zimball, Ms. Sparrow, and the Royal Court swept in grinning, Marissa slid to the edge of her seat, no doubt hoping her sister pulled some strings and got her voted on. Grace scanned the room for me, flashing me a secret thumbs-up as soon as she caught my eye. My stomach lurched.

"This was so hard, everyone. You are all such amazing young ladies," Ms. Sparrow said. Her eyes met mine and darted away again. "However, I'm pleased to announce we've made a decision."

Chapter Eleven

(Dis)orientation

When Lauren Sparrow announced that Danica and Denise Delgado were the first new royal pages in the 125th anniversary Winter Sun Festival Royal Court, they jumped up and exchanged some sort of special, crazy twin handshake that—not surprisingly—shook their spaghetti straps loose.

I don't know if it was because their shrieks were so loud or because I was determined to tune out my certain humiliation, but I was still mesmerized by the over-the-top Delgado twin celebration going down when the girl next to me nudged me. "Don't they mean you?" She jerked her head to the front of the room where Grace was already shaking hands with Mr. Zimball and Ms. Sparrow.

As I walked up in a daze, Sienna Connors leaned into

the microphone. "And, lastly . . . uh, Bottoms?" she read, squinting uncertainly.

"That'd be Trista," Lauren Sparrow said with a smile that looked more like a worried cringe. "Trista Bottoms."

As Trista picked up her helmet and marched forward, Marissa heaved a sigh so forceful it might have actually propelled distant sailboats across Luna Vista Bay. "Figures," she hissed.

"We're thrilled to have some true Luna Vista heroes serving our Court this year!" Mr. Zimball added.

"Thanks to all of you for trying out," Jardine said. "This was totally not easy."

"I'd even say it was superhard," Kendra added, shooting her sister a helpless look.

"You were all crazy awesome?" Sienna lied, her voice tilting up. "But let's hear it for our new royal pages!"

Stray raindrops spattering against a window would have been louder than the crowd's applause.

When my family pulled into the Ridley Mansion's long horseshoe-shaped driveway the next morning, the queen and princesses already stood on the terrace steps, the breeze rippling against their skirts as they giggled excitedly and posed for pictures with the tons of high school friends who'd come to see them off.

"I'm so proud of you, Sophie!" my dad said, beaming as my mom pulled our minivan to the curb.

"I always knew we'd see a Young in the Festival one day," Grandpa added with a nod.

My stomach twisted into knots as I spotted Ms. Sparrow walking toward our car, smiling and waving. There were roughly three million things I wanted to do more than get out of that minivan. Eat live worms. Drink rancid milk. Roll in a thicket of poison ivy.

I thought of Mr. Zimball's relaxed, clueless smile and steeled myself. That morning I'd heard my parents talking about how Mr. Lee still hadn't been released from the hospital. They were puzzled about why he wasn't stable yet, but my mom reminded my dad about an AmStar colleague who'd spent three solid days in the hospital when he'd collapsed from dehydration and overwork. I could hardly expect them to jump to theories about slow-acting poison, but still, it reminded me that if a killer really was out there, the adults wouldn't realize anything was wrong until it was too late. I had to go into that mansion.

"You know, I always regretted not trying out for royal pages," my mom said, unbuckling her seat belt and turning around to look at me. A lock of her brown hair fell over her eyes, and she brushed it away again. "My senior year in high school, every single girl chosen for the Court had been a page in middle school. I didn't stand a chance."

Grandpa reached out from the seat next to me and patted my shoulder. "Good tactics, soldier. Leaving your options open."

"Question," Jake piped up from the way back. In one five-minute ride, he'd managed to make the entire van smell like feet. It was a talent of his. "If Sophie's royalty now, does that make me a duke or something?"

"More like a dork," I mumbled.

"Watch it, Soph," My dad twisted around in the passenger seat and looked stern. "You're a role model now."

Jake made a face at me as soon my dad turned away. I smiled a sickly sweet smile that I hoped conveyed I'd be sneaking into his room to de-alphabetize his vinyl record collection the minute I was home—which couldn't be soon enough.

Grandpa slid open the van door and hopped out like he was still a paratrooper dropping behind enemy lines, which is exactly what spilling out onto that mansion driveway in last summer's purple sundress felt like. He wrapped me in a hug that left me smelling like Old Spice. "Remember,

Sophie. *Semper Fidelis*," he said. "Always loyal." Grandpa hadn't been a marine, but his army regiment in the Korean War had had the same motto, and he quoted it a lot. I was a little confused about why he was saying it then, though.

"You bet, Grandpa," I said, playing along. Then he pressed something into my hands. I looked down and felt a little teary. He'd given me the metal dog tags he'd worn in the army.

"I know these will come in handy," he said while my dad looked on doubtfully. "Now knock 'em dead!" Then, perhaps realizing someone had recently literally been knocked dead, he added, "Er, I mean—show 'em what you're made of!"

"Page Young! Welcome to the 125th Royal Court," Ms. Sparrow swept one arm out in greeting. If I hadn't have heard her in the hall after auditions, I never would've known she was worried about me fitting in. "I knew you had great taste," she added with wink, looking down at her own purple sundress.

As she chitchatted with my parents, reassuring them that she'd be staying with us on the mansion premises at all times, Grace and her parents pulled in. I waved, but Grace was sunk low in her seat, as if she were a celebrity hiding from paparazzi. When she finally emerged, she kept her head ducked, eyes darting toward the high schoolers. Dread seeped through me as I tried to figure out what was so off about her. I'd never seen such a strange look on her face. Had she found out something awful about Harrison Lee?

I heard a hiss of tires on pavement and turned to see Trista Bottoms' family humming past in an electric vehicle prototype that they were testing for AmStar. Trista's little sister, Tatiana, practically flew out of the car before they parked, then pirouetted around the Ridley Mansion lawn like she was auditioning for a dance show. Apart from her ripped ballet tutu and sparkly T-shirt, she was a perfect seven-year-old version of Trista's mom, who was tall and willowy and had light-brown skin that was always darker after they came back from vacations visiting her family in Brazil. Trista had her mom's mane of dark-brown curls and complexion, but apart from that she looked exactly like very wide, very white Mr. Bottoms.

I was still trying to read the strange expression on Grace's face when I noticed the Delgado twins spilling out of their family's SUV. Their mom appeared and hovered over them, fixing their already perfect hair while their father strolled over to talk to some Brown Suiters helping with luggage.

I looked over at Grace. She held her arm around her mom's waist like Dr. Yang was a balloon that might drift away and shrink to a speck in the sky. I turned back to my own mom—her blue eyes shining as she helped me wheel my luggage to the steps. A knot swelled in my throat as it hit me: Grace was scared. Maybe she'd crowed about freedom and how perfect it was that our parents were supposed to back off and let us "bond," but she sure didn't feel that way now. And neither did I. I was scared, too. Scared everyone would think I was a loser, like Ms. Sparrow had thought. Scared of spending every minute with all these older girls— these cooler girls who expected us to serve their every need. But it wasn't just that. I hated the idea of being away from my family for a whole weekend. No playing Uno with Grandpa after finishing my homework. No trying to do the crossword puzzle in the morning with my mom. No listening to dad's totally exaggerated stories about work crises. No Jake being Jake. Sure, maybe when he heard I'd made pages he snorted so hard that an actual booger flew out of his nose and onto my shoes, but I was going to miss him and our silly wars over nothing. Smelling his feet was probably a zillion times better than filing down calluses on Kendra's.

Add in the potential for a homicidal maniac to be lurking somewhere in the mansion, and I was already homesick.

"Mom?" I glanced nervously at the high schoolers milling behind us. Jake was joking around with them.

"Yeah?" Her eyes filled with concern.

"This sounds really dumb, but I'm a little scared because—"

"Oh, Soph, you're going to have the time of your life," my mom interrupted with a wave of her hand. "With your best friend? A whole long weekend? Being taken around to fancy events?" Her eyes sparkled. "It's not really just about serving the Court, you know."

She smoothed my hair behind my ear and planted a kiss on my cheek. "You'll be home in no time, sweetie."

Just then I noticed Grace signaling to me. She still looked frightened, but now there was a determined gleam in her eye.

Front steps, she mouthed, jerking her head to the mansion.

Trista caught our eyes from the lawn, where her mom and dad were basically running a professional photo shoot with her and Tati. She quickly said her good-byes, slung her army-green duffel bag onto one shoulder, and marched over, leaving her mom and dad looking a little sniffly as they watched her go.

"Thanks, mom," I said as the rest of my family gathered around for one last farewell. I wanted to give them all big sloppy hugs, but I felt the eyes of all the high schoolers trained on us. It was mortifying enough standing there in my too-small dress that my mom had dug out from deep in my closet. "See you guys at the Festival!" I called out cheerfully and ducked away, following Grace up the steps and joining her behind the pillar right in front of the mansion door.

"What is it?" I whispered, darting a nervous glance toward the Brown Suiter placing a vase of Coral Beauty roses onto the table in the marble entryway.

"We need a plan," she said.

Trista joined us. "So," she said, casually but not at all quietly. "What's first? Need me to monkey with the alarm system? I already know the code: 1890. Year of the Festival's founding. The Brown Suiters have been tossing it around all week like nobody's business."

"Good to know," Grace said. "I'm thinking we hit up Mr. Steptoe's office first."

"Won't that look suspicious?" I asked. "As soon as we get in, we're snooping around the victim's office?"

"Not if we play it right," Grace said. "We have to be on alert for openings. First chance we have, see if you can get some cleaning supplies and meet on the third floor. We'll act like someone asked us to do some tidying up."

"Roger," I said.

Trista looked impressed. "Sounds good. And, just to be clear up front, there's not a chance in the universe I'm going to put on a dress and ride that float on parade day. Like, never. Unless they drug me and tie me to one of those dolphins."

"Don't worry," Grace patted her on the shoulder. "No one will make you."

Heels clip-clopped behind us on the steps. We turned to find Danica and Denise. The three of us stared at them. They stared back just as awkwardly.

"Page Bottoms." Trista broke the silence and extended her hand to the twins.

Denise—I think Denise was the one who always wore pink hair-clips—limply took Trista's hand but looked at her sister as if she were introducing herself to a sea slug.

"Um . . . yeah," Danica said with a giggle. "We know who you guys are."

"Town heroes!" said Denise with forced excitement.

"Yay!" Danica said in a falsetto.

Grace flipped her hair over her shoulders and shot us a look just before Ms. Sparrow floated toward us, smiling. She gestured to the flowers on the table inside the open door. "Such a beautiful arrangement! And Coral Beauties, too. Please thank your parents again," she said to Grace. "I bet they smell as good as they look," she added, sneezing a very cute, polite sneeze that could only have come from her. She turned and clapped her hands to get the crowd's attention.

"Our pages have all arrived and are ready to take on their official Royal Court duties!" she sang out. "Let's give them a warm welcome!"

A loud cheer rose up as everyone on the steps whirled in our direction and applauded. My face flushed. My mom waved and blew a kiss. My grandpa gave a thumbs up. This was it. We were going inside. And I wasn't ready. Not even close.

Ms. Sparrow waved over Kendra, who'd been laughing with a group of her friends as she practiced a parade float wave. "Princess Kendra, will you do the honors of escorting the girls to their rooms and acquainting them with the morning's schedule?"

Kendra's smile collapsed for a second before she pasted it back on. "Sure thing!" she said brightly, but she rolled her eyes at her friends when Ms. Sparrow wasn't looking. There was no way she was over our nudging Marissa out of her rightful place as royal page—and I wasn't sure she ever would be. She came over and let out a heavy sigh, her blond bangs fanning up in its breeze as she clicked past into the mansion and motioned for us follow. I took one last look at my family, swallowed down my fear, then turned and hurried after her.

"Welcome to the Ridley Mansion!" Kendra said breathlessly to Danica and Denise as if we weren't even standing there. As she guided us through the entryway, the dog she had shoved in her purse burst into an ear-splitting yipping. "This is Pookums Pritchard. He's a pure-bred Pomeranian," she announced. It sounded like she was practicing tongue twisters. She plunked the dog onto the marble floor in front of us. "His great-grandfather took Best in Show at Westminster," she added. Pookums immediately started sniffing the floor as if searching for a good place to relieve himself, then gave up, and licked his rear end instead. He wore a pink canvas vest that kind of looked like a tiny life jacket. "You'll be taking care of my Pooky when my royal obligations don't allow me to be the best dog-mother I can be." Kendra pouted as she looked directly at me.

Trista sneezed and fished out her inhaler as Ms. Sparrow breezed past us in the hallway. She called out a bless you and handed Trista a crisp white handkerchief, then bonded with her over the nightmare of having allergies at a flower festival.

As soon as she'd left, Grace looked down at Pookums. "Do they really let you bring a dog—?"

"Pooky's a therapy dog," Kendra snapped. "My emotional state is very fragile right now."

Pookums growled fiercely at an umbrella stand as Kendra opened up the entryway closet. A small safe hung open on a shelf. Her pink manicured fingernails gleamed as she pointed inside. "Phones in here. House rules."

Trista looked like she was handing over her younger sister to a death squad as she watched her phone—and access to TrigForce Five—disappear into the black hole of the safe.

"The Royal Court has a long history. We need to uphold tradition," Kendra said proudly as if she'd been born and raised in the mansion herself. "Your parents have been asked to keep communication to a minimum while you're here. We ask the same of you. Part of the pledge you make as royal pages is to be present for us and for one another at all times. Like family." She shut the safe door and twisted the dial, then shoved her purse at me. It was a good thing I had developed those tai chi reflexes, or it would've dropped on my toes like a bowling bowl. It was about as heavy as one too.

"And we are family. Festival family," she added, giving Danica's shoulder a little squeeze while completely ignoring us. Danica and Denise's eyes were shining in awe.

"Ms. Sparrow has requested the presence of the Court

for our first lessons. You'll report for duty with us in a half hour. In the meantime, let's get you settled," Kendra continued, beaming as she started up the majestic staircase. We followed. "You'll find your schedule in your rooms along with the Royal Court mix-and-match wardrobe binder," she said when we reached the landing. "The outfits are sooo awesome! Study the combinations carefully, so you can put them together right." She paused, and a starry look came over her. When she finally finished imagining herself sashaying down fashion runways in various dresses—or wherever else her mind had wandered—she nodded down the hallway with her chin. "Your rooms are right next to the Queen and Court sitting room," she explained. "Ms. Sparrow will issue you each radio headsets. You are to wear them at all times. You never know when we might need you." She smiled. I pictured flushing my radio down the toilet as soon as Ms. Sparrow issued it to me, then running out the big double doors and all the way home.

"Denise, Danica, and Sophie, the three of you are right in there," she pushed open an ornately carved wooden door. "Trista and Grace, you're next door. Follow me."

Grace and I exchanged a look of terror. We weren't rooming together? The possibility had never even occurred to me. Suddenly it felt like the hallway was closing in on itself. The stripes on the wallpaper blurred. This was awful. This was worse than awful. I watched helplessly as Kendra ushered them down the hall, leaving me with Denise and Danica. They'd never looked more alike than that moment, as they flashed me twin looks that made it clear they, too, assumed I'd be rooming somewhere else. Danica struggled to smile.

"This is so exciting," she said, her voice as forced as her grin. She gripped my hands and gave them a shake that made one of her sundress straps fall. "We're going to be roomies!"

Chapter Twelve

Poise and Posturing

The Ridley Mansion hummed with constant activity that morning. Brown Suiters rushed up and down the grand staircase to and from offices on the third floor. Caterers flitted around bringing coffee and pastries to meetings. Workers tromped across the Oriental rug runners in the long dark hallways, straightening the portraits lining them and tightening loose doorknobs. Tour guides led Luna Vista VIPs through the rooms, entertaining them with colorful stories about the Ridley family past.

"Kendra, screwing in the lightbulb is the Queen Mother wave. You've got to 'wipe the window.' Nice, smooth long strokes," Ms. Sparrow called out as we helped the Royal Court with Walking and Waving, their first lesson of the day. They'd channeled all their excitement that morning into taking Ms. Sparrow's instructions very, very seriously.

"There we go! Excellent!" she exclaimed. "Now hold that smile and let your legs do the walking. Glide with pride." She showed them how it was done, clicking across the floor in cute purple heels that matched her dress.

I'd never realized walking required so much moral support. Granted, I was just happy to be out of the room I was sharing with the twins. Within five minutes, Denise had claimed the bunk beds and filled up the entire dresser with their clothes while Danica had sprayed Axe body spray around the room like she was trying to kill oxygen. *It reminds me of my camp boyfriend*, she'd said, sucking in a deep breath.

Luckily, the foyer smelled of both oxygen and flowers. I gulped in all the breathable air I could before Danica's next Axe-travaganza. I didn't even mind scuffing the Royal Court high heels with sandpaper so they wouldn't slip on the marble staircase. I did mind, though, when all of a sudden Grace became a Court celebrity.

"Oh my god. That is the *best*. I need one of those, like, yesterday," Jardine said, pointing to Grace's messenger bag in the corner. Grace had made it from recycled corduroy pants and jeans, and used a cool old Chinese coin as a button to fasten the flap. The rest of the Court and Danica and Denise were just as into it too. As I watched Grace being pulled into the whirlpool of their circle, I wondered if she would ever get out again—or if she'd want to. Even Ms. Sparrow joined in. "I should hire you to make me something!" she exclaimed, and Grace looked down at Ms. Sparrow's shoes and suggested she make her some tiny Coral Beauty rose button covers out of pink ribbon for parade day.

Things only got worse when, during the water break, they all snapped pictures of each other with the disposable cameras the Festival had given us since we couldn't use our phones, but no one posed with me and Trista. It started to sink in how long three days really could be.

It wasn't until Ms. Sparrow started in on Poise and Posture that I realized I might have worried too soon. "How about Trista, Sophie, and I get some books from the mansion library? You know, for balancing?" Grace asked Ms. Sparrow. She outstretched her arms and pretended to have a stack of books on her head as she walked, then secretly flashed us a look.

"Good idea!" I played along. "They'll be able to really"—I tried to remember the phrase—"glide with pride." Ms. Sparrow had barely agreed and pointed the way before we'd grabbed Trista and headed down the hall.

The smell of musty paper and polished wood greeted us as we stepped inside the library and shut the heavy paneled door. Bookshelves rose almost all the way to the room's high ceiling. Leather armchairs were nestled into reading nooks, and a few dark wood study tables were set up around the room. Grace plunked her messenger bag down on one of them and flapped it open. "Last night I downloaded these layouts of the mansion interior from the Luna Vista Historical Society website," she said, pulling out several printouts. "I mean, we know the basics—but this has everything." She darted a glance to the door, then, for cover, grabbed some books from the shelves and laid down the plans on their pages. "We're staying here, on the second floor." She tapped the paper. Certain rooms were labeled with letters in brightly colored marker in what seemed to be some kind of a code. "All the VIPs' offices are one level up. Except Sparrow. Looks like she's got an office off her bedroom suite down the hall from us."

"What's with the letters?" Trista frowned.

Grace pulled out three small index cards. "So, Sophie was telling me about this cool code," she began. I beamed. If I'd had any doubts about why she'd been so into us being pages, they were gone now. "It's like Morse, but better than Morse . . . ," she said, smiling knowingly at me as she echoed my exact words in the float barn.

". . . Because not many people know about it," I finished.

"It's called a Polybius code or cipher. Prisoners used it in the olden days." I pointed to the square on the index card Grace had handed me.

	1	2	3	4	5
1	A	B	C	D	E
2	F	G	H	I/J	K
3	L	M	N	O	P
4	Q	R	S	T	U
5	V	W	X	Y	Z

"Let's say you have an emergency and need to send an SOS," I continued. "You find *S* on the grid—it's at row four across, three down." I tapped one of the books four times, paused, and hit it rapidly three more times. I think it was the first time I'd ever had to explain anything to Trista.

Grace's hair fell over her radio headset as she leaned forward. "You have to pause longer between letters so it's not confusing," she explained to Trista. "So before tapping out the numbers for *O*, you'd wait a few beats."

"Got it," Trista said, almost impatiently. She quickly rapped out the three across, four down pattern for *O*, waited a long second, then tapped out *S* just like I had. "Guess you can signal with a flashlight like Morse too, huh?"

"Yep. Anything," Grace replied. "Honking. Clicking.

Whistling." She pointed to the letters on the layout. "I made letter codes for places in the mansion and the grounds so we can call meeting spots over the radio. And I listed the codes on the back of the card." She flipped one of them over proudly.

Trista nodded, impressed. "So, let's see . . . *RG* stands for Rose Garden, that'd be—"

The door to the library burst open just as Trista was making extremely loud fake beeping sounds with her mouth. Danica and Denise stared back.

"Um . . ." Danica looked at her sister.

"You caught us!" Grace smiled so wide I thought she might sprain her lips. "Playing spy games, again." She pretended to roll her eyes at her own silliness. "You guys want a secret code map?" She picked up one of the printouts.

I leaned my mouth closer to the mike of my radio headset clipped onto my shirt. "Roger, wilco two-two-four-ten-twenty-one. We've got intruders. Twelve o'clock. Do you copy?"

"Whoa," Denise said. "You're really into this."

Grace shrugged. "Passes the time."

"Ten-four," barked Trista.

Danica nodded slowly. "Well, uh, ten-four, one-niner, whatever . . . You might want to actually turn those radios on? Ms. Sparrow was wondering what held you all up."

Danica and Denise barely had a chance to close the door before the three of us practically fell on the carpet laughing. "Close call, team," Grace said.

I slapped them both five. "Over and *out*."

A half hour later, I was upstairs in the royal suite, struggling to figure out which color codes went with the outfits detailed in the Royal Court mix-and-match wardrobe binder. Next to me Trista was already elbow-deep in Jardine's closet, hangers screeching as she flipped through dresses like a department store saleslady during prom season. At least I was faster than Danica and Denise, who stopped every other minute to hold up dresses and twirl for each other.

Trista had just finished whipping Jardine's closet into shape and was jumping in to help me when static crackled over our headsets in a clear pattern. I slipped the index card from my back pocket and sneaked a look as I listened. *Psht-Psht-Psht-Psht* came four rapid bursts, then a pause, then three more. *S* for Steptoe's office. Time to put our plan in action.

As Danica and Denise started oohing and ahhing over outfits again, I made eye contact with Trista and excused myself to the restroom. Trista gave a single nod and turned back to Kendra's closet, hangers jangling and screeching again as she flipped through them double-time.

I grabbed a roll of paper towels from the bathroom off the Queen and Court sitting room and headed to the third floor. Grace was at the top of the landing, pretending to dust a glass case displaying past Royal Court tiaras and dried bouquets. A spray bottle of window cleaner hung from her belt.

"Trista's coming." I held up the paper towels and shrugged. "This is all I could find for cover."

"That'll work." Grace tucked her feather duster into her belt next to the spray bottle, then set one of the vintage watches she wore on her wrist—the digital one. "There's a huge Festival meeting in the living room—all the officials. We should have enough time. Etiquette doesn't start for twenty minutes. "

I cocked an eyebrow. "Twenty minutes Festival time?"

"Uh," Grace's watch chirped as she reset it. "Make that fifteen."

"You sure we're alone up here?" I peered down the long hallway.

Grace twisted her ponytail into a messy bun and checked herself out in the display case reflection. "Don't worry," she said.

I worried. I worried a lot. Officials had been dashing up and down the stairs all day. Electricians rattled around with their stepladders, checking light fixtures. And every time I passed a window, it felt like I was jumping at yet another silhouette of a window washer. The last thing we needed was for someone to catch us on our very first mission.

A clattering on the stairs interrupted us, followed by a grunt and muttered curse. Grace's mouth fell open as Trista rounded the corner battling with the hose of a vacuum cleaner as if she were in a fight for her life with a boa constrictor. She'd strapped the vacuum canister to her back like a leaf blower, and a dust mask hung from her neck.

"All set!" she boomed. "You think you're going to need me to pick the lock?"

We cringed. She might as well have yelled directly into Barb's megaphone.

"Nah, we're probably fine," Grace whispered back. She hesitated a moment—probably weighing the risk of telling Trista to bring it down a notch or five—then leaned out to look down the long carpeted hall. "Coast looks clear. Let's go!"

She darted forward like a cat, slowing at each open office door then jetting past it. There wasn't much point. With Trista's vacuum rattling the whole way down the hall, we might as well have been trying to spy with a one-man band trailing behind. Grace shot us irritated looks, but she kept going.

Finally, we stood in front of the thick paneled door of Mr. Steptoe's former office. Engraved letters on a brass plaque greeted us: Festival President.

Grace swallowed hard and looked at Trista and me. "Ready?" she whispered.

We nodded.

"Okay. One, two—" Grace reached for the knob. The door swung open first. "—three," she finished faintly as her head tilted up to the figure in front of us.

Chapter Thirteen

Otter Beware

Principal Katz stared back at us, dazed.

A minimum of seven centuries passed before any of us spoke.

"Just clearing out some things I left behind," Katz said. He tightened his grip on the white file box he carried and smiled at us like my dad smiles at our neighbor's Rottweiler. Next to me, Grace stiffened.

"Ms. Sparrow sent us to do some cleaning up," she said, eyeing the glass paperweight poking out of the open box. "And to see if you needed any help?"

Mr. Katz looked even more startled. It was hard to believe this was the same man who'd once glared over his glasses at me from behind the principal's desk at Luna Vista Middle School. "Why that's, uh, awfully nice of her. I didn't realize"—his face turned a blotchy, sunburned pink—"but no, thanks, I've got it covered." He pivoted and scooted down the hall. If he'd had a tail to tuck between the legs of his brown polyester suit pants, he would've.

The three of us traded looks.

Grace folded her arms. "He was demoted two weeks ago, at least. What's he doing clearing out things *now*? Looks a lot like someone removing evidence from a crime scene to me."

Trista nodded toward the wide-open office door. "Guess I won't need to pick the lock?"

"Or remove any police tape," I pointed out, my stomach hollowing. If police were secretly investigating, the last thing they'd want was people cruising in and out of the victim's office whenever they liked. That could only mean one thing: they weren't.

"C'mon!" Grace's bun shook loose as she charged ahead. "We don't have much time."

A hush fell over us as we entered the office. A triangle of sun blazed through the gap in the beige linen drapes, lighting up dust motes like an old-time movie projector. The off-white walls looked anything but inspiring without Mr. Katz's framed posters of golf courses and rainbows. There was even something a little bit creepy about the tiny nails still jutting out of the wall where'd they once hung.

Mr. Steptoe's desk looked bare without him sitting at it,

even though it was lined with various trinkets and souvenirs. A calendar counting down to the Festival leaned next to several framed photos. One was of Rod and his family standing with him in front of the Luna Vista Aquarium. As a bachelor without kids of his own, Mr. Steptoe probably thought of the Zimballs as family, I realized.

Grace dragged Mr. Steptoe's black swivel chair over to block the door, then tossed us pairs of the latex gloves she'd stolen from the beauty closet in the Royal Court sitting room. "People wear them for dyeing hair," she explained. "But they'll keep us from leaving prints."

Trista winced as she snapped on her gloves. "One size fits all: greatest myth of the twenty-first century," she said with a snort.

"Right next to 'flesh colored,'" Grace held up her own hand. Next to her skin, it was Mickey Mouse–glove white.

"Tell me about it," Trista rolled her eyes, then headed for Steptoe's computer. "Password hack might be tough," she said.

"Then again . . ." I pointed. One shelf of the bookcase behind the desk was practically a shrine to sea otters—including sea otter salt and pepper shakers, a sea otter snow globe, a small stuffed sea otter wearing a T-shirt that read "Otterly Awesome." "We *otter* be able to make an educated guess."

Grace giggled. "No kidding. The man loved his puns. This otter do it?" She held up the keyboard and tapped a Post-it note taped under it. "UnderTheSea-Sixty-Three," she read out. "Right where my parents keep theirs."

Trista rolled her eyes. "You guys ever wonder how adults even survive, let alone run the country?" The keyboard clattered as her fingers flew across it.

"All. The. Time." Grace sighed.

I leaned down to pick up a pink piece of paper that'd fluttered to the floor when Grace had flipped the keyboard over. *Miyamoto Jewelers*, read the fancy lettering across the top. *Fine Craftsmanship since 1913.*

I froze.

"Are you okay, Soph?" Grace frowned and leaned over my shoulder. "Oh, wow." She tapped the paper. It was a delivery receipt—the delivery receipt—for the official tiara of the 125th Winter Sun Festival. "Time stamped 10:45 p.m. That means he died sometime between then and the next morning. Good find."

I pictured the tiara spiraling into view in its velvet display case, its rose insignia filling the giant outdoor screens—Harrison Lee, all choked up, announcing it as "Jim's final gift to us all." Locking that tiara into its secret compartment had probably been one of the last things Mr.

Steptoe had ever done. I stared at his spindly signature at the bottom of the receipt until it blurred.

"Whoever delivered that tiara was one of the last people to see him alive," I said.

"If not the last," Grace said. She held out an open Ziploc bag for me to drop it in. "Any record of who delivered it?"

I shook my head. "Shouldn't be too hard to figure out, though."

"Whoa," Trista interrupted. She shook her head at the computer screen and let out a low whistle. "Check it out."

Grace and I leaned in to look. On the screen was a picture of a puppy and kitten curled up together, followed by a poem about enjoying life to the fullest that actually rhymed *sweet* with *feet*. The email asked Mr. Steptoe to forward the message to nine animal lovers, then, in case he needed extra encouragement, detailed all the horrible tragedies that struck people who didn't. Freak accidents involving Ferris wheels, barbecues, corn threshers, mountain ledges . . .

Everything but death by giant marshmallow, basically.

Grace covered her mouth in horror. "That's it. I'm forwarding every chain email to everyone ever, forever. And ever."

"Me too," I said. "Twice."

"That's the sad thing." Trista pointed to the screen.

"Dude actually forwarded it."

"No!" Grace gasped.

Trista sighed wearily. "The outbox doesn't lie."

We observed a moment of silence at the unfairness of it all.

"Well." Grace spoke at last. "What else have we got?" She ran her finger down the list of sender names in Steptoe's inbox. "Spam, spam, World Wildlife Foundation . . . oh, hey, Harrison Lee? Click on that."

I skimmed quickly over her shoulder. The email seemed to involve something about Festival money and was cc'ed to Mr. Zimball:

Hey, Jimmy,

I'll have the expense spreadsheet ready for you by Friday. The account's looking low, but no worries. We have plenty to cover budget. Just a temporary issue. Thanks for your offer to take over bookkeeping given everything I'm balancing at work. I'll let you know if it gets to be too much, but I've got it under control. Quick coffee meeting Fri. at 9?

—Harrison

"Talk about shady," Trista said. "He's all, 'There's no money in the account. But, no worries, I don't need any help!'"

Grace and I both glanced to the door. Trista's imitation of Harrison Lee's booming voice was more booming than any spy's ever should be. My skin crawled remembering that—at any moment—the murderer could burst in and find us snooping.

Grace lowered her voice to a whisper. "Classic. Business-man gets caught stealing, then kills to keep the secret." She nodded.

"An even better motive to kill than being Festival Presi-dent," Trista added, completely ignoring Grace's volume cue. "Two get-rich-quick schemes in one."

"It's like the plot of every cop show I've ever watched with Grandpa Young," I said, but in my head I pictured Lee on the stretcher at the Beach Ball, his face racked with pain.

"There's just one thing. He can't be the killer *and* a vic-tim."

Trista's mouth twisted as she thought about that. "Unless he's faking. If the police are still investigating, you know who they wouldn't suspect? A victim."

We looked at each other. A shiver tingled across my back. It was possible. "He's also the only one who knew there was a chance the police were going to investigate this as murder," I said, picturing him call out to Officer Grady all buddy-buddy, trying to convince him to speed things along. Then I shoved the thought away again. "Or . . . ," I added, "he did really collapse from dehydration and stress."

Grace raised an eyebrow. "Know what's stressful? Murdering someone!"

It seemed just crazy enough to be true. After all, it wasn't like Harrison Lee was some hardened criminal. He was a man with a used car business and screaming loud plaid pants who'd maybe gotten himself into some deep water. Or shallow soup, as the case was.

Trista turned back to Mr. Steptoe's inbox and groaned. "We need to search these emails for keywords or something. There's too much."

"Maybe his web search history has some clues?" I offered.

"Good thought," Grace said.

Sadly we found nothing but some links he'd followed to videos of seals and sea lions frolicking in the ocean. His desk drawers didn't turn up anything, either, except that he, too, must've been hoping for a little Pretty Perfect magic to make his wrinkles disappear. He'd stocked up on three different kinds of moisturizer.

"Guess that was kind of a waste." Trista sighed, and I wasn't sure if she was referring to the search or to Mr. Steptoe's skin-care regimen. I suppose both were true.

Grace popped open one of the jars of moisturizer and rubbed it into her cheeks, using Mr. Steptoe's magnetic paperclip holder as a mirror. "Isn't it nice when a man really cares about his appearance?" she asked, looking at me pointedly.

"You know Jake slathers his hair in gel instead of washing it, right?"

Grace shook her head at me sadly. "You just don't understand him," she said, sighing.

"All right, all right," Trista said. "I think we should get back—"

"Wait a minute," I interrupted. "Remember how you joked about how Ms. Sparrow would probably slick down Mr. Steptoe's hair every day if they were an item?"

Grace squinted. "Yeah. . . ."

I pointed to the jar she was holding. "Would she also want to make sure his skin was nice and soft?"

Grace's eyes lit up. "Oh my gosh, Soph, you're right. Lovers after all, you think?"

Trista pursed her lips and nodded. "Could be."

We jumped as the radio suddenly squawked with feed-back.

"Princess down! We've got a princess down! Code Red!" The voice squealing through the static was unmistakably Kendra Pritchard's. "Pages! Emergency! Report to the front foyer immediately! Bring the first aid kit!" Kendra's voice blasted over the radio again.

"Uh-oh," I said, grabbing the paper towel roll and delivery receipt before turning to the door.

"Bring your tweezers." Trista sighed and rolled her eyes. "She's probably got a splinter in her pinkie."

"Quick," Grace whispered to Trista. "Print out everything in Steptoe's mailbox from at least the last couple days."

"Hang on." I shoved paper in the tray. "Okay, go for it."

As the printer hummed into action, Lauren Sparrow's calm voice floated through our headsets. "Just need some ice, pages. Maybe an ankle-wrap. Kendra took a little spill, that's all. Those high heels are tricky!"

I rolled my eyes. "Leave it to Kendra to report her own 'emergency.'"

"A walking emergency," Trista said. "Let's think about that a minute."

I reached for my radio mike.

"Hold up!" Grace interrupted. "Let Danica and Denise

answer first. It'll buy us some time."

"Oh, man," I said, catching sight of the next page the printer spit into the tray. My heart started to race.

Grace grabbed it. Her face turned two shades lighter. "Oh, man, is right."

"What?" Trista leaned over our shoulders.

The subject line stared back at us in bold all caps:

YOU ARE DEAD . . . !

The hairs on my arms lifted.

"Barbara Lund, four oh seven p.m.," Trista read aloud. She fumbled for her inhaler and drew in a long breath.

Grace looked back at us, eyes wide. "I think we know where to find our murderer."

I gulped. "Let's hope she doesn't find us first."

Chapter Fourteen

Stepping on Toes

We turned to leave but a loud rap on the door stopped us cold. Grace's hand flew to her mouth as Mr. Steptoe's swivel chair creaked forward.

"Who's in there?" a deep voice rumbled.

Grace and I whirled to each other in panic. Trista ducked down, flicked on her Dirt Devil, and hoisted it onto her back. As the vacuum roared to life, Grace tossed me the feather duster we'd left on the desk and whipped out her Windex bottle like a gun from a holster. I grabbed all the emails from the tray, folded them lengthwise, and stuffed them in my back pocket as she raced to the door. She opened it only the tiniest crack and peered out like a suspicious old lady eyeing a door-to-door salesman. "Oh, excuse me, Mr. Zimball!" she said. "We're doing some cleaning up." She pushed Mr. Steptoe's swivel chair aside, pretending it weighed roughly the same as a midsize sedan.

Mr. Zimball stepped inside. He blinked, bewildered. Trista's vacuum howled. It was loud. Indy 500 loud. That is, if the Indy 500 was raced by portable vacuums.

I picked up a ceramic sea otter and dusted it so intensely that actual feathers started to shake loose from my duster.

Mr. Zimball cupped his hand next to his mouth. "Ms. Sparrow and the Court are looking for you!" he called out.

The vacuum shifted into an even higher whine as Trista, back still to the door, leaned over to clean the underside of the couch cushions.

"Pardon me?" Grace shouted.

"I SAID," Rod's dad yelled, "MS. SPARROW AND THE COURT . . ."

At that moment Trista pretended to finally notice we weren't alone. She spun around, her dust mask covering the lower half of her face. Her vacuum whimpered slowly to silence just as Mr. Zimball finished his sentence: ". . . ARE LOOKING FOR YOU!" He blushed as his voice echoed against the blank walls. "They're downstairs," he added quietly.

I made a big show of pulling out my radio earpiece and shaking it. "Did they radio? We didn't hear it."

"MUST'VE BEEN TOO LOUD!" Trista shouted as if the

vacuum was still roaring. She held up the hose, in case he missed the point.

"Right, well . . . ," Mr. Zimball said. His eyes traveled to Mr. Steptoe's desk, taking in the framed photos, the calendar, the dolphin-shaped pencil holder. I could feel the sadness rolling over him. He looked away again and cleared his throat. "This area's closed."

❧ ❧ ❧

The stolen emails in my back pocket rustled against my shirt as we followed Mr. Zimball downstairs. The halls buzzed with other Brown Suiters hustling back to their offices after their morning meeting. They nodded respectfully to Mr. Zimball as we passed, and I felt doubly awful for lying to him—even if it was for his own protection.

We put away our cleaning supplies then followed the sound of the Court's voices in the living room.

"Are they"—Grace knitted her eyebrows—"singing?" she asked, as if not quite sure if they might be meowing instead.

They were singing. Chanting, really. Their voices became clearer as we walked down the hall.

"Handle in your hand and your fingers on top! Handle in your hand and your fingers on top!" they called out, and I half-feared that we'd round the corner to the dining room and stumble upon some sort of ritual sacrifice.

Instead we discovered the Court around a table loaded with enough silverware to sink a schooner. They gripped their forks awkwardly, as if using never-before-seen tools from an ancient civilization.

Ms. Sparrow laughed and flipped her hair over her shoulder. "I know it's silly, but the song totally works. Right? Now loosen those death grips, and keep those forks from clanking."

Kendra Pritchard sat sulking at the opposite end of the table with her leg propped up on a chair. She winced melodramatically as Danica pressed a bag of frozen peas to her hurt ankle.

"Oh, pages!" Ms. Sparrow waved us in. "You're just in time."

Her friendliness caught me off guard. If Barb were in charge of the Royal Court, we'd be listening to a lecture about respect and how Kendra's leg was going to have to be amputated because we hadn't arrived in time. Of course, it would have probably been delivered with a lot of weird slang, bowing and curtseying, and proper royal-addressing. No matter how she felt about Lily not being chosen as Sun Queen, I was pretty sure that Barb was still dedicated to Festival tradition.

"We're learning how to eat," Sienna added, smiling

goofily as she lifted her fork.

"And you all thought you already knew how," Ms. Sparrow gave a sideways smile.

"Now the real challenge," Ms. Sparrow said, eyes twinkling. "Meatball subs without licking your fingers or smearing your lipstick! Pages? Can you bring the sandwiches in from the kitchen for your princesses? Don't forget a big stack of napkins."

"The vegan one is mine," Jardine warned with a glare. Her tone made me wonder if certain vegans were actually totally fine with murder.

We served the sandwiches, and on the way back to the kitchen to eat our own lunches with Danica and Denise, Grace ducked into the pantry. "We could use a little reorganizing in here, don't you think?" she shouted to me and Trista.

"Looks fine to me," Trista said.

"What a mess!" I called out at the same time, shoving Trista inside and pulling the door shut.

"Ow. Hey!" she called out. "What do you think you're—? Oh, right, sorry," she added as I pulled Barb Lund's email out of my back pocket and held it up.

Grace took it from me and began to read aloud. "'You are dead . . . wrong if you think you can drive me out.'"

I breathed a sigh of relief, the pantry's smell of tea and

spices calming me. "Thank God. Just a figure of speech."

"'You ruined Lily's life over this—I will ruin yours,'" Grace continued in a whisper, stiffening. "What is it they say? Eye for an eye.'"

"Some figure of speech," Trista rasped. I felt the blood rush from my face. Hesitantly, we leaned over Grace's shoulder as she read the rest. Filled with mistakes and those same weird abbreviations my mom texts when she thinks she's being cool, the email looked like it had been typed on a smart phone and sounded more like an angry kid's:

To: Jim Steptoe <jimsteptoe@wintersunfestival.org>

From: barbararlund@wintersunfestival.org

Subject: YOU ARE DEAD . . . !

. . . wrong if u think u can drive me out. You ruined Lily's life over this—I will ruin yours. What is it they say? Eye for an eye. You sure have the right name cuz I am tired of u stepping on my toes. Ive shut up and just taken it until today because Lily deserved her shot at being Queen, but now it doesn't matter does it? You all have taken care of that.

Ive done this for 22 years now and never had any problem and I have kept things on schedule and everyone always thinks my floats are the best and now u come along, and its change this, change that, its not safe like this, it needs to be like that? Well, its going to take alot more to make me quit. I swear on my Ridley ancestors grave that you will not live to see that day.

U say its time for me to go, I say its time for YOU to go! And u will, mark my words.

We looked at each other for several long seconds. Hands shaking, Grace folded the email and gave it back to me.

"'You will not live to see that day . . . ,'" I repeated hoarsely.

"'I've shut up and just taken it,'" Grace quoted. She bit her lip. "When Lily wasn't queen, that was the final straw. She snapped and . . ." She made a slitting sound effect as she dragged her finger across her neck.

"Would she be stupid enough to send this first, though?" My voice shook almost as much as Grace's hands had when she had handed me the email.

"She did make it to middle age without knowing 'a lot'

is two words," Trista pointed out.

"My mom says they didn't teach grammar and spelling in the eighties." Grace said matter-of-factly. "Not that I'm arguing."

"Sure looks like she wrote it fast, at any rate," I said. The email crinkled as I stuffed it back into my pocket. "A death threat. Hours before he shows up dead. If we hand this over to the police, they'll have to look into it."

"Just like they had to conduct a really long, detailed murder investigation?" Grace shot back sarcastically.

Just then the door creaked open.

Grace lunged for the shelves and started rearranging soup cans. I turned and nearly cried out. Lily Lund stood in the doorway.

Grace dropped a soup can with a thud. My stomach lurched to the floor with it. How much had she heard? I put my hands behind my back and shoved the email deeper in my pocket.

"Found them!" Lily called back to someone, and a sudden image of Barb lurking behind the corner wielding an ax flashed in my mind until I heard Danica and Denise's voices in the kitchen.

"My mom specially requested you three to come help in the float barn," she said. Her eyes looked big behind her dark-framed glasses. Her bangs weren't curled, for once.

We all watched as the soup can started a slow roll toward her, wobbling across the hardwood like a badly thrown bowling ball.

She frowned at us. "Is something wrong?"

"Nope!" Trista cried out.

"Sounds fun," I said, trying to smile though my heart was about to rip through my chest. "But, uh, you know"—I shrugged and gestured to the pantry—"We have our page duties."

"Ms. Sparrow gave the okay. So, come down?" She stopped the can with her foot and handed it to Grace. "I mean, when you're done here." She looked around at the perfectly ordered shelves.

"Sure, we'll be right there," Grace said, her voice shaky.

As soon as Lily left, I shut the door and leaned up against it, breathing so hard it felt like my lungs were collapsing. Trista held out her asthma inhaler helpfully. I waved it away. "I'm all right," I wheezed.

"It's just a coincidence," Grace said. She muttered it to herself two more times, as if that would somehow make it true.

Chapter Fifteen

Staying Chill

When Barb Lund greeted us in front of the Root Beer float, she didn't cross her arms and glare. She didn't snap her gum. It was far worse than we ever could have imagined.

She smiled.

I almost screamed and ran.

"Page Young, Page Yang, Page Bottoms." Lund bowed her head in greeting as she addressed each of us individually. I swear she curtsied. She wiped her hands on her flower-stained overalls, carefully avoiding the Winnie the Pooh patch on the front, then turned to Lily, who was standing next to her with her eyes fixed firmly to the floor. "Talk about the bomb dot com! Now they can help out the *real* Festival royalty, right?" She patted Lily on the shoulder and smiled. "Okay, first things first." She gestured to our headset radios as Lily reached out a Tupperware container. "Let's get those buggers in here. Don't want them to get damaged in the petal dust."

We reluctantly dropped them in. As Lily stared at us and sealed the lid with a *thwomp*, the air rushed out of my lungs, too.

"What's with the long faces? We're here to have fun," Barb smiled, exposing a row of teeth that were as tiny as they were terrifying. "Great-Great Grandpa R's got some gigantamundo holes in his britches." She jerked her head to the towering half-decorated figure of Willard Ridley on the Root Beer float. "As if he hasn't had to suffer enough indignities this Festival!" Her mouth curled into a sharp frown as she looked over her shoulder in the general direction of the mansion. "Anywho, better cover those up with some straw-flower before it gets too breezy in those unmentionables." She shoved a cardboard flat at me.

I looked around the float barn, dazed. If it weren't for the small detail that a potential killer had asked us report to her, it actually might have felt fun to be back. Shouts echoed in the rafters as volunteers scrambled to their decorating stations, trying to fill in the last of the dry petal-and-seed color-base before the fresh flowers would be put on. Another of Barb's crazy eighties songs was blasting. It encouraged everyone to "shake their bodies and do the conga."

I didn't know what the conga was, but I was pretty sure Barb Lund couldn't murder us to those crazy beats, right there in front of everyone.

Could she?

"Watch your step," Grace muttered as we headed down the main aisle of the float barn. "We might be accident prone, if you catch my drift."

The skin on the back of my neck prickled. I turned and glimpsed Lily lingering not far behind us.

"I can't believe how friendly Lund's being," I whispered. "So creepy. She knows we know, doesn't she? She's acting nice to fake us out."

"Could be. But don't forget. We're royalty to her," Trista reminded. "This is a woman with a collection of dried flowers from every Sun Queen's bouquet from the last twenty years. She's going to show her respect and curtsey to royalty no matter how mad she is. And judging from that crack about 'real royalty,' she definitely still is."

"She should show her respect by dialing down that slang a notch," Grace mumbled.

"I guess she couldn't already know we're onto her, anyway. I mean, she requested us *before* Lily could have overheard something," I pointed out.

"But our last-minute sign-ups for royal pages might have tipped her off. Pretty suspicious," Grace said.

"Chill, people," Trista said. "It really might be a coincidence she asked for us."

"I guess we'll see," Grace said ominously.

I looked up, praying sudden death wasn't in our future, when I caught sight of Rod three levels above the warehouse floor, gluing onion seed onto one of the ten black sheep enjoying the fake Ferris wheel on the Sheep Family Thrills float. My heart skipped. He spotted us, waved, and started climbing down.

Grace smiled knowingly and bumped her shoulder against mine. "We'll give you two some privacy. Right, Trista?"

"Sure." Trista shrugged and strode toward the storage bins at the back of the warehouse.

Rod swung down from the scaffolding, his sneakers squeaking as he landed off balance. It still sort of seemed like a superhero move to me.

"How's it going?" he asked, his eyebrows tilting toward each other hopefully. I couldn't help but notice that they made the cutest indentation in his forehead. It matched his dimple.

"Great," I said, feeling the email in my pocket and

wondering if I should tell him.

"Cool." He flashed a sideways smile. "Haven't had to wear your skirt yet?"

I slapped my hands on my jeans and grinned. "Sticking with these."

He laughed. "Nice! So . . ." His eyes darted around the float barn, then he leaned in. For a panicked second I thought he was going to kiss me. It didn't matter how crazy a thought that was; the entire surface of my skin felt like it was bursting into flames. I must've turned redder than the cherry on top of the float's sundae.

"Um. Are you okay?"

I mopped my completely dry forehead with my sleeve. "It's really hot out, isn't it?" Unless someone developed a cure for massive full-body blushing by our wedding in 2027, Rod and I were definitely going to have to skip the kiss in front of everyone.

"No kidding. They're, like, breaking child labor laws having us volunteer today." Then he added, quietly. "Hey, so. You haven't seen anything strange, have you? My dad thinks it's dumb for me to worry that he's in charge now, but . . ."

"I know," I said, glancing toward Grace. She and Trista were handing up boxes of chopped red strawflower petals to an assembly line of volunteers filling in Willard Ridley's pants. "Listen . . ." I hesitated, knowing I'd never be able to take my words back. "We're scared too," I finally said. "And I think we've found something really important."

"Seriously?" The crease in Rod's forehead deepened.

I nodded. "We have to talk."

Just then Barb Lund's voice blared from behind us. "Hear ye, hear ye! Royal pages!" She made a fake heralding trumpet sound into her megaphone. From across the room, Trista shot me an I-told-you-so look. "May I request the favor of your presence?" Lund squawked.

I shuddered, desperately wishing for a taste of the gruff, command-barking Ms. Lund who I knew and—well, didn't love, exactly—but who I was at least a hundred times less terrified of. She strode toward Grace. "We need a quick supply run," she said.

Rod's face fell. "Wait, Sophie." His voice was low and urgent. "Don't go yet."

Ms. Lund's gaze locked on me. She held up her megaphone and whooped its siren twice. "Page Young?"

I looked Rod helplessly. "Meet you by the port-a-potties in ten?"

I cringed. Leave it to me to suggest meeting at toilets

when a gorgeous rose garden was a few steps away.

"Uh, okay?" Rod squinted. "I'll bring the air freshener?"

❧ ❧ ❧

Barb and Lily sent us with a list to the old refrigerated cargo container the Festival used for extra flower storage. It was far down the path, past the herb garden and the tennis courts. The sun beat down. I fanned my T-shirt to get a little air, wishing there was more of a breeze from the ocean that stretched beyond the jagged bluffs down the hill in the distance. "Is it me, or is she now talking to us all British, too? I mean, 'Request the favor of our presence?'" I said. "I guess she really is just into this royalty stuff."

"She thinks we're dumb enough to relax if she's all polite," Grace said darkly, her Converse slapping on the path as she strode ahead.

"Well, whatever it is, we're not relaxing, are we?" Trista said. She sneezed a sneeze that sounded like a lion roaring. "Man! This better be the last run before we go back to the Mansion. If she doesn't kill us, this pollen will. I didn't think I'd need to take my allergy meds this morning."

Grace glanced nervously over her shoulder. "Watch your backs. They didn't have to send us all the way down here. The tents still look fully stocked," she said, her voice

173 ❧

swallowed by the noisy hum of a generator set up to run the air-conditioned white tents on the lawn outside the float barn where a lot of the flowers were kept.

My legs felt shaky as we headed farther down the path. The mansion was barely in view anymore when we reached the refrigerated compartment. Trista heaved open its door and hooked it in place. As we stepped inside, Grace lifted up her arms and spun around to drink up the chilled air.

"Ahhh . . . coolth."

"And serious flower power," Trista said, rubbing her watering eyes. Flowers burst from every shelf and corner. The sickly sweet smell made me dizzy. It reminded me of the time I rode twenty-six floors up in an elevator next to a lady who smelled like she'd spent the last two weeks snorkeling in a vat of my grandma's perfume.

"Sure you don't want to wait outside?" I asked Trista, remembering she once fainted at school after a bad allergy attack.

"Nah," Trista said. She puffed on her inhaler, then pounded her fist against her shoulder and raised it. "Royal solidarity. 'We are family,' right?"

Grace bumped her own fist against Trista's. "That's what I'm talking about."

She looked down at Barb's list then at the blooms packed

on the shelves around us. "This is going to take forever."

"Check it out. You can see your breath." I blew out a puffy white cloud. Grace wrinkled her nose and fanned it away. "Ew. Did Barb force-feed you one of her tuna and pickle sandwiches?"

I laughed.

"You two done playing around?" Trista shoved a bunch of pampas grass into a bucket. "Because I think we have more serious things to discuss."

Grace's smile fell. "True. And not much time." She plunked down her bucket of snapdragons and pulled out her black notebook from her shorts pocket. "All right. So Barb couldn't take Mr. Steptoe all up in her business, and finally lost it when Lily wasn't queen."

"So maybe Mr. Lee wasn't a target? He really is just sick from exhaustion?" I said, hopefully.

"Uh, Lee was on the Royal Court judging committee too," Trista pointed out.

Grace tapped her finger on her notebook page. "Yup. More likely that Lund is taking the other committee members out, one by one. Maybe with Lily's help."

"Who else were judges?" Trista asked. "Steptoe, Lee, Sparrow . . ." She counted them out on her fingers.

"At least two past queens . . . ," Grace began. She didn't

want to say the obvious out loud.

"Rod's dad," I added, my voice small.

"And Rod's dad." Grace cringed apologetically.

"All targets," Trista said. "And two of them are down."

"Maybe Mr. Zimball will listen to us now?" I said. "We have to take that chance."

"On the other hand, there's a possibility it's just . . . *Achooo*!"—Trista let out another massive sneeze. She pulled out her inhaler and took a puff. "Anyway, what I meant was maybe Lund was just firing off a really angry email."

"That's one angry email," I scoffed. "'You won't live,' 'you are dead,' 'I'll ruin your life'?"

"We know she has a temper. There's no doubt she wrote that email fast." Trista rearranged some irises in her bucket.

"Or Lily did, using her mom's account. Tough to tell with all those mistakes," I pointed out.

"Either way, 'ruining' is not 'killing,'" Trista said. "Don't forget. We have other suspects. Katz, for one."

The compartment door slammed shut with a metallic clang.

"Dunh, duhn, *duhn*!" Grace laughed. "It's a sign!"

"He is pretty sketchy," I admitted. "What do you think he had in that box he was carrying out?"

"Guess we know what our next mission is," Grace said

as she went to open the door back up. "And you saw him at the Beach Ball talking to Lee, right? He looked like he was going to punch something he was so mad." Grace looked at the door and frowned. "Um. Am I crazy? Where's the handle?"

Trista's face clouded over. "Uh-oh."

I walked over and pushed against the door. It didn't budge. "This can't just close and lock. Can it?"

"Yes," Trista said. "It can." Her voice sounded quieter than I'd ever heard it.

"There's got to be a latch here somewhere. Maybe a button?" I ran my hands across the cold metal.

Grace felt around on the wall as if stumbling for a light switch in the dark. "Nothing here," she said.

The handprints I'd left when I pushed the door looked ghostly as they faded. I shuddered, picturing Festival officials finding us, days later, icicles hanging from our noses.

"Hey, I hooked that door into place. No way the wind could've blown it shut," Trista said. Her breath quickened. So did mine. I'd never seen her nervous before.

"Are you saying what I think you're saying?" I shivered.

Trista nodded and drew in deeply on her inhaler again.

Grace ran her hands through her hair and paced. "Who else knows we're down here right now?" Grace asked, her voice rising in panic. "Tell me someone else knows."

I pictured Rod. My last hours on earth, and I left him waiting for me at a row of port-a-potties. The stink of sewage and eye-watering disinfectant fumes would be his final memory of me. I closed my eyes and concentrated all my brain waves on sending him a message to come find us, then I wheeled around and pummeled my fist against the door as hard as I could. "Hello!" I cried out. "Anyone there?"

"This place is ventilated, right?" Grace's question came out all in a rush. "Like, we're not going to run out of air?"

I rubbed my bare arms. "Pretty sure we'll freeze to death first."

Grace raised a warning finger at me. "Don't you dare joke about that."

Behind us, Trista coughed again. Grace looked back. "Are you okay?"

Trista nodded. "Totally fine. Stupid allergies! Ugh, why didn't I take my medicine? Just need another . . ." She trailed off and looked at her inhaler. "Puff." She held it up, squinting at it like it was some alien artifact that she'd stumbled upon amid the flowers. "Uh-oh."

"What?" I asked.

"It's empty," she said in disbelief.

I banged on the door again until the heel of my hand

stung. "Open up!" I shouted. My breath left another foggy trail, but nothing about it was funny this time. Not one thing.

Grace turned to Trista hopefully. "Maybe you've got a refill in one of your pockets?"

"'Course I do," Trista said, unzipping one cargo jacket pocket after another and feeling around. "I always do."

"You won't need them. We'll be out of here in a sec," I said, trying to sound calm. I scanned the room. My heart thudded against my chest like it was trying to escape.

"If we could somehow get that vent open"—I pointed to a square grate in the ceiling next to a giant cooling fan—"I might be small enough to fit through it."

"I'll lift you up!" Grace said. Flowers spilled over as she shoved buckets aside to make shelf space, then she boosted me up as high as she could. The shelves rattled as I hoisted myself higher. I felt like I was on the float barn scaffolding again, closing in on my target.

"It's got to be around here somewhere," Trista muttered to herself, searching her pockets again, her breathing ragged.

I tried to keep my own breaths even as I wriggled toward the vent. Up close, it looked way too narrow for me to fit through—but I had to hope. "Listen, lots of people saw Barb send us off," I said, hoping I sounded more sure than I was. Rod was probably at the port-a-potties right that second. Would he worry?

"Let's hope you're right," Trista said, her voice so much fainter than usual.

I slipped my fingers through the vent grate and tugged. Screws held it tight at every corner. I stuck my thumbnail in one and tried to turn it. My nail snapped. "Ow," I muttered to myself. Jardine Thomas knew nothing about real nail-breaking emergencies.

"How's it going, Soph?" Grace tried to sound casual. She wasn't fooling anyone.

"Great! I think this could work!" I called back cheerfully. "Hey, you guys see anything around we could use as a screwdriver?"

Trista started to look around, but Grace held up her hand. "I got it. You take it easy," she said before tearing around like a robber ransacking the place. She spilled over more flower buckets. She looked under the shelves and riffled through a burlap bag in the corner. She flung open a big rectangular cooler and toppled over a jar. Red cranberry seeds hissed as they poured to the floor.

"What about your—?" Trista rasped faintly, raising one finger.

Just as I figured out that she was pointing to my dog tags from Grandpa Young, a sound like an airtight jar opening made us all turn to look.

The door banged open. Warm air rushed in with the blinding sunlight.

We squinted at the two silhouetted figures in front of us.

Chapter Sixteen

Warming Up

"They *are* in there!" Ms. Sparrow cried out. The sun reflected in her coppery hair like a halo, making it feel like an actual angel was sweeping to our rescue. When my eyes adjusted to the light, I caught sight of something even more angelic: Rod stood right next to her.

"You guys all right?" he asked. His voice cracked, but relief washed over his face.

Ms. Sparrow's eyes widened as she spotted Trista breathing heavily.

"She needs her inhaler," Grace called back.

"It's in my top drawer," Trista wheezed.

Ms. Sparrow waved Grace toward the mansion and told her to hurry back with it. Grace shot forward like a runner out of a starting gate, gravel flying, while Ms. Sparrow offered a nonstop stream of soothing words as she and Rod helped me lead Trista to a bench by the path. "I used to have asthma too," she told Trista, who seemed to be catching her breath again. "Now I'm just stuck with these allergies. I take one step in the float barn and, ugh!" As calm as Ms. Sparrow's tone was, she had trouble hiding her worry.

"I'm just lucky I didn't faint," Trista said.

"I'll say," Ms. Sparrow replied, eyes wide.

"That happens if I have a full allergy attack sometimes," Trista explained, waving off Ms. Sparrow's shock. "Don't worry. I'm good as long as I take my meds."

Ms. Sparrow turned to me. "Sophie, are you okay?" she asked, her voice shaking the way it did the morning she told us about Steptoe. It made me feel even more shivery, though the sun was warming my back.

I nodded. I couldn't find my voice yet.

"Sophie and Rod, take the flower refills to Ms. Lund, please." She motioned to the buckets inside the refrigerated compartment, her voice still wobbly as she asked us to have Lund send the Festival medic to take a look at Trista. "Please reassure Ms. Lund that everything's fine," she added. "I don't want her to . . ." She trailed off, looking a little sheepish.

"Overreact?" Rod finished helpfully. Ms. Sparrow nodded, relieved we'd gotten the drift. It was true. If Barb Lund hadn't been the one to shut us in the fridge, she probably would have called the marines, a SWAT team, and several ambulances—not to mention a K9 search and rescue team. Pookums would've loved that.

I turned to go back in the shed, but Rod flung his arm in front of me the way my mom does when we stop short at a traffic light. "Lemme bring them out to you," he said, already lurching forward.

If my cheeks weren't still numb from the cold, I would've smiled. Rod quickly finished filling the buckets and loaded me up. Then we dashed along the path as fast as our lungs let us, buckets thumping against our sides. As we rounded the corner to the float barn, we had to stop to catch our breath.

"That was crazy scary, Soph," Rod said, panting. He explained he'd waited for me for a while then figured Lund had sent us off somewhere else. His eyes turned dark. "Then, when Ms. Sparrow said she'd been looking all over for you—"

"Wait," I interrupted. "Didn't Ms. Lund tell her where we were?"

Rod frowned, trying to remember. "I guess not."

"Listen. Trista says she hooked that door in place," I said, gulping for air. "Someone shut us in there on purpose."

Rod's eyebrows shot up. "Why would anyone—?"

"We think it might be Ms. Lund," I whispered. "Maybe Lily."

The squirrels behind us squawked and scurried after each other up a tree as Rod took in the news. "You serious?" he asked at last.

I darted a nervous look around as I pulled Lund's email from my jeans pocket. Up on the terrace, the Royal Court were practicing their waving and walking in full wardrobe, their occasional shrieks of laughter echoing down the hill to us. Danica and Denise hovered nearby, handing them mini-bottled waters and snapping pictures with the Festival disposable cameras.

My hands trembled as I handed over the email. "Oh, I'm serious, all right," I said.

Rod stared at the paper long enough to read it at least twice. He shook his head slowly. "Where did you find this?"

"Trista thinks it could just be an angry email," I said, hoping he didn't notice I'd ignored his question. "But look at the time. Mr. Steptoe was found dead twelve hours later."

Rod squinted toward the float barn. "Steps from her office. On a float."

"Exactly. Nobody knows those floats better than Lund." I clenched and unclenched my hands nervously. "We think she knows we're onto her. She or Lily shut us in to scare us or maybe . . ."

". . . worse," Rod finished for me. He tugged at a curl at the back of his head. "I'm really freaked out, Sophie. How are you not freaking out right now?"

The truth was, if I'd actually eaten lunch, it would have come back up and landed on his shoes right then. But I stood up as straight as I could. "Because I know we'll figure this out." I stopped myself before adding "in time." He didn't need that reminder.

Rod nodded uncertainly. "Maybe my dad will finally listen." He tapped the email. "I can keep this to show him, right?"

I looked toward the mansion and hesitated. It didn't feel right not to hand it over. It was his dad's life at risk, after all. "Yeah . . . I think so," I said. Then, a little louder: "Sure."

Rod crammed the email in his pocket and pointed to the buckets of flowers. "I'll take care of these. Pretty sure Lund's the last person you want to see right now?"

I grinned. "Good guess."

He loaded himself up and turned to leave.

"Oh, and Rod?" I called back.

"Yeah?"

There had to be some other way to say it—some words

that would mean more than the same phrase people used if someone poured them lemonade or held a door open. But if there were, I couldn't find them.

"Thank you," I said. The words sounded even smaller than I thought.

Rod shrugged. "No problem," he said, and turned toward the float barn, buckets rattling against his knees as he headed off.

❧ ❧ ❧

I hurried down the path back to Trista but ran into Grace on the way. She rushed toward me and grabbed my hand. Hers was still ice-cold.

"The medics checked out Trista and took her up to our room to rest." She panted. "She's totally fine."

"I'm not sure I am." I shivered a little.

"Me neither." Grace looked back down the path toward the shed. A truck creaked down the side driveway toward the float barn, where volunteers were streaming in and out with supplies. "You think Lund locked us in? It had to be her or Lily, right?"

"Lots of people saw her send us down there, though."

"Sophie, whoever it is, they're definitely onto us. We don't have much time."

"Don't worry. We might not even need it," I said.

Grace cocked her head. "What do you mean?"

"I just talked to Rod and told him we were shut in. He's as scared as we are. He's taking Lund's email to his dad, and he's pretty sure Mr. Zimball's got to take this seriously now."

Grace was silent for a long time. She let her hand drop from mine. "You just . . . gave the email to him?"

"It's his dad were talking about. You know that. How could I not tell him?"

Grace's lips clamped together. She shook her head and fixed her eyes on some rose petals that had scattered from the arbor onto the path. "Well, you could have waited and asked, you know," she said after another long pause. "We're a team. We're running an investigation. You can't just up and hand over our evidence to everyone."

"'Everyone'? I gave it to Rod. Not 'everyone.'" An odd thick feeling filled my throat. "Grace, we need help," I said quietly. "And this is our best hope right now. You have to admit that."

Grace scuffed the toe of her sneaker against the path and shrugged, then jerked her head up as a clatter of footsteps rang out behind me. "Oh my god, are you guys all right?" Kendra asked breathlessly as we turned to find a cluster of very worried royal faces peering back at us. In their bright-pink business suits and silk neck scarves, Jardine, Sienna, and Kendra looked like flight attendants who'd just hopped off a flight from Bora-Bora. "We rushed from Scarf-Tying as soon as we heard," Kendra added. As silly as her words sounded, I was a little touched.

"So freaky," Denise said, her brown eyes wide, and the rest of them agreed. Sienna reached out and ruffled my hair. "Jake would've killed me if something happened to you on my watch." She smiled. "Glad you're okay. For both of our sakes."

"We heard someone shut you in," Danica said. The sparkly blush she must've been experimenting with shimmered in the sun.

"Wow. Rumors spread fast." Grace shot me a look and sighed.

"The door just shut by accident." I shrugged. "No big deal." My supposedly casual shrug probably looked more like a spasm.

"Everyone thinks some jealous seventh grader shut you in because she thought you shouldn't be pages," Denise said. Her eyes flicked to Kendra, and I wondered if Denise was talking about Marissa. Then she rushed to tack on: "But that's so stupid! I mean, obviously, you guys are the best."

"And no one would think you don't deserve to be pages," Danica added, flicking her hair over her shoulder. "Ever."

I was beginning to understand why Danica and Denise's child acting career in LA never panned out.

"C'mon," Jardine said, almost sweetly. "We've got our first photo shoot on the terrace. We're definitely going to need your help. If you're up for it?"

Grace promised the Court we'd join them after we cleaned up a bit, and we practically sprinted back up to the mansion. As soon as we were inside, she tugged me toward the first floor powder room and shut the door.

"I'm sorry, Grace. I swear Rod would have never run off and told everyone we were shut in. He—"

"Of course he wouldn't." Grace waved her hand. "They're just being them. Listen, we'll talk about that later. Let's see if we can find anything else in those emails. If Mr. Zimball's going to help—and I sure hope you're right about that—maybe there's something more we can hand over." She pushed aside the bottles of Pretty Perfect lining the vanity to make more room. It was funny to think that a day ago I'd been in that same bathroom, steeling myself for clipping

Kendra's toenails or whatever I thought it meant to be a royal page. Little did I know that being a page was going to be the easy part.

I fanned out the emails we'd printed out from Mr. Steptoe's office on the marble countertop and we sorted through them.

There was lots we didn't understand. Various officials wrote confirming meetings, orders, and Festival plans. An email exchange between Mr. Steptoe and Mr. Katz caught my eye:

Hi, Josh,

As you know, your things are still in my office. I must say, I'm going to miss your inspirational posters—I've needed the encouragement. Still, it's been two weeks now. I'd appreciate it if you can move the remainder of your things today before you leave. I'll be here till midnight, at least. Miyamoto's is delivering the tiara for the big unveiling tomorrow, then I'll be doing my float rounds. Come by anytime! Doesn't matter if I'm in the office or not.

I know it's not fair it had to shake out this way. I'm

deeply saddened it's affected our friendship. It really

shouldn't.

Fondly,

Jim

I could feel Katz's anger seething in his reply:

Had to shake out this way? It didn't, Jim. You know

that. But fine. I'll be there tonight.

My hand trembled as I reached the email over to Grace. "Check this out."

"Wow. Not exactly a friendly email," Grace said, her expression darkening. "It sounds like he even thinks Steptoe could have stopped his demotion, doesn't it?"

"And that 'I'll be there tonight.'" I shivered. "It sounds . . . threatening."

Grace squinted at the page and read it again. "And if he went that night, what's he doing carrying out his stuff today?"

"Especially since he had to have stopped by that night.

All of his posters were gone." I pictured the empty nails jutting from the blank walls in Mr. Steptoe's office, like rows of accusing fingers. "What time did Steptoe send that email?"

Grace looked down at the page. "Five oh five p.m.," she said.

"You have that notebook in there?" I pointed to the messenger bag she'd grabbed from kitchen on our way in. Grace nodded and pulled it out. My handwriting looked a little shaky as I wrote:

MR. KATZ SENT ANGRY EMAIL.
VISITED VICTIM BETWEEN 5:05 P.M. AND HIS DEATH.
ARGUED WITH POTENTIAL VICTIM #2 AT BALL.
SPOTTED LEAVING VICTIM'S OFFICE WITH BOX THE NEXT DAY.

"With a *glass paperweight*," Grace added in a hushed whisper as she read over my shoulder. "Talk about a possible weapon. Remember?"

I nodded. As I wrote it down, a thought hit me. "Grace, at the Beach Ball, when Lee and Katz were talking. Katz didn't go back into the ballroom right after. He went . . ."

". . . Back to the kitchen," Grace finished, stiffening. "Oh my gosh, you're right. Maybe Mr. Steptoe wasn't killed by that s'more, after all."

Next to my note about the paperweight, I added:

HAD ACCESS TO "WEAPON"/PEA SOUP IN KITCHEN?

I felt a tingling at the base of my neck. "Steptoe, Lee, Sparrow, and Rod's dad were all judges. But they were also all involved in the decision to push Katz out," I said.

"Exactly." Grace nodded.

We sifted back through the emails. I looked at the one from Harrison Lee about not needing help with accounting again. It was shady, for sure. And Grace could be right. If it was stress that laid him up, the stress might not have been from taking over the Festival presidency. Still, the longer he was lying in that hospital bed, the surer we could be that he was a victim.

There wasn't much else. A schedule for the Royal Court public appearances. Questions about bleacher set-up on the parade route. Some boring emails from Rod's dad about ticket sales.

"I didn't see any love notes from Sparrow," I said. "If they were an item, there'd be tons, you'd think."

 194

Grace frowned. "I saw something from her when we searched his inbox. I'm sure of it," Grace shuffled through the papers again. "Yes! Here!" She flipped down the toilet seat and sat cross-legged on it as she bent over reading. "Not what I'd call a love note, though. . . ." She handed it over.

To: Jim Steptoe <jimsteptoe@wintersunfestival.org>

From: Lauren Sparrow <msprettyp@prettyperfectfaces.com>

Subject: SUPPLIES

Just a note to say thanks again. I can't believe you all managed to get a double order delivered on time! No wonder they've put you in charge. I know how tough it is for you to keep everything on track in this season, as it is. I really do hope that alternative sourcing routes come through soon. Last breeding season already produced a far smaller crop—and, obviously, the harvesting is hardly environmentally friendly. Of course, beauty has its price. And no one can argue with gorgeous results! Still.

Please do alert me if you anticipate any slowdowns.

You're a dear. Feeling lucky to have you in my corner—

All my best,

LLS

"She does call him a dear." The printout crackled as I handed it back. "But, yeah, it's not exactly romantic. Why are she and Steptoe talking about flower orders, anyway?" I said, cocking my head. "That's Lund's department."

"Right?" Grace said. "And why is she so lucky to 'have him in her corner'? Do you think she and Mr. Steptoe were taking over control of the float decorations?"

I rubbed the back of my head. "It kind of makes sense, when you look at Barb's email. 'You say it's time for me to go,' she said."

"After twenty years, I can see them wanting to change things," Grace said, standing up suddenly. She began to pace, stopping to fix her ponytail in the mirror.

"Especially if she's trying to tell them who should be on the Court," I added. "If Steptoe and Sparrow were trying to shove her out? It must've driven her crazy."

"Crazy enough to kill?" Grace's eyebrows lifted.

I pictured Ms. Sparrow's tight smile at Lund in the living room the day she broke the news about Mr. Steptoe, and wondered if she knew she could be a target. I swallowed hard. "On the judging committee *and* she's trying to topple the Floatatorship? She might as well have a bull's-eye painted on her."

"Then why didn't our Floatator try to take out both of them?" Grace said, rubbing her temples. "Instead she poisons Harrison Lee's soup? It makes no sense."

"*If* she tried to poison Harrison Lee. We don't know that." I shrugged. "All we know is this might give Lund even more motive for murder, don't you think?"

"And it means Ms. Sparrow could be in serious danger," Grace said grimly.

Just then someone knocked at the door.

Chapter Seventeen

Dead Wrong

G race and I looked at each other in panic. "Someone's in here!" she called out. I flattened myself against the wall behind the door.

"Is that you, Grace?" a muffled voice called out. "It's Lily."

My reflection in the mirror over the sink stared back at me, eyes bulging, chest heaving.

"My mom forgot to give you and Sophie your headsets back?" Lily said, her voice tilting up. "I don't want to leave them. I'll wait for you out here."

"Just a sec!" Grace said. As she scrambled to gather up the emails from the vanity, half of them scattered to the floor with a loud rustling. We froze.

"Are you doing okay? After . . . everything?" Lily asked.

I leaned down and, as quietly as I could, gathered up the papers.

"What? Yeah!" Grace said, way too enthusiastically. She flushed the toilet, then motioned for me to stay against the wall, took a deep breath, and poked her head out the door.

I cringed as Lily's eyes immediately met mine through the gap between the door hinges. The toilet let out a final swish and burble as I stared back.

Lily's forehead creased. "Hi, Sophie."

"Hey," I said. The mess of papers in my hands crinkled as I hugged them tighter to my chest.

"You guys are hard to keep track of," she said slowly, her eyes flicking between us. She handed our radio headsets to Grace. "These should make it a little easier."

She smiled, but as she pivoted on her heel and walked away, a chill ran down my back.

❄ ❄ ❄

We shoved the emails in Grace's messenger bag and headed to check on Trista when we ran into Mr. Zimball striding down the hall toward us. "There you are, ladies. I've been looking all over for you. Glad to see you in one piece! Can I steal you for a chat?" he asked. Warm relief rushed through me as I spotted a folded white paper poking up from his shirt pocket. Barb's email. Rod had talked to him. Finally, we'd get help.

"Sure," Grace replied. As we followed Mr. Zimball down

the hall, she smiled at me, and I could sense how relieved she was too. When we reached the living room, Mr. Zimball slid open the paneled door and invited us ahead.

We stepped through the doorway and froze. Parked on the sofa, still wearing her grungy work overalls, was none other than Barb Lund. The pattern of the Oriental rug in front of us blurred dizzily as I willed my legs to follow Grace to the long sofa facing the fireplace. As soon as we sat down, Grace started nervously twisting her hair.

"We wanted to check in. You doing okay?" Mr. Zimball plunked down in his armchair and leaned his elbows on his knees. His face was filled with concern.

"Oh, definitely," I lied. My eyes darted to the email in Mr. Zimball's pocket and back to Lund. A drop of sweat shimmied down my forehead like a raindrop across a windowpane. A pretty suspicious look for someone who'd spent the afternoon in a freezer.

"That's a relief. I hear Ms. Sparrow has some fun and games planned tonight. That should be nice for you. Nothing like some hot cocoa at craft night to warm you all up nicely," Mr. Zimball said.

Hot cocoa! Maybe I'd nearly died in a fridge, but right then I wanted to live on an iceberg. In an igloo. With all ice furniture. Wearing an ice hat. Drinking iced tea. I pretended to rub my eye but mopped my forehead with the back of my hand instead.

"Royalty should never miss out," Ms. Lund said through clenched teeth as she stared right at Mr. Zimball. I realized she must be commenting on Lily's snub.

I eased back into the sofa. That paper in Mr. Zimball's pocket had to have been something else. There's no way he could have read it and invited us to a little sit-down with Barb Lund.

"We were worried you all might have gotten yourselves a little worked up," Mr. Zimball continued.

Grace stopped jiggling her heel and leaned back, too. "We're really okay now," she said. "It was just a little scary."

Mr. Zimball reached up and pulled out the paper from his pocket. The pit in my stomach opened into a canyon. "No. I mean about this." He held up Barb's email.

The ticking of the grandfather clock in the corner suddenly seemed so loud I was sure some tiny person was crouched next to it holding it up to Barb's megaphone.

Barb looked at us, arms folded.

"After what you girls went through in October, I can see where you might imagine danger lurking around every corner," Mr. Zimball said gently. "We're all very upset by Mr. Steptoe's passing. He was family to me. And Festival family to all of us." He gestured as if the room was full of people, and I saw his hands were trembling. "An accident this tragic is hard to take in."

I stared at the email and sank lower into the sofa. I realized that to him, it looked like Barb fired off an angry rant with lots of crazy figures of speech. He hadn't heard Officer Carter telling Lee how long a murder investigation would take. He wouldn't trust twelve-year-old Trista's explanations any more than the police who supposedly "looked into it," even if we told him. We were just town heroes who'd gotten ahead of themselves.

"I wanted you all to have an opportunity to chat in order to put your mind at ease," Mr. Zimball said, nodding to Barb. "And Ms. Lund wanted to have a chance to clarify some things. Right, Barb?"

"I'll say. You all must think I'm battier than a bedbug," she said, slapping her hands on her knees. "I would have thought the same thing at your age, I promise. I would have taken that note right to my spy club." She sighed sadly, and her voice grew quieter. "I'm very, very sorry I sent it. Those were my last words to Jim. I'm going to have to live with that," she said, and I realized it was the first time I'd ever seen her look sad. Of course, we knew by then that she could act, even if she was just pretending we were royalty. "I've been known to lose my temper and go a little overboard from time to time."

Grace let out an involuntary puff of air that sounded suspiciously like a snort. Lund didn't seem to hear it. She explained that she was angry, and her "colorful language" was exaggerated.

"Mr. Steptoe and I didn't see eye to eye on a lot of things. I was very upset about Lily being denied the crown, and I'm not going to lie, I still am," she declared as if Lily had been poised to rule an actual country. Her eyes shifted to Mr. Zimball and back. "But me! Sending a death threat!" She shook her head as if that were the silliest thing she'd ever heard.

"I think that clears up a lot. Thank you, Barbara," Mr. Zimball said. "Agreed, girls?"

There wasn't much use in arguing. Grace and I mumbled a yes.

Then Mr. Zimball frowned and ran his hand through his hair the same way Rod did when he was brushing petals from his curls. "There's something that concerns me. Rod also said you thought someone shut you in on purpose?"

My heart froze midbeat. Barb flinched.

"It did seem really weird," Grace said at last. "Trista hooked the door in place. There wasn't any wind. And then boom, it slams." She added, hurriedly: "But I guess we were wrong. It was just an accident."

Lund and Mr. Zimball traded long looks.

"If someone shut you in there, that's serious business." Mr. Zimball leaned forward. "Kids need to understand how dangerous pranks like this can be."

"And un-ac-*cept*-able," Barb added. She folded her lips over her teeth in disapproval. Her resemblance to the grim-faced Ridley relatives scowling from the portraits above the fireplace had never been so startling.

"Ms. Lund and Ms. Sparrow are going to talk to the volunteers as soon as Ms. Sparrow wraps up the terrace photo shoot. Bullying's an important issue to us and, frankly, we have concerns about it every year." He let out a long sigh. "A lot of girls want to be on the Royal Court. Some get upset." He avoided looking at Barb Lund, who shifted uncomfortably on the sofa.

"I had my fair share of knocks in middle school," she blurted, no doubt trying to turn the spotlight back on bullying. "'Four-eyes,' they called me. I had glasses twice as thick as my Lily's. I begged for contact lenses but when you've got the Ridley dry-eye curse, you're up the creek." She sighed. "You all might think Lauren was our beauty queen, but she took her lumps, too. I wonder if the people in this town buying up her beauty creams by the vat still remember when they called her "crater face" because she had pimples. Now she's got her empire, and I got the ol' laser eyes now." She widened her eyes at us. "They're practically bionic."

She wasn't kidding. Nothing got by her now. As Ms. Lund delved into a little too much information about her eye surgery, I thought about Lauren Sparrow. It was weird to imagine her ever being bullied. Suddenly a lot about her pretty perfectness made sense, though. Her expensive-looking matching outfits. Her copper waves of hair, always gorgeous and styled, even when she was going for a "casual" look. Her endless cute shoes, with their different buttons and buckles. She was making up for something she didn't have. Now I understood why she had been so worried about Trista and me when we were auditioning and—even though the tips of my ears still burned when I thought about it—I forgave her. She'd been trying to look out for us.

"I can't help but wonder if Lily had been Sun Queen whether we'd be seeing this same sort of trouble. Good leadership counts for so much," Ms. Lund huffed. "I shall personally be supervising all runs to the flower shed from here on out," she added. "We will not tolerate pranks on our Festival royalty."

Mr. Zimball cleared his throat. "I hope we've cleared this up for you. And I hope the message is coming through." A hard edge crept into his voice. "It's simply not safe for you to be running around hiding and snooping—in Mr. Steptoe's office or elsewhere. I don't want to hear one more breath about you all spying. Not even if you're just playing. Does that make sense?"

Grace and I glued our eyes to the floor and nodded.

"Good." Mr. Zimball smiled sadly. "Times like these can make the best of us lose our heads. But rest easy knowing that we're doing all we can to keep you safe."

"We sure are," Lund said. She broke into the broadest smile she could, which wasn't very broad at all.

Chapter Eighteen

Knock Knock

"It's a cat-and-mouse game now," Trista said darkly after we raced back upstairs to update her. She'd recovered but she was still resting in bed. "Either Lund wins, or we do." She propped herself up on her pillows and nudged a stuffed tiger out of the way as if it were some random object someone had placed on her bed, but it looked seriously well-loved.

"We need to tighten up operations," Grace nodded from her own bed. "We get caught spying now and we're done."

"If the killer doesn't catch us first," Trista added.

I felt a sad sinking in my chest and looked around the room to avoid Grace's gaze. Trista's side looked like what I'd imagine a military school dorm room would be like. The few toiletries she had were lined up in a neat row on her dresser, and a green duffel bag had been placed neatly at the foot of her bed.

"I'm so sorry, guys," I said in a small voice. "I should've asked you before I gave the email to Rod."

"Aw, don't be so hard on yourself, Soph," Grace said. She scooted over on the bed to make room for me. "I totally overreacted. As soon as I saw Mr. Zimball in the hall, I realized I would have done the same thing." She hugged her knees to her chest. "I think I was—I don't know. It felt like you and Rod were suddenly in this together without us or something. And I know how much you like him, and . . ." She dragged her fingers through her hair and looked away.

"I'd never be in something together without you guys." I grabbed the dog tags hanging around my neck, leaned toward her, and showed her the imprint on them. "*Semper fidelis.* It's Latin for 'always loyal.' That was Grandpa Young's army regiment's motto," I said, letting them fall to my chest again.

Grace smiled. "By the way, those look awesome. I'm totally jealous. Vintage is your style. There's just one thing I don't like about them." She scooted closer and lifted the tags. "They cover up your yin." She shifted the tags so my half of our split yin/yang pendants showed again.

"Maybe I could split up these dog tags and share them between the three of us." I looked at Trista.

"Nah," Grace said. "They're perfect for you, 'soldier,'" she said, imitating Grandpa Young.

Trista spoke up. "And thanks, but I prefer not to distract from my flair." She pointed to the bedpost, where her cargo jacket plastered with Girl Scout badges hung. "Besides, check out that chain your Grandpa put on them. No way you're getting those tags off. What is that, a titanium alloy? Practically indestructible." She got up from her bed and walked over to us. "But we're still a team, promise," she said as she reached out her hand, palm down. We looked at it, puzzled. "Well, c'mon, put your hands in! Like how they do in sports. Before a game? Isn't that what they do?"

"Oh!" Grace said as she slapped her hand on top of Trista's. I did the same.

"Ready . . . break!" Trista called out, and we lifted them again, wriggling our fingers. "I mean, we could totally have a secret handshake, but we don't have time for that."

"We sure don't. Soph and I need to go fan the Royals at their photo shoot or something. Rest up. Meeting at Location A after lights-out." She pointed to the floor. "That's here. I'll knock a Polybius code on the wall."

Later that night Ms. Sparrow gathered us all together in the Queen and Court sitting room to kick off our first night in the mansion with some hot cocoa and fun bonding activities to give us all a chance to get to know each other. The Festival had wisely canceled the traditional opening s'more roast around the far garden fire pit, given the general feeling about marshmallows those days. Ms. Sparrow had arranged for a craft night instead, pairing us up to decorate white T-shirts for each other. We were supposed to interview each other, find a creative way to represent that person with our T-shirt design, then share with the group while we sipped our cocoa.

"T-shirts! Right up my alley!" Trista beamed after Ms. Sparrow finished describing the decorating activity that night, and I don't think she was acting. Trista had a real thing for T-shirts, especially ones with slogans she loved. My favorite of hers was a faded green one that read "PROUD TO BE AWESOME" across the chest. "You've been paired with the right person," Trista told Sienna matter-of-factly. "If you want to represent me, I'd go with a 1996 Ferrari 550 and the character Memnon from TrigForce Five. Paint him with horns, please. So,"—she reached for a blue puffy paint pen—"what things do you like?"

"I play soccer?" Sienna said hesitantly, looking

overwhelmed by Trista as she twisted her light-brown hair around a finger.

Lauren Sparrow had us help her lay out a sheet of plastic over the carpet and the flower-patterned sofas to protect them, then we spread out on the floor in our pairs. I was matched with Jardine. Grace was with Danica.

After we served ourselves mugs of hot cocoa (without marshmallows, of course), Jardine and I laid out our white T-shirts and paints. "No yellow," she announced to me before we even started interviewing each other. "I don't look good in yellow."

"No problem." I missed the Jardine who was worried for us when we got locked in the shed. "Maybe green?" I asked, looking at the silky wallpaper's broad two-toned green stripes.

"Sure," Jardine said, smoothing out my T-shirt. "So, you're really into this tai chi thing," she said, struggling to sound interested. "That's Chinese or something, right?"

Grace jerked her head up and looked at us. Jardine had said the word Chinese like it meant Martian. I could feel Grace wondering if I was going to set her straight, or if she'd have to.

"Right, it's a Chinese martial art. You're making it sound like it's really strange!" I said, feeling blood flow to my face.

It was hard to stand up to Jardine. "Like, a quarter of a billion people do tai chi every day." I explained that it could be used for self-defense or for exercise and focus.

Grace surprised me by chiming in, then. "Soph's interested in Chinese culture in general," she called across the circle. "It's really cool."

"But I got a little too into it," I smiled. Grace smiled a little too. She'd once pointed out that me quoting Chinese philosophers and babbling about feng shui to her would be like her dancing jigs and dressing like a leprechaun and thinking she knew something about being Irish. I'd since taken it down a notch or five. "I focus on my tai chi now," I told Jardine. "We're training with staffs and ropes, which is pretty fun."

Jardine seemed to think that detail was interesting enough for a symbolic T-shirt and got to work, but after only a few minutes she got distracted by the TV on the wall above a wood desk in the corner. Ms. Sparrow had hooked her laptop up to it and was showing clips from her Pretty Perfect "how-to" web series on make-up and skin care. If we finished early, Ms. Sparrow had suggested that for fun we watch and try out some of the techniques with the products she'd laid out.

"Oh my gosh. Who is that?" Jardine pointed to the

screen where a man stood bundled up in a jacket in front of some kind of Arctic-looking landscape, his longish jet-black hair whipping in the wind as he talked about Pretty Perfect products. "So. Gorgeous. I can't even." Jardine turned back to the group. "Check him out, ladies."

Raúl Jiménez—Pretty Perfect Enterprises—Chief Chemist, said the caption on the bottom of the screen.

The rest of the girls got giggly, especially Danica and Grace. "Sooo cute," Grace jumped in as if she'd loved Raúl her whole life long and Jake didn't even exist.

"And Raúl." Jardine swooned. "The most perfect name ever."

I wondered if one day I'd go crazy over every remotely good-looking guy on TV, even if he was, like, thirty. Maybe that was a thing you just grew into suddenly. It sure seemed to have happened that way for Grace.

Trista was the only other one who wasn't swept up in Raúl. She was already finished with Sienna's T-shirt. She'd simply scrawled, **"I LOVE SOCCER. GO RIPTIDES!"** in blue across the chest, laid it out to dry, and disappeared behind a battered copy of *Teen Vogue* someone had left behind. Considering her favorite magazine was *Car and Driver*, she looked surprisingly interested in it.

Jardine oohed at the screen again, this time at the

adorable baby white seals playing on an iceberg in the background. "Where is that? Canada? Pages, book me a flight there ASAP!" she joked.

"I love his voice," Grace chimed in, then lowered her own to imitate his deep bass. "'We put together a unique blend of proteins—a secret recipe of sorts.'" She hammed it up, arching one eyebrow debonairly, and everyone laughed. It almost felt like she was purposely trying to rub in how easy it was for her to fit in when she wanted to.

"Secret recipe?" Sienna giggled at the TV. "I want to know his secret recipe."

"Ladies! Enough!" Ms. Sparrow finally scolded. "You can watch the videos after you make your T-shirts," she said firmly. Her face turned tomato red, and I realized that she thought Scientist Raúl was handsome too.

I wasn't the only one who noticed Ms. Sparrow's blushing. The girls all flashed each other knowing looks and shrank back. Suddenly, it occurred to me she worked with this Raúl Jiménez guy every day. Could he even be her boyfriend? If so, we could forget any wild theories about a romance gone wrong with Mr. Steptoe. Perfect Raúl was definitely a better match—and Lord knows she loved matching.

"Sorry," Sienna said quietly before turning her attention

back to her T-shirt. Drawing a Ferrari with paint-pens sure looked hard.

Jardine flopped down next to me and asked me to paint baby seals all over her T-shirt. I flinched, thinking of Mr. Steptoe and his otters. He really would have been touched if we'd made him a T-shirt with seals on it, too. I looked back to Ms. Sparrow and felt a sharp prickle run across my skin. What if Barb was targeting her next?

While I made a smeary mess trying to paint seals in green, across the room Grace and Danica were huddled next to a velvety ottoman whispering, giggling, and making smooching sounds that either had something to do with Raúl or Danica's camp boyfriend, I didn't know which. They sure were getting along well. I guess Grace didn't mind the smell of Axe.

Jardine took a pad from an end table next to the couch and started practicing signing her married name. "Jardine Jiménez," she said aloud, pronouncing her "new last name" with such an over-the-top accent you'd have thought she'd spent a year abroad in Acapulco. "Hee-MEN-nez," she practiced. "JJ! J-Squared!" She beamed at the group. "Or Jardi-J? I love it!"

She sighed as Ms. Sparrow came over and finally reminded her to get painting my shirt. I'd finished Jardine's seascape. It was a total mess. The seals looked more like eels. As I laid it out on the plastic to dry, Jardine looked at it and wrinkled her nose before forcing out a cheerful, "That's great, Sophie! Thanks."

The night was far from pretty perfect. And I had a feeling it was about to get worse.

I was right. Just then we heard the thud of footsteps out in the hallway.

"Who is that?" Kendra said, cocking her head. Everyone looked at each other uncertainly. The rest of the Festival officials had long since left for the night. The door behind us creaked open the rest of the way.

"Knock, knock!" a voice sang out.

Chapter Nineteen

Burning Questions

"Hallooo there, ladies!" Mr. Lee crowed. My stomach dropped. He was back. Grace, Trista, and I traded dark looks across the circle as the room burst into a chorus of cheery hellos and sighs of relief.

"Didn't you work enough this afternoon, Harrison?" Ms. Sparrow asked, and I realized with a jolt that he had *been* back. He looked happy, healthy, and rested—and not at all like a man who'd spent over twenty-four hours lying in a hospital bed.

After Lee muttered something about have a lot to catch up on and Ms. Sparrow made him promise not to work too hard, he rolled his eyes sheepishly and made an exit with a goofy double-handed wave. "Welp, ciao, my Coral Beauties!" he called out. "Just wanted to personally welcome you to the Festival family!"

Grace pretended to casually walk over and borrow one of my paint pens.

"From Victim Number Two to Suspect Number One," she muttered to me as she leaned over. "Listen for the signal."

When Grace knocked the Polybius code later that night, Danica and Denise were still giddily wide-awake. They knocked back. Soon, they'd roped me into playing a version of "name that tune" entirely in knocks, which would have been kind of fun if I a) didn't have to catch a killer, and b) wasn't playing with near-telepathic twins. After the umpteenth time they guessed each other's "songs" right after three knocks, they finally went to sleep.

Still, I held my breath as I eased open my door and tiptoed next door, Mr. Zimball's firm warning echoing in my mind.

"Sorry, guys," I whispered as I shut the door gently behind me. A bedside lamp they'd covered in a sheet cast a ghostly glow over the room and sent eerie shadows across the patterned wallpaper. "I thought they were never going to stop."

I shielded my eyes as they turned their flashlights toward me.

"That last one was totally "Happy Birthday," wasn't it?" Grace asked. She was sitting cross-legged on her bed in plaid boxer shorts and a T-shirt from her Chinese summer day camp.

I shook my head. "Kumbaya."

"Told you," Trista said to Grace.

"Double or nothing for tomorrow night's round," Grace fired back without skipping a beat. The way they joked around, it felt like they'd been roommates forever.

"You mean if we make it through another night," Trista said as she sat up in her twin bed. She was wearing a matching set of baby blue flannel pajamas dotted with cartoon sheep.

Grace chewed at her lip. "We've got work to do, don't we? Let's run down the facts." She pushed her black notebook toward me and reached out a pen. "Want to be secretary again?"

"Okay," I said as I sat down cross-legged on the bed next to her. "So. Lee is back on the list," I began. "We have one supershady email from him and a good motive."

"Right," Trista nodded. "I'm pretty sure stealing money from the Winter Sun Festival ruins you for life in this town, even if they don't throw you in jail."

"And we know he was at the mansion earlier today," Grace added. "Early enough to have shut us in that fridge? We'll need to find out."

"Problem," Trista interrupted. "He can't be the same person who locked us in the flower shed. He didn't even know we're spying, so how could he have known to scare us off?"

"Or kill us," Grace reminded her almost proudly. "Whoever it was might have been trying to kill us."

I shivered and moved to close the window next to Grace's bed, but I knew it wouldn't help. The night air outside was perfectly still and soundless. Not even a breeze rattled through the leaves.

"Actually, Lee *could* know we're spying," I said, remembering Grace's float faceplant the morning they found Steptoe. "He could have seen us run out of the float barn after we eavesdropped on the police and him that morning."

"Or . . . overheard you and me talking at the Beach Ball," Grace added with a wince, remembering how careless we'd been. "Then, boom, he fakes a collapse to throw everything off." Grace flung up her hand and bumped her flashlight. It lit up her face spookily as she leaned forward. "Like Trista said: No one suspects a victim," she whispered dramatically.

"Maybe." Trista squinted at us. "But I'd say the lady who basically wrote 'I'm going to kill you, Steptoe,' and then sent us to die in a fridge is still probably the number one suspect."

Grace grabbed her pillow to her chest and sank back on the bed. "Point taken, Page Bottoms. You're getting this all down, Soph, right?"

I nodded. "That meeting with her and Mr. Zimball got me thinking too. Steptoe was on her case all the time, right? But Mr. Zimball is always jumping to help her. If she wiped out Steptoe and Lee, she'd get revenge for Lily *and* have her man in charge."

Trista and Grace exchanged a look, and I felt like I'd said something dumb, so I hurried to add a new idea. "And then there's Lily. She's everywhere. It's like Lund sent her to track us twenty-four/seven."

"We can't forget that Lily could be acting alone," Trista said. "How much do we really know about her except that her mom has prepped her since the Paleolithic era to be the Queen? And that she *hunts*?"

I pictured Lily and her stringy dull hair standing next to her friends back in the float barn earlier that week and realized what it must have felt like to be her. I was afraid of living with the Royal Court for three days. She'd had a lifetime of growing up surrounded by smiling photos of Sun Queens with long legs and shiny hair that looked nothing like hers—and her mom worshipping it all.

"Hard to picture her hunting by s'more," Grace deadpanned. "But let's do some countersurveillance and see what we can dig up. Speaking of which, I've updated our Polybius squares with a few new codes for meeting spots." She handed new index cards to us.

"'PP' for 'meet in the pantry'?" Trista read aloud, the lines around her eyes crinkling. "You're giving *me* a hard time about being a bad spy? What top secret agent is, like, 'Breaker-breaker, I'll meet you in the pee-pee place!'"

I covered my mouth, trying not to laugh.

"Shhh!" Grace giggled. "Roll with it."

"I move that 'PP' stand for the first-floor bathroom," Trista said. "Makes more sense."

"I second the motion," I said, raising one finger officially. "I've already asked Rod to meet me in one pee-pee place. He won't be surprised when I do it again!"

The room fell silent except for a faint buzz coming from Trista's flashlight. Grace and Trista traded glances again.

I frowned, puzzled. "I mean, I should copy a Polybius square card for him, too, right? He's in with us now," I said, my eyes darted back and forth between them.

"Trista and I were talking . . . ," Grace started with a wince, as if by feeling uncomfortable about what she was about to say she would somehow make it gentler, when really the opposite was true. I pictured them huddled together, discussing me, and it felt like something inside me was crumbling. "The thing is . . . ," she tried again, twisting and untwisting a lock of her hair around her finger.

"Rod needs to stay out of the loop," Trista said flatly. It felt like she'd slammed a book down on the nightstand. "At least until we can confirm an alibi for Mr. Zimball."

"Alibi?" My voice squeaked higher like I'd been sucking helium.

"Sophie, Mr. Zimball caught us spying," Grace said in a pleading tone. "He told us to back off. He knew we were at the float barn decorating and could've seen us go to the refrigerated compartment. And he sure is helpful to Barb."

"He has no motive," I pointed out. The bed creaked as I flung up my hands.

"If Lee had died too, he'd be Festival President," Grace whispered gently. "His motive is almost as good as Mr. Lee's."

Shadows of tree branches outside clutched the wall like bony fingers. I remembered Mr. Zimball's conversation with Ms. Sparrow on the day of auditions. Could he have been trying to keep us out of the Court? My throat tightened like a fist.

"I mean, it's Rod's dad, though," Grace added quickly. "We know it's not him! It's just—we've got to rule out all possibilities."

"Right." I straightened and flipped to a fresh page in Grace's notebook, trying to wipe from my mind the image of the two of them pacing the bedroom, making decisions about me. I guess it made sense that they'd talked about the note. And it was true that Mr. Zimball couldn't be ruled out as a suspect. But even when I cleared my throat, the sadness stayed caught inside it. Reluctantly, I jotted Mr. Zimball's name at the bottom of our suspect list so we would remember to clear his alibi.

"So. What else do we have?" Trista asked. She got up and rolled her desk chair over to Grace's bed and hovered over the spread of emails.

Grace plucked Lauren Sparrow's message about flower orders from the top of the pile and handed it to her.

Trista's eyes flicked across the page. She wrinkled her nose. "What's Ms. Sparrow doing emailing Mr. Steptoe about float flowers?"

"Exactly," I tapped my pen against the notebook. "We think they might have been working together to push Lund out or take over." I explained that Grace and I thought Barb might have been trying to take them out to avoid losing her control over float decorating. "Sparrow could be in serious danger."

"Or . . ." Trista rubbed her chin. "Something went wrong between Steptoe and Sparrow, and he wasn't 'in her corner' anymore."

Just then a muffled thud echoed from down the hall. We flipped off our flashlights and froze. After a long minute, Grace turned on her light again. "Probably only Ms. Sparrow going to bed."

I felt like I could still hear all of our hearts pounding at once, but it was just my own pulse thudding in my ears. As it clunked around in my chest like sneakers in a dryer, I steadied my hand and summarized our main suspect details in the notebook:

#1—BARBARA RIDLEY-LUND
MOTIVE: LILY REJECTED FROM COURT. BATTLES WITH STEPTOE.
ALIBI: UNKNOWN
#2—LILY LUND
SAME AS ABOVE. MIGHT BE ACTING ALONE.
ALIBI: UNKNOWN
#3—HARRISON LEE
MOTIVE: FESTIVAL PRESIDENCY. POSSIBLY COVER-UP OF

SHADY DEALINGS.
ALIBI: UNKNOWN
#4—JOSHUA KATZ
MOTIVE: REVENGE/SHAME OVER POOPER SCOOPER DEMOTION.
ALIBI: UNKNOWN
#5—SPARROW
MOTIVE: ROMANCE GONE WRONG OR STEPTOE AND HER IN SOMETHING TOGETHER.
ALIBI: UNKNOWN
#6—DAVID ZIMBALL
MOTIVE: FESTIVAL PRESIDENCY.
ALIBI: UNKNOWN

Trista butted in. "Listen, people. We're on borrowed time." Her chair squeaked as she sat up suddenly. "No matter what, the killer thinks we're onto him. Or her."

"And the murderer could strike again at any time," I said, swallowing hard. I glimpsed our reflections floating like bluish ghosts in the dark windowpane behind us and a chill rippled down my back.

Trista rolled her chair back to her desk and riffled through her pink orientation binder. She pulled out the next day's schedule. "Tomorrow kicks off with a 9 a.m. photo shoot at the Luna Vista Rancho and Stables," she read. "That's Outfits 2C, D, and E, by the way," she looked at us chidingly. "Horse-riding clothes."

"Yee-haw," I said sarcastically, circling a pretend lasso in the air. Then something dawned on me. "Wait, no, seriously: Yee-haw!"

Grace realized what I was saying. "The overflow float barn! The Girl Scout float's got to be there, doesn't it?"

Since not all of the Festival floats could fit in the warehouse at the Ridley Mansion, several were parked inside one of the covered riding rings at the Luna Vista Rancho and Stables a couple of miles down the road. Half of it was sectioned off and served as a graveyard of parts from past years' floats. Though we couldn't be a hundred percent sure, chances were the Festival officials had probably towed the (not so) Beary Happy Family float over there to disassemble it.

"I think so," I said, feeling a sudden lightness.

Trista kicked back and forth in her desk chair. "I might be able to get permission to work on my remote-control programming in the float barn tomorrow," she said, explaining that everyone really wanted to roll out the first driverless float for the anniversary year. "We're at least a full day behind. The team's stressed. If Ms. Sparrow lets me skip the hoedown photo shoot or whatever it is, I could try to gain access to Lund's office while I'm there."

"Perfect." Grace clapped her hands together. "Soph and I will try to sneak into the overflow barns."

A minute ago I'd been shrinking from the weight of everything that lay ahead, but now a hopeful feeling bubbled through me. I looked down at the list I'd jotted down neatly in the book. As long as all our plans fit between ordered lines, it felt like nothing could go wrong.

Of course, that was when we smelled the smoke.

Chapter Twenty

Fired Up

The scent was faint, like burning toast.

"Do you guys smell that too?" Grace wrinkled her nose.

"I'm probably never going to smell anything again." Trista sighed. "These allergies, man."

I got up from the bed, crouched by the open window, and sniffed again. At the same time an alarm began shrieking. We pressed our hands to our ears, but nothing could dull its wail or the shouts and pounding footsteps in the hallway.

"Fire! Fire!" girls screamed. My heart started to race.

"Wait," I said as Trista reached for the doorknob. "You have to feel for heat." Suddenly I was trying to remember the story Grandpa told all the time about how, after the war, he got stuck in a barracks fire in Korea right when he was about to be shipped home. I felt under the door. "It's not hot," I said. "Get wet towels!"

Trista dashed to the bathroom, soaked a towel and washcloths and threw them our way. I put one of the wash-cloths over my nose and mouth and peered in the hallway. "All clear. Let's go!"

I turned to see Grace, frozen in the center of the room, face pinched. Her thin, long legs reaching out from her plaid boxer shorts suddenly seemed like fragile twigs that would splinter if she took a step. I thought of the last time I'd seen her looking so terrified, on the beach below the bluffs. Twice in her life Grace had faced death and barely escaped. It was no wonder she was so scared now.

"Are you all right?" I asked, letting down my face cover.

She shook her head slowly.

"It's safer out there, Grace. We've got to go." I motioned to the door.

Trista extended her hand in front of both of us. It took me a moment to understand. Then I slapped my hand on top of hers. We looked to Grace. She gave a weak smile, then laid hers on top, too.

"Ready, team? And . . . break," Trista said. We flung our arms high; then I hooked mine through Grace's and headed for the door.

Out in the hall everything was chaos. Red lights flashed across the ceiling and distant sirens wailed. Grace clung to me as we made our way down the dark hall. The air was clear except for the burning smell, but the Royal Court sounded like a herd of wild coyotes yipping as they rushed from their suite. An unearthly howl rose up from the end of the hall, and I soon realized it was Pookums, tucked like a pink purse under one of Kendra's arms. With the other, Kendra dragged her half-open rolling suitcase, which spit out scarves, underwear, and tank tops as it bounced down the steps. Jardine yelled at her to leave it behind and waved her on.

Lauren Sparrow materialized at the top of the staircase in a green silk bathrobe that was basically fancier than anything I've ever worn. "Everything's going to be fine, ladies." Her voice was calm but her eyes bulged. "Just head out to the front terrace."

Dew soaked the hems of my pajama bottoms as we gathered on the lawn. Sienna, Jardine, and Kendra stood with their arms around each other, staring in shock back at the mansion. Trista—who wouldn't have dreamed of leaving behind her cargo jacket, especially now that she'd sewn asthma refills into the lining—threw it over Grace, who was shivering in her boxer shorts and T-shirt. Kendra noticed.

"Over here, ladies," she said gently, waving us over. "We'll warm you up."

The three of us shuffled over and joined their group-hug circle. Sienna slung her arm around me, and Jardine asked if we were okay. Scared, and huddled together on the wet grass in their pajamas, their hair all messy, for once they didn't seem like royalty at all, but more like big sisters. I felt a stab of guilt remembering all the mean thoughts I'd had about them. Maybe I was seeing something closer to their real selves.

Danica and Denise, in matching purple pajamas, joined our circle too. "Where were you? We were freaking out!" Denise said to me, worriedly.

"Shh," I said, eyeing Ms. Sparrow. "Snuck out for a little slumber party."

They nodded but traded suspicious looks. Meanwhile Pookums yapped and ran dizzy figure eights through our legs, nearly tripping Ms. Sparrow as she checked in on us. So much for Pookums providing soothing therapy in times of distress.

I froze at the sight of two figures tramping toward us from the side path next to the mansion. I didn't have to wait until the motion-detector floodlights clicked on to know it was Barb and Lily Lund.

The mood in the mansion the next morning was anxious. The number of workers hustling around seemed to have doubled. Brown Suiters directed them to fling open windows and set up fans. Every outlet seemed to house a floral air freshener plug-in. As Grace, Trista, and I set the breakfast table, we heard the cooks muttering about the Festival curse. I felt like breaking into the cell phone safe to call my parents—or just plain running home.

The adults might have been muttering about Ridley cursing the Festival, but I was more and more sure a different Ridley was behind it all. One who was very much alive. Last night as Barb Lund helped Ms. Sparrow wrangle us all on the lawn while the firefighters thudded through the mansion, she'd mentioned how lucky it was she'd been working in the float barn late so she could "be there for our Royal Court in their time of need." She stayed with us until the firefighters gave us the all-clear signal to go back to bed.

"Ms. Sparrow said it was no big deal, but have you seen her? I didn't look that pale when I saw an actual dead body," Kendra said—with an odd sense of pride—at breakfast. Her mouth flapped open as she chewed a piece of bacon. Apparently they'd skipped a pretty important chapter in that etiquette class.

Jardine looked irritated. "Can you not . . . ?" She held out her hand at Kendra and pinched her fingers together to mime a closing mouth. "Thanks."

Sienna ignored the showdown and took a sip of coffee. It seemed so adult to sip coffee, but Sienna looked like she'd been drinking it since third grade or something. "I'm not surprised. Can you imagine if she hadn't woken up? The fire was right in her office. They say it started when the curtains blew into a scented candle that she forgot to blow out before bed."

Grace kicked me under the table. I kicked back. It was almost impossible to imagine Ms. Sparrow, the same woman who organized books on shelves by order of height, forgetting a detail—let alone one like that. Sparrow had seemed run-down and distracted lately—by her usual standards, at least. Did she know she was being targeted? I kept remembering her strange expression when Lee had thanked Officer Grady at the royal announcements for his speedy "closure." Was it fear or surprise? Or both?

"Her own smoke detector didn't even go off! No batteries in it!" Kendra said. She pushed aside her plate, probably not wanting to risk any more scolding from Jardine. "I heard her tell the firefighters last night."

I pictured Barb and Lily Lund tramping into view from the shadows the night before, and my toast and eggs felt like they were going to climb back up my throat. A fire in Ms. Sparrow's room. A smoke alarm without batteries. Lee, Barb, and Lily all lurking nearby.

Grace widened her eyes at Trista and me and dropped her fork against her plate with a clatter. Then she drummed her fingers on the table like a heartbeat. Tap tap, tap tap. I stopped midchew and leaned closer as Grace paused, then repeated the pattern twice more. Tap tap, tap tap.

I slid my index card into my lap and sneaked a glance. PP! She wanted us to meet in the pantry! Or wait—did PP mean the first floor bathroom, after all?

I got my answer when Trista darted a look toward the hallway that led to the powder room, then I stacked everyone's breakfast plates into a Leaning Tower of Pisa and hauled them away.

A minute later we were huddled around the porcelain sink. Grace's eyes flicked nervously from Trista to me and back again. "Are you guys thinking what I'm thinking?" she asked, her breathing uneven.

I nodded, picturing the lacy curtains in Grace and Trista's room. The air had been so still that night that they hadn't so much as twitched. "There was no breeze last night," I croaked. "How could the curtains have billowed out into a candle?"

"A candle Ms. Sparrow doesn't even think she lit," Grace said. "I don't think there's any doubt about it. This was an attack." She rolled her eyes. "A breeze! Talk about 'hot air.' Someone set that fire."

"And they took out the smoke-alarm batteries first," Trista said, clenching her fist nervously.

"Steptoe, possibly Lee, and now—Ms. Sparrow," I said, tapping the marble countertop at each name. "All Royal Court judges." I shuddered.

Grace nodded slowly. "We're back to our original theory: Lund. In the float barn. With a giant s'more."

There was only one problem. This round of Clue was no game.

Chapter Twenty-One

Horsing Around

As we stepped from the Festival van onto the grounds of the Luna Vista Stables that morning, the breeze fanned my hair against my face, its smoky scent mixing with the earthy stink of hay and horse manure. Not a good smell—but it was a relief to be away from the constant dizzying scent of flowers. In fact, it was a relief to be away from the mansion in general. Safer, too, I thought as I watched Ms. Sparrow hop out of the van, brush off her spotless dark-blue jeans, and cinch her plaid shirt more tightly around her petite waist.

I looked down the hill to the large covered riding ring where the overflow Festival floats were parked, its aluminum siding reflecting the sun. A wide-open dusty path circled it like a moat. How would we ever slip away to it without being seen?

"Don't worry," Grace whispered, reading my mind.

"We'll pull this off. Promise."

"Pages! We need footmen!" Ms. Sparrow said with a wink, gesturing to the hard plastic step Danica and Denise had placed in front of the van's open passenger door.

"Hands off the jacket," Jardine snapped, waving us off as we attempted to help her down. She was back in royal form after being so nice to us after the fire. That day's photo shoot was for next year's Festival calendar, and each Court member was dressed in a different ridiculously overdone horse-themed outfit. Jardine was an English dressage rider, complete with black jacket, white breeches, boots I'd shined myself that morning, and a black riding helmet. She'd refused to carry the long riding whip that went with the getup, of course. I was relieved. Given her mood that morning, chances were high she'd have used it on us.

Jardine wasn't the only one on edge that morning. Just when I'd started to kind of have fun with the Court, they'd turned around and started being difficult again. I told myself it was from lack of sleep. Sienna, of course, was still friendly. She jumped down from the van with a giggle and a silly "giddy-up!" In her Western wear, with her two golden ponytails cascading over her fringed vest, she made the perfect cowgirl. Kendra tottered out next with Pookums, wearing a polo helmet. Kendra immediately gave a panicked cry, afraid the dust Sienna had kicked up was going to get on her bright white polo uniform—a surprising turn of events, considering the fit she'd thrown earlier about wearing it in the first place. It wasn't until we'd taken a blue Sharpie to turn the royal-blue number one stitched onto her pocket into a three that she'd finally put it on. One was her unlucky number, apparently.

"I got you covered, Princess Kendra," I said, reaching inside the quilted Queen and Court supply bag for a towel to dust her off. We had enough to worry about without Kendra tantrums.

"You've got Pooky's treats in the bag, right?" Kendra said, tightening her grip on her polo mallet.

In a single swift motion, I tucked away the towel, grabbed a bacon treat from a Ziploc bag, and tossed it to a delighted Pookums. "All set," I said. Kendra's braces gleamed as she smiled.

"Follow Mr. Diaz, ladies," Ms. Sparrow motioned for us to join a Brown Suiter coming up the path. "He'll give us a brief tour, we'll meet the parade horses, and then it's time for your close-ups!"

"And time for our close-up too," Grace muttered to me, eyeing the overflow barns. "Watch for my signal," she added.

"Ten-four," I said, my stomach turning inside out as I caught sight of Mr. Katz in his brown blazer striding toward the stables. If we got caught spying again, it was over.

I slung the pink supply bag over my shoulder and followed, ready to bust out with make-up, water bottles, or outfit changes at any time. Grace walked beside the Court, misting them with a spray bottle and handheld battery-powered fan. Danica flanked the Court on the other side, offering to counteract the stink of manure with some squirts of Axe, while Denise hustled behind with an overloaded picnic basket. Everyone made sure to keep a healthy distance from Kendra, who swung her long polo mallet over her head so casually and so frequently that I was fairly sure at least one of us was going home with a concussion. Pookums, never far from Kendra's heels, was the likeliest victim. Too bad he wasn't wearing his own tiny polo helmet to soften the blow.

"In a moment you'll see our Parade Route Integrity team in action! Of course, you probably know them as the Pooper Scooper Brigade. They're practicing now," Mr. Diaz explained as we followed him down the path and along a large outdoor ring enclosed with a white fence. Inside, a ranch hand stood exercising a speckled horse on what looked like a long canvas leash. Jardine winced as he cracked a long whip at the horse's heels. I turned toward the sound of thudding hooves and saw a line of parade riders trotting toward us on tan horses, their blond manes so thick and shiny that they'd probably make Kendra and her friends wish for hair transplants. On the path behind them, Rod and several other kid volunteers in white mechanic's jumpsuits shoveled up the horse droppings and dumped them in the gray rubber trash can on wheels that they towed along.

Rod's eyebrows lifted in surprise when he saw us.

"Solid round, Route Integrity," Mr. Katz called out halfheartedly to the volunteers, looking like a washed-up country star in his jeans and cowboy boots paired with his brown suit blazer. He flipped up the dark sunglass lenses he wore over his square wire-framed glasses and reset his digital watch with a beep. "Let's try to shave off a few more seconds next time! Success comes to those who persevere," he said. I recognized the slogan from his office poster of a kayaker paddling against a river current.

Grace caught my eye. She must've been thinking of Katz's email too. The words sounded so angry: *Fine. I'll be there tonight.* Had he been angry enough to kill? My scalp prickled as I watched him direct the Brigade to empty the gray trash can. Meanwhile Rod leaned his shovel up against the stables and made his escape, ducking into our group while Mr. Diaz introduced us to the parade riders and their horses.

"I'm really sorry, Sophie. I was so sure my dad would take it seriously," he whispered.

"It's not your fault," I mumbled, my eyes darting to Grace and back again. Somehow, I was going to have to find the courage to ask him what his dad had been doing the night Mr. Steptoe died. In the meantime I pretended to listen with great interest as Mr. Diaz lectured us on the history of Palomino horses in the Winter Sun Festival. Even the Palominos themselves were stamping their hooves in boredom.

"I'm here for back-up." Rod jerked his head toward the barns. "I've got my bike here. I've got my phone. My parents are totally wrapped up in Festival stuff. I can tail Lund, investigate, whatever you guys need."

Just then Kendra spun her polo mallet yet again, startling one of the horses. It flattened its ears, jerked its head wildly, and backed up, sending a ripple of whinnying and shuffling through the pack that nearly toppled one of the riders. While Mr. Diaz lunged for Kendra's mallet, Pookums lowered his head and growled as if ready to take on all of us, and possibly an entire team of Clydesdales to boot. In the chaos, Grace noticed Rod and me lingering behind the group. She pointed to Rod and mouthed something. I didn't have to be a good lip-reader to know what it was: *Ask him*.

"Who thought it was a good idea to give her a weapon, huh?" Rod smiled and nudged me as everyone settled down. Then his expression clouded. He cocked his head. "You okay? You haven't said a word."

I cleared my throat. "Oh, yeah. I'm fine. It's all going to be all right." I kicked the toe of my sneaker in the dust as Mr. Diaz droned on about proper horse grooming. "Listen, about your dad . . ."

Rod's brow furrowed. "Yeah?"

"We were going over everything last night, kind of checking everyone's alibis, you know, and . . ."

"Alibis? Wait." Rod stepped back as if I'd pushed him. "Are you saying what I think you're saying?"

"Oh no. I mean . . . we know your dad could never . . . would never . . . ," I sputtered as if I were drowning. I felt like I was. "But, we were—"

"You think my dad is a *suspect*?" Rod could hardly keep his voice to a whisper. Ms. Sparrow twisted around and hushed us, pointing to Mr. Diaz who'd moved onto giving an entire rundown of Winter Sun Festival horses who'd gone on to careers in Hollywood Westerns.

"I don't," I whispered. "Promise. It's just . . ." I glanced over to Grace. Rod followed my eyes.

"Oh, I get it," he said, his gaze hardening. "And you didn't tell them they were out of their minds?" My body burned with shame as he shook his head at me in disbelief. "I really thought you were different, Sophie." He sighed and tossed up his hands. "Look, if you really need to know, my dad was with me and our neighbors that night. They had this huge plumbing emergency we helped with."

"Zimball!" Mr. Katz called, eyeing me. "There'll be time to charm the ladies later! Maybe after you take a shower?" He made a face and waved his hand in front of his nose theatrically. Some of the Pooper Scoopers burst into laughter. Danica and Denise chimed in with an *ooo* that upset the horses again, probably because they sounded a little like nervous cows. Rod's ears blazed red and he shot me one last disappointed look before turning away and hustling back to the group.

I kept my eyes rooted to the ground. My insides felt like they were collapsing. Behind me, Mr. Katz lectured the Brigade on the importance of not leaving even a little horse dung on the parade route, otherwise it could get caught in the float tires and kick into the float drivers' compartments.

As if inspired by Mr. Katz's description, right then one the Palominos shook loose a thick string of slobber that helicoptered directly toward me, landing with a wet splat across my forehead.

"Photo time!" Ms. Sparrow chirped, pointing us to the photographer setting up by the paddock fence.

I sighed and searched for a baby wipe in the supply bag to clean off the mess.

Photo time was as miserable as I expected. We spent the next half hour sweating in the sun, fanning the court, bringing them water, and waving carrots at the horses so they'd turn toward the photographer. When I swatted a fly circling Kendra, Jardine looked like she might tackle me to the ground for animal abuse. Mr. Katz continued to run his Parade Route Integrity practice nearby. Rod went about his work, jaw set, never glancing my way. I'd given up watching for Grace's signal. The entire day felt like a bust. That is, until Pookums gave us the best gift ever.

It happened as Kendra was posing for her solo shots. While she was distracted, Pookums made a break for the hefty manure pile the Pooper Scooper Brigade had dumped nearby. Panting with excitement, he belly flopped into it like a kid diving into pile of fall leaves. Then, he rolled. And rolled. When he finally shimmied to his feet again, his tan fur was a stinking mass of dark-green matted clumps. Wild-eyed, he turned and—a maniacal smile pulling at his cheeks—bounded back toward Kendra in her perfect polo whites. Grace's face froze in horror.

"Pooky, no!" Kendra shrieked.

"Guess we know why he's called *Poo*-kums," Jardine quipped from the bench where she and Sienna were resting.

I acted fast. The Ziploc bag of Pookums' treats was in the supply bag I'd put under the bench. "Pookums!" I called in my best soprano, squatting next to Jardine and grasping a whole handful of bacony treats tucked in the outer pocket. "Over here, Pooky!"

Sienna gagged from the stench as the tiny abominable Poo-meranian skidded short and scampered over to us instead. I caught Grace's eye, and all at once it came to me in a flash. This was our chance.

"Oops!" I cried as I stood up, letting the bacon strips slip from my fingers and spill into Jardine's lap. "I'm so sorry!"

The sudden direct contact with pork would've probably made Jardine scream as it was, let alone fielding poo-covered poofball Pookums. As he snarfed one bacon bit after another, she squealed and pushed him away as gently as she could, smearing brown trails down her white riding breeches. She stood, frozen, arms outstretched, as Pookums waddled around in giddy circles.

I picked up the supply bag, grabbed Jardine's arm, and shot Grace an urgent look. Forget watching for her signal. It was time. "We'll get Jardine a change of clothes right away, Ms. Sparrow!"

Jardine didn't even have a chance to object before we were whisking her off to the stable restroom.

"Oh, perfect. Take your time, ladies. We're ahead of schedule," Ms. Sparrow called back. "Danica, Denise? Can you clean up Pookums? We'll take a quick lemonade break. Come find us by the west corral when you're done!"

Danica and Denise stared helplessly as we raced away. It was perfect. If Ms. Sparrow took everyone to the west corral, we might actually get to the overflow barns without being seen. I whipped out a fresh pair of riding breeches from the Queen and Court supply bag and handed them to Grace. She hurriedly opened a bathroom stall door, slung the pants over it, and invited Jardine inside like a fitting room attendant. "We'll give you some privacy, Jardine! See you in a few!" she sang out, nudging me toward the exit.

"That was so genius of you," she whispered to me. "Overflow barns, now! Run for it!"

We jetted out of the bathroom and down the long row of stalls, horses rustling in alarm in our dusty wake as we made a break for the wide-open door at the end of the stable. But just when we were about to sprint through it, a bubble of laughter and voices rose outside. Grace whirled back and grabbed my arm, and we dove for cover behind a trash can seconds before a cluster of white jumpsuits passed right in front of us. The Pooper Scooper Brigade.

Grace leaned against the barn wall and sighed. "Close call," she panted.

I watched as Rod passed, dragging his shovel as he trailed glumly behind Mr. Katz. "Listen, Grace . . . about Rod . . ." I told her his dad's alibi, and how upset Rod had been that I'd asked for it, then made my case for letting him in on everything. "We could really use someone on the outside. Think about it," I said. "We can get the letter back. He has his bike here. He could ride to Miyamoto's and try to talk to the tiara deliveryman, see if he saw anything that night." My words tripped over each other as they came out all in a rush. Grace listened, frowning. "I mean . . ." I shrugged. "I guess we should make all decisions as a group, but . . ."

"And Rod should be part of that group," Grace said. "Trista thinks so too. We talked about it last night. We needed Mr. Zimball's alibi, that's all. And now we have it." She nodded confidently. "Like she said, sometimes a person needs to make a quick decision and hope it's a good one. Right?" She looked up at me and smiled.

"Exactly," I said, grinning back. I darted a glance outside

to check if the coast was clear and stood up. "Ready? Three, two, one . . ."

"Liftoff!" Grace whispered. And we were off.

I jutted my chin high, pumped my arms, and didn't dare look back until we skated to a stop in front of the big rusty sliding door to the overflow float barn. Grace gulped to catch her breath as she handed me a pair of latex gloves like the ones we'd used in Steptoe's office. "We don't want to contaminate the crime scene," she said, snapping her own pair on.

We tugged on the rusty door handle as if we were unsealing an ancient tomb. The door creaked and thundered on its tracks as we shoved it open and stole inside, blinking as our eyes adjusted to the dim light. It was a tomb, of sorts—a graveyard of floats. Thin shafts of light struck them at odd angles. A forklift in the corner seemed to be lying in wait like a sleeping beast, its headlight eyes catching the light. The float barn smelled damp, like a basement, and a hollow *drip-drip* echoed from a far corner.

Parked to the side was the Beary Happy Family float, still wrapped with police tape, the bears' overly enthusiastic grins looking like crazy clowns' leering over the half-assembled bodies of the floats. Not far away were newly decorated floats that didn't fit on the Ridley grounds. Their mix of colorful cartoon character heads and giant rainbows looked so cheerful next to the empty metal frames of all the old broken-down floats next to them.

"Here goes," Grace said, her whisper echoing eerily as she squeezed my hand and tiptoed ahead. We wove our way past piles of wooden pallets and stacks of scaffolding, linking arms as we crept up to the Girl Scouts of America float.

An icy chill seeped through me as we lifted the police tape and ducked under. As we stepped up to the campfire circle, I could see how everyone missed seeing Mr. Steptoe's body that morning. The campfire logs, already fully decorated with brown bark, crisscrossed chaotically over each other, creating small hidden spaces in between. The giant s'more loomed not far off. The hard-plastic marshmallow, still undecorated, swelled out from between two graham crackers dusted brown with what was probably crushed cinnamon. It threw an eerie shadow over the campfire "pit," which wasn't a pit at all but a dip in front of the logs that held a gas pipe where a small burst of flame would fire up like the gas flames in the Ridley Mansion living room.

I pulled out my disposable camera I'd squirreled away from our orientation welcome basket, set the flash, and took a picture. Grace helped me up onto the float, and we crept around carefully to inspect the logs themselves. The more we poked around, the more it felt like we were wasting time. While we were staring at glued-on lentils hoping to stumble across something, a killer could be striking.

"Oh." Grace made a sound like air leaking out of an inflatable mattress. She crouched down by one of the logs.

"What is it?"

Grace waved me over and pointed. Caught in a bit of exposed chicken wire on one of the fake logs was a small round navy button with a blue thread trailing from it. It looked like the kind of medium-sized button from the cuff of a men's blazer. Judging from the pained look on Grace's face, she and I were struck by the same awful thought.

"Mr. Steptoe's?" I rasped.

"I think it might be." Grace nodded sadly. "It could have pulled off when they, uh . . ." She had trouble finding the words. "Removed the body."

Even the click of her disposable camera as she took a picture sounded flat and empty.

"Could be our killer's, though," I said hopefully. "Or one of the officers'?"

"Could be," Grace said weakly. Her face looked gray in the dim light.

She stopped my hand as I reached out for it. "Don't forget. Pictures only." We had agreed the evidence was pointless if we tampered with it before we went to the police.

A metallic ping and thud rang out behind us. I jumped. Why hadn't we checked to see if anyone had followed us? Grace stifled a scream, and I bit my lip as I turned, expecting to see a human head rolling in front of us like a bowling ball. I don't think I'd ever have imagined being so relieved to see a fat oval-shaped rat skitter across the concrete, its hairy tail disappearing under a stack of boards.

Grace clung to my side.

"We got this, Grace. Let's wrap it—" I glanced back at the campfire and jumped. Two tiny beady eyes gleamed back at me.

Grace leaped away, nearly tripping over the bark-covered canoe jutting from the side of the float. She grasped at her neck. "Don't freak me out like that, Soph!" she wheezed.

Still clutching my own chest in fear, I gingerly leaned forward to look more closely. The little black eyes were not real. They were shiny and smooth and blueberry shaped. I had a very strong suspicion they . . . Yes, that was exactly who they belonged to, I realized with a chill.

Chapter Twenty-Two

Nothing to Pooh-Pooh

"Is that Winnie the Pooh?' Grace said, her brow wrinkling. She crouched next to the campfire to get a better look.

I nodded. It was Winnie the Pooh. A very tiny stuffed Winnie the Pooh that could have fit in the palm of my hand. He was almost unrecognizable. His yellow fur had melted into nubby patches all over. His mini red T-shirt was singed. Half of his body was charred light brown.

Grace looked back at me in shock. My heartbeat swallowed every other sound in the float barn.

"It's a key chain," I said, voice shaking.

"If it's burned, it had to have been there before the campfire pyrotechnics test that morning," Grace said. She grabbed my arm and squeezed it tightly. "You know what this means, don't you?"

"Barb Lund," I said. It came out as a whisper.

"The Grand Pooh-Bear," Grace said, but she definitely wasn't joking.

I looked to the jumble of logs in front of the campfire pit where Kendra had discovered Mr. Steptoe. My mind was whirling, grasping for some other reason Barb Lund's key chain had ended up feet from his body. I couldn't think of any. Barb Lund wasn't even responsible for overseeing the Girl Scout float.

"We're getting closer, Sophie." Grace whipped out her disposable camera and started snapping pictures from every angle. I looked up at Goldilocks and her Beary Happy Family staring out wide-eyed above us, as if dazed by the camera flashes. Their smiles looked like grimaces.

"Okay, that should do it," Grace said, tucking her camera in her pocket. "Now, let's get back before they freak out that we're gone."

Grace and I bolted through the graveyard of junk and parade floats to the door. After a panicked struggle to heave the rusty door shut again, we finally raced across the wide-open path and had just rounded the bend to the stables when a silhouetted figure stepped out of the shadows directly in front of us. My heart froze.

It was Mr. Katz.

A cloud of dust billowed around us as we skidded to a stop.

He flipped up his clip-on sunglass lenses and peered at us suspiciously. "Where have you been, ladies?" he asked.

"Oh, just the overflow barns," Grace said as casually she could, but her chest was heaving from our run.

Mr. Katz's gaze swept across our faces like a police searchlight.

"We had a staff meeting, you know," he said. "I understand you've been snooping around?" His eyebrows disappeared under the shock of gray hair that hung on his forehead.

Several horses craned their necks from their stalls curiously. I looked around, suddenly aware of how quiet it was.

I said nothing and blinked, hoping my freckles made me look innocent.

"You'd think after all you've been through, you'd make safety more of a priority." He flipped his sunglass lenses down again so fast it made me jump. "It's dangerous to be running around here," he said firmly. "I'd hate for anything bad to happen to you girls." Then he jabbed his finger ahead. "Back to the west corral, please. The Court needs your help."

Grace and I hustled forward. We didn't make it ten steps before he called after us.

"Oh, and girls?"

We turned back.

"I'll be reporting this at our Festival meeting tonight," he said gruffly. He spun on his heels and strode away, cowboy boots crunching in the dirt.

Grace and I hurried past the stalls toward the corral, pausing to catch our breath outside the tack room. Up ahead we could see the Court striking their poses for the photographer along a bright white fence.

"If Lund finds out we're still spying—" I broke into a cough before I could finish. The fine dust we'd kicked up on our sprint coated my throat.

"We've got to stay calm," Grace said, but her voice rose in panic. She brought her fist to her mouth and fixed her eyes on the ground. "We've got to think."

"If he tells the Festival officials he caught us spying, he's telling the killer—even if it's not Barb. They'll know we're on their trail. Or . . ." I pictured Mr. Steptoe's email asking Mr. Katz to collect his things and shuddered. "He just found out himself."

"Listen," Grace called out suddenly, clapping her hands on my shoulders. "No matter what, we've got time.

Not much. But we've got it. Trista might've found something on Lund today, too. We might have enough evidence to go to the police this afternoon, even." Her eyes looked hopeful.

"Okay, okay," I said, trying to slow my breaths and center myself like we did in tai chi class. "You're right. Maybe Trista managed to slip into her office somehow, maybe—" I cut myself short as I pictured Trista—Trista who brought rattling vacuum cleaners on spy missions, Trista who didn't know how to tiptoe—attempting a solo stealth office break-in. My breathing turned shallow again. "Oh, man, Grace. Trista doesn't slip in anywhere. Ever. What if . . . ?" I broke into a sweat as I realized that we'd probably sent our best friend, alone, to spy on a killer.

Grace's throat bobbed as she swallowed hard and looked at me with wide eyes. "We can't worry yet, Sophie," she said. Then her lips turned up in weak smile. "She is Trista Bottoms, after all."

I don't think in the history of mankind that there was ever a photo-shoot that felt longer. Only when I spotted Rod did the images of Lund catching Trista stop spinning through my head. He was carrying his shovel back to the Route Integrity supply shed. I caught Grace's eye. She nodded and took my place handing out snacks to the Court while I hurried over to him.

When he saw me, he tightened his grip on his shovel and kept walking.

"Rod, wait–" I called out, jogging after him. "Can we talk? Please? Just for a second? It's really important," I said.

He must have heard the fear in my voice. He hesitated, then turned, his lips pressed together impatiently.

His expression finally softened as I babbled apologies. "Everything's just been so crazy," I finished, slapping my arms to my sides. "It's like we're trying to get everything right and we"—I looked right into his eyes—"lost track of what's really important."

I didn't pull my eyes away. I kept right on looking. I noticed that he had a spray of small freckles on his nose. Not obvious ones, like mine. But teeny-tiny faint ones probably brought out by the sun. I finally understood why people thought freckles were cute.

"I get it, Sophie," he said quietly. "I really do." He kicked his boot against his shovel and sighed. "I'm going crazy too. When you asked me for his alibi, something snapped, you know? If I can't count on you, who can I count on?"

"Oh, you can count on us," I said, squaring my shoulders,

 258

not sure if he meant me specifically, or the three of us together. "The things is: we need you, too."

I reached out the copy of the Polybius code square like a peace offering. He took it from me hesitantly, then cocked his head, puzzled.

"Page Young!" Kendra's screechy voice rang out behind me. "Can you bring me my sunscreen, please? I'm turning into a lobster out here!"

I sighed. "Listen—there's a lot to explain and no time," I said, darting a glance over my shoulder. It was probably better not to freak him out by telling him about the key chain yet, anyway. In a hushed voice I asked him to try and get to Miyamoto's Jewelers to see if he could find out anything from the person who delivered the tiara that night. I pointed to the code square. "We use this tap code to communicate. There's a list of abbreviations for our emergency meeting places on the back. If you have anything to report—or need us for any reason at all—use it to call a secret meeting, okay?"

He nodded hesitantly.

"Don't worry. We got this." I smiled back. "Together."

Rod broke into a grin and gave a salute. "Ten-four. Over and out."

Even if Grace and I hadn't already had very good reasons for speeding home to the mansion that afternoon, we would have been silently willing the van to move faster. As soon as the driver pulled away, the Court began belting ballads from Disney musicals at the top of their lungs. I couldn't believe I'd escaped permanent ear damage from Barb Lund's megaphone only to have Kendra's ridiculous vibrato finish the job. Ordinarily after two days of bonding, we might have actually had fun singing along too. Instead Grace sat next to me, eyes closed, squeezing my arm the whole way. We finally pulled into the mansion as the chorus of *Frozen*'s "Let it Go" crescendoed to a full-blown shout.

"I thought we'd never make it," Grace muttered to me. Then her face lit up. I followed her gaze out the window and melted in relief. Trista was sitting on the lawn with a bunch of AmStar employees, eating lunch.

"Trista!" I exclaimed way too enthusiastically as she strode over to help us with our footman duties. I felt like throwing my arms around her and singing my own ear-splitting chorus. A hallelujah one. Danica and Denise shot each other an odd look. "I mean, it's great to have your help," I said, more normally, handing her Kendra's polo helmet as Pookums yapped near our heels.

"No luck," she said as she took it from me, forgetting to whisper.

Sienna made a face as she hopped down and pulled off her fringed vest. "No luck with what?"

"No luck getting into—" Trista started.

"Still having trouble with the remote control programming, huh?" Grace interrupted, widening her eyes at Trista as she covered for her. "You guys will pull it off. I know you will."

"Of course we will," Trista said, sounding irritated, as if she thought Grace was expressing real sympathy.

Kendra, whose ankle injury had miraculously turned into a crippling disability after having been nonexistent for over a day, pretty much demanded Danica and Denise lift her from the van while Jardine handed a rolled-up pile of clothes at me. The stench was unmistakable. The horse-poo breeches.

"Better go soak those, Page Young," Jardine said.

"I'll help you with that," Grace called out hurriedly. "So will Trista!" She huddled closer and lowered her voice. "Emergency meeting. Our room. Now."

We shut the door and gathered on Grace's bed. Trista stroked her chin and listened as we told her everything, then nodded slowly. "Man, I wish I could've gotten into that office today," she said, at last. "Police can't arrest her with just this, but it's all lining up, isn't it? Who knows what she could be planning for the parade." Her expression darkened. "Besides Zimball, though"—she nodded at me and smiled—"we haven't ruled out any other suspects."

An uneasy feeling spread through me as I thought of going to the police about Barb. If we were wrong—or even if the evidence was too shaky to make an arrest—a different killer could go scot-free. Meanwhile, everyone would be busy laughing at the "town hero" drama queens who saw suspects everywhere they looked. Nobody in town would ever believe us again.

Grace nodded. "We've got to be on high alert this afternoon, people. For possible suspects *and* victims." She turned to me. "Soph, you have the emails and our notebook still, right? We may need to refocus the investigation fast. Do a last check through and call an emergency meeting if you find anything—or if Rod gets back to you with anything on Miyamoto's," she said officially. "We might even find something else on Lund that way."

"Roger," I answered, wondering how she always made things sound so easy.

Trista seemed lost in thought. She pursed her lips and

stared at the floor. "That button. It was navy blue, you said?" Trista asked.

Grace nodded. "Like a button from a man's blazer," she replied.

"Could be anyone's, really." Trista said. "But a Winnie the Pooh key chain, now . . ." She made a face.

"Exactly," Grace said. "Let's see what else might be hiding in that office of hers then, shall we?" Grace said. "Midnight mission tonight. Last ditch effort. It's all we've got. Listen for the code." She rapped her knuckles on the nightstand.

I nodded as we headed out the door. "Let's hope Danica and Denise don't hear it, or I'll have to lose ten rounds of 'name that tune' first."

Chapter Twenty-Three

Truth or Dare

O rders blared fast and furious over our headsets that afternoon, keeping us racing to pack "emergency" beauty kits, fix runs in stockings, set up make-up and hair stations in the Court sitting room, not to mention help the Court primp for the Festival Eve barbecue. We barely had a chance to use the bathroom, let alone puzzle over other evidence or meet. Still, the Court's mood was light and happy. I kind of liked running around with Trista and Grace, headsets in our ears and Brown Suiters buzzing past, bringing the Court water and snacks and rearranging their clothes. If it weren't for the constant thoughts of Barb Lund and our midnight mission throbbing through my head, I might have even thought it was fun.

By the time I walked into the Queen and Court sitting room later that night, I barely had any "pep" left for the

Festival pep talk Ms. Sparrow had told us to gather for. The Court were lounging in the puffy flowery armchairs, looking casual in their orientation T-shirts and flannel pajama pants as they bopped their heads to the music playing from speakers on the mahogany desk. Ms. Sparrow's Pretty Perfect "how-to" videos ran on the TV with the volume down while Danica and Denise painted the Courts' fingernails and played rounds of twenty questions, which—thanks to their twinlepathy—were ending lightning fast. I made a mental note to never, ever play charades with them.

"Where's Grace?" I asked, frowning.

Sienna looked up from her magazine. "Oh, she's with her parents."

A burst of panic jolted me. "Her parents?"

Trista shot a look at me. My stomach twisted.

"Uh-huh," Sienna nodded absently, looking at her newly pink nails. "They heard about the fire and flipped out, even though everyone assured them it was totally nothing. They think the Festival officials are being careless, I heard them say. They want to take Grace home. Pull her from the parade, even. It was kind of turning into a scene."

I cringed as I pictured the Court walking directly by Grace, her cheeks blazing as her parents asked to check smoke detectors.

Kendra shook her head sadly, no doubt horrified that the "house rules" and Festival family–only tradition had been violated by a visit with actual family members.

"Can you imagine?" Denise's eyes bulged. "The night before the parade? To have to go home?"

"Taylor Swift!" Danica blurted out suddenly. Everyone except Denise looked at her like she was insane. "That's who it is, right?" She beamed at Danica expectantly. "Your celebrity?"

"Yessss!" Denise high-fived her. Jardine shook her head at them, smiling.

Kendra shot them an annoyed look. "Ms. Sparrow's talking them down, though," she explained as if she and Ms. Sparrow had consulted about it personally. Then she added, "I hope she can stay. She's really good at covering up this beast." She pointed to the microscopic scab on her forehead from her run-in with Jardine's tiara. "And she's awesome, of course," she finished. Everyone murmured in agreement, and I was surprised to find I wasn't jealous at all, like before. I felt maybe even a little . . . proud?

"Did you know she was going to make tiny roses with ribbon for Ms. Sparrow so she can match the Coral Beauties tomorrow?" Kendra continued. "And now . . ." From the sorrow in her voice, you would have thought we hadn't faced any other tragedies that week.

"Oh my gosh, how perfect! Do you hear that?" Jardine exclaimed. She jerked her head to the speakers on the desk. "Turn it up! I love this song!"

Denise and Danica burst into giggles when they realized it was Taylor Swift's "You Belong with Me." They got up and started singing along and whirling around, and this time there were no spaghetti straps falling every two seconds, just their big smiles and the T-shirts we made at orientation billowing around them as they spun. Kendra, Jardine, and Sienna jumped up too—holding up outstretched hands both to wave their manicures dry and dance around like crazy people.

"C'mon, Sophie! C'mon, Trista!" Jardine yelled. "Get your groove on!"

"You belong with meee-ee-ee," Sienna shout-sang as she motioned for us to join on the "dance floor."

Trista and I looked at each other. She shrugged and smiled.

Before I knew it Jardine was tugging me and Trista into their circle. I shot one guilty look toward the door, but soon I was twirling around, laughing and singing as we thumped against the ottoman and puffy couches like bumper cars. As I looked around at their beaming faces and silly moves,

I thought back to the way they'd huddled around us so worriedly after we'd been locked in the fridge—and how Kendra had pulled us into their circle the night of the fire like we were their little sisters, not their servants. Sure, the three of them could be such royal pains—literally—but they were *our* royal pains. Even Kendra's weird vibrato seemed more funny than annoying right then, and I found myself wanting them to like me.

Trista stood frozen in the center of our circle for a verse or two, but when the chorus hit she suddenly thrust two fists above her head, and rocked her whole body forward and back in a superfast wave motion, her butt waggling behind her. The Court went nuts, hooting and cheering as they formed a dance circle around her. I cheered, too, wishing so much Grace would burst in and do our crazy dance moves so we could all forget everything for half a second and just have fun.

"Ladies!"

We stopped cold at the sound of Lauren Sparrow's shout echoing from down the hall. Kendra dove for the speaker volume like an Olympic gymnast, her ankle injury miraculously cured in time for our dance party. The rest us slumped down guiltily as Ms. Sparrow appeared in the doorway, her hair looking flatter and messier than usual. She frowned, her eyes dark—and even a little wild. She looked seriously stressed out. For the first time I realized she must've been under a lot of pressure to keep us all safe with everything that was going on, even without the Yangs showing up to ask questions.

"Shhh!" Ms. Sparrow hissed, not sounding at all like herself. "I'm in a meeting downstairs. And I don't need this racket right now. I'll be up in a minute. And in the meantime? Behave!"

"Yikes," Sienna said as Ms. Sparrow stormed off. Kendra looked like she might cry. She hated disappointing Ms. Sparrow—and Ms. Sparrow had never looked angrier.

We looked a little wilted, like flowers left outside the float barn too long. Danica and Denise looked at each other; then Danica nodded and said, "I know, guys! Why don't we all play twenty questions together?"

The rest of us shared a look.

"Or"—Jardine flashed a mischievous smile—"truth or dare."

"I don't play that," Kendra said. "Well, just not the dare part," she said.

"Me, neither," I said, remembering the gritty taste of liver-flavored Whiskas from the last time I'd gotten suckered in.

"Truth, then," Sienna said, her eyes lighting up. "Why don't we all tell our most embarrassing stories ever?" she suggested, mentioning that it'd totally bonded her soccer team at their sleepover before last season's playoffs. "I don't think it's an accident the Riptides took the league title," she finished. "Besides, that's why we're here tonight, right? To get pumped?" She pointed at Jardine. "Queen first!"

Jardine sighed and leaned back her head. "Oh my gosh, which one? Here's one from last month. The. Worst." She sucked in a breath like she was diving into cold water. "You know, Lucas? The blond guy. Baseball pitcher?"

Everyone but me and Trista nodded.

"So I was texting my friend, right . . . ," she began. "And I was going on about Lucas and how I wasn't sure if I should ask him to prom or not. And like, how cute he is . . . You know where this is going, right?"

"Oh, no," Kendra gasped. "You didn't."

"Yep." She flung up her hand and looked at the ceiling. "I was texting it all to Lucas. Totally spaced." A spray of gasps and laughter rose up as Jardine shook her head at herself. "Okay," she said, waving her index finger around the room. "I choose . . . Kendra!"

The stories went on, one better than the other, all involving crushes. That is, until we came to Trista, who stood up and—after letting out a high-pitched giggle I'd never heard come out of her—told us that at summer science camp her model rocket had shot off sideways and plunked into a lake. "Mixed up metric with US standard measurements. Threw the newton-second calculations all out of whack," she'd said, shaking her head at herself as her cheeks colored. "Mickey Mouse—mistake."

The Court *awwww*ed as if they understood perfectly. Kendra even patted Trista on the shoulder as she sat back down.

"That leaves you, Sophie!" Danica said, clasping her hands together.

"Go, Sophie!" Denise whooped as the Court leaned forward. They were counting on me to end with a bang. I felt it—and I didn't want to let them down.

"Sooooo many to choose from," I lied, trying to mimic Jardine's dramatic opening.

"So. Picture it. Sleepover at a friend's house. We're all on her bed, laughing." The Court nodded. "And . . ." I drew in a breath. "I crack up so hard that I pee my pants a little."

There was a long pause. "Ha!" Kendra barked, but it—and every other chuckle in the room—was forced.

"Some got on her comforter," I added, hoping that was more interesting.

"Ew," Jardine said, wrinkling her nose. The rest of the Court looked away awkwardly. Sienna yawned and checked her watch. I guess only Trista could get away with telling a story not involving boys. A sinking feeling came over me, and suddenly I was desperate to make up for my lameness.

"But," I raised one finger. "If Grace were here? She has an *amazing* one."

The Courts' heads tilted up to me, eyes shining. I froze. The words had flown out before I'd even thought about it.

"You'll have to ask her about it," I backpedaled.

"But she might not even come back!" Kendra erupted. She sure was over her sadness awfully quickly.

"Oh, tell it! Please tell it!" Denise called out.

I shook my head, panic rising. "I can't, guys. I mean, it's her story, right? I won't do it justice."

"She'd totally tell it. We all told ours," Danica said it like she'd known Grace since kindergarten. "We're bonding!"

"Never mind, guys," Jardine rolled her eyes. "She's not going to tell it." She sighed as if I'd just confirmed she'd lost any sliver of hope that I could ever possibly be cool.

"Well, maybe for, you know, group bonding . . . ," I began. Maybe it wouldn't be that big of a deal, I told myself with a shrug.

"Yes!" Sienna called out with a pump of her fist. She

leaned forward in her chair.

There was no going back. Seconds later the whole story was tumbling out of me. It went over better than I ever, ever could have imagined. I felt giddy as they clutched their sides, in stitches, while I dramatically acted out the time that, at a barbecue at my house, Grace had come back from the bathroom with her skirt completely tucked into the back of her underwear. As they laughed harder, something came over me and I couldn't stop. "And get this, guys," I said, breathless, my words tripping over each other, "She was low on clean laundry, so she was wearing way too-small underwear that rode up her butt." I tucked my shirt into my pants and pretended to be walking around with a wedgie. "And not just any underwear. Too small *Wonder Woman* underwear." As the girls howled, I went in for the kicker, "And guess who saw it and told her?"

"Oh no. No, no, no!" Kendra exclaimed. "Don't say your dad. Please don't say your dad."

"So much worse," I said.

"Your brother?" Danica cringed.

Jardine gasped. "Oh my gosh, your brother is Jake Young. Jake Young had to tell Grace to get her dress out of her Wonder Woman underwear. I. Am. Dying!"

"Jake! He's so cuuuute, too!" Sienna said. Then she

clapped her hand over her mouth. "Oh, sorry, Sophie. Don't tell him I said that, okay?"

I'd totally forgotten Jake was in Sienna's math class. A cold, slithery feeling ran through me as they kept laughing until they were gasping for breath. Kendra sounded close to another hyperventilation fit. I could only imagine how they would have howled if I'd told them Jake was Grace's secret older crush. *At least I left that out,* I told myself. It wasn't much consolation, though. I'd just sold out my best friend.

As their laughter faded, Trista looked at me from across the room, chewing on the side of her lip. I felt hollow as I pictured Grace downstairs, begging to stay while we all danced around and told stories. Stories about her. What had I been thinking? I wished I could gather all my words and shove them back inside me.

Before the Court could burst into another chorus of the Wonder Woman song, I distracted them by pointing out that the Pretty Perfect interview with Mr. Handsome himself, Raúl Jiménez, was on Ms. Sparrow's video loop. To my relief, Jardine was all over it. She started singing out the variations on her married names. When she petered out, I scrambled to find the pad she'd written them all down on to keep her going. I found it on the end table by the couch and was about to run it to her when my eye caught something that made me smile. Right there next to J-Squared, J2, and Jardi-J were the letters JJim. Jardine had dotted her *i* with a heart. A spark of warmth lit up somewhere inside me, and I felt like "Jim" himself was sending me a sign that everything—the story, the night mission, even the Festival itself—was going to turn out all right. As I looked around the room at the Court's shining faces, I realized how much Mr. Steptoe would've like this Festival Eve pep talk, and maybe even the sparkly heart over his *i*.

Just then Ms. Sparrow appeared at the door. She smoothed down her hair and forced a smile. "Okay, I'm ready for you all. Now, what is it you always say, Queen Jardi? 'Let's get this party started?'"

The Court was quiet as Grace passed by in the hall behind her, sniffling.

We all exchanged looks. Finally, Danica asked the question on the tip of my tongue:

"So, is Grace going to get to stay?"

Chapter Twenty-Four

Flash in the Night

Ms. Sparrow nodded and broke into a grin. Kendra gave an over-the-top cheer. I slumped in relief, only for my heart to start racing when it hit me that our mission was definitely on—and how dangerous it could really be. As Ms. Sparrow made a fun game out of quizzing us on the key points of walking, waving, poise, posture, and etiquette, her voice faded to background noise behind the staticky rush of panic in my head. Before we charged ahead that night, I had to review our notes one last time. Grace was right. With the parade kicking off at noon the next day, if we were wrong about Barb, we'd only have a few hours of mansion access to get anything on other suspects.

Ms. Sparrow gave a detailed overview of the next morning's schedule, gathered us all for a group hug, then sent us off for an early lights-out. "Call time at eight a.m., ladies!" she sang out as the Court shuttled to their rooms. "That's eight a.m. Festival Time," she emphasized. "If you're on time, you're late. Gotta hurry up and wait!"

I shivered as I remembered Barb Lund singing the same jingle to Grace and me in the very office we'd be breaking into that night.

Just before I was about to follow Trista into her room to check on Grace, Ms. Sparrow shooed me playfully to bed. "Uh-uh-uh!" She wagged her finger. "You've got to get your beauty rest!"

Little did she know how ugly the next day could be if we actually did.

As Denise and Danica brushed their teeth in the bathroom, I tucked my flashlight, the emails, and the suspect note-book under the covers with me. My stomach somersaulted with worry, and it wasn't just because of the night mission. I had to keep shoving away the image of me tucking my oversized T-shirt into the back of my sweats to imitate Grace's anything but *wonder*ful moment. I had to tell Grace and apologize—as soon as I could. But first, I had to focus.

I waited until I heard Danica and Denise's twin snores, pulled my covers over my head like a tent, then carefully clicked on my flashlight and looked over our notes and emails again.

What was it Grace said? Motive and opportunity. We needed both. Katz and Lee still had no alibis and plenty of motive. I reread Harrison Lee's email, moving my lips silently along with his puzzling words: "Thanks for your offer to take over bookkeeping . . . but I've got it under control." Maybe he had it so much under control, he'd been stealing. It seemed very possible that Mr. Steptoe could have uncovered some shady business. Would Lee have killed to cover it up?

I flipped to the email exchange between Steptoe and Katz. "I'll be here until midnight," Mr. Steptoe's email said. Sometime after Steptoe sent that email at 5:05 p.m., Mr. Katz had to have picked up his posters at least. If not, he would've been carrying them—not the white file box with his glass paperweight sticking up like a dagger—as he'd scooted out of Mr. Steptoe's office.

I read Ms. Sparrow's email to Mr. Steptoe again. Why would she be emailing him about "breeding seasons" and "harvesting"? Ms. Sparrow not only wasn't involved with flower orders, she seemed to actively avoid flowers at all costs. I remembered that she'd even told Trista she couldn't step foot in the float barn without taking allergy medicine first. Steptoe and Sparrow both couldn't stand Barb. Maybe they weren't lovers, but could the two of them have been in on something together? Something that went really wrong? Even so, the pollen-filled float barn had to be the last place she'd have picked to take him out.

I clicked off my flashlight and pushed aside the papers. The questions swirling in my brain hid the fact that only two potential killers had a clear motive to attack not just Steptoe, but Lee and Sparrow, too. And that night we were headed straight into their lair.

I started drifting off as I waited for Grace's knock signal only to be jerked awake again by a strange bird or owl hooting outside in the usually dead-quiet night. I was about to get up and shut the window when a pulsing light flashed several times across the ceiling, then went dark. I froze. The light came again. *Flash flash.* Pause. *Flash, flash.* The room went pitch black, and the bird hooted again. It almost seemed to be imitating the rhythm of the lights.

It *was* imitating the rhythm of the lights! I flung back the covers and crept to the window, scanning the dark shapes and shadows for any sign of Rod. He had to be hidden in the side garden.

The light flashed again, and I counted carefully. Four quick flashes, a pause. Two more. I felt around for the jeans

I'd slung over the bedpost and reached for the Polybius square in the back pocket. *Flash, flash.* Pause. *Flash, flash.* A long silence followed. As I waited for the "bird" to hoot the same pattern, I checked the card and ran my finger down the grid. Four and two intersected at *R*. Two and two at *G*.

RG. Rose Garden. My heart hammered wildly. Rod wasn't coming to the mansion to play flashlight games. Something was up, and it couldn't be good. I had to act fast.

I pulled on my jeans, tossed on a hoodie over my over-sized pajama shirt, and dragged my fingers through my hair, cursing myself for even caring how embarrassed I'd be when Rod saw me.

I tiptoed to the door, twisted the squeaky knob with a wince, and slipped down the hall to Grace and Trista.

As soon as they caught onto what was happening, they darted out of bed. Trista threw on her cargo jacket over her lamb pajamas. Grace had already changed into jeans and a sweatshirt for spying. Downstairs Trista punched in the 1890 alarm code the Brown Suiters had been so careless with, and we headed out into the darkness.

The night was cold and pitch-black except for the stars winking above us like pinpricks of light shining through a velvet curtain. The air burned my throat as we slunk across the terrace and made our way down the path to the rose garden. No sooner had we stepped through the vine-covered arch into the garden than a shadow flickered beside the stone table and stood up.

It was Rod, of course. He brushed dirt off his jeans and stood up as Grace pointed her flashlight his way. "Thank God," he said, his face pale. "Any more hooting and flashing and I was going to get caught for sure."

I couldn't be sure in the darkness, but his eyes looked puffy, as if he might have been crying. His Adam's apple bobbed as he swallowed hard. "My dad just left to meet Barb Lund at the overflow float barn. Alone."

Grace drew in a sharp breath. I felt the blood drain from my face.

Rod kept calm as he explained that Barb had called his dad and told him she needed his help very urgently, refusing to take no for an answer. "She was totally flipping out about moving all this stuff out of the way to clear a path for the floats before tomorrow," he said. "You know how she is. She always manages to rope my dad into something."

"So true," Trista said with a heavy sigh, as if Mr. Zimball might want to reconsider being so nice.

Rod shoved his hands in his jacket pockets and looked at us pleadingly. "He wouldn't listen to me. He says I'm being ridiculous." With a cringe, he added: "He thinks you guys have gotten me all worked up."

"We have. But for a good reason!" Grace cried. She started to pace, gravel crunching under her feet.

I pictured Barb Lund lying in wait for Mr. Zimball in the dark overflow float barn.

"Did you call the police yet?" I said, wishing I'd already told him we'd found Barb's key chain on the float. "We have to call the police."

Rod shook his head. "I knew they'd need to hear it from someone they'd believe," he said. He pulled out his phone and handed it to me.

I stared at its blue-green glow, paralyzed as scenes flashed across my mind from the night I begged Officer Grady to get down to Luna Vista Middle School to capture Deborah Bain. It felt like I'd been flung back in time. It was all starting again.

"Quick, Sophie," Rod said, his voice cracking. "By now he's already there."

I imagined Mr. Zimball stepping into the dark, shadowy barn again. A burst of adrenaline surged through me, and I grabbed the phone. Rod, Grace, and Trista kept their eyes locked on me, waiting and listening as the 911 operator came on the line.

"There's an emergency at the Luna Vista Rancho," I said.

"Is anyone hurt?" the woman on the line asked.

"Please send an ambulance and police," I said as if I hadn't heard her. "And is it possible to connect me with Officer Paul Grady?" I said. "Tell him it's Sophie Young."

There was a long pause.

"Sophie Young," the operator repeated, a spark of recognition in her voice. "I can request his call back, but . . ."

"Please," I whispered, avoiding Rod's eyes. "It's a matter of life or death."

I'd thought Rod was wasting time by coming to us first, but now I realized how smart it was. I wasn't some twelve-year-old freaking out. I was Sophie Young, Luna Vista hero. I could feel her deciding what to do.

"Stay on the line, please," she said, at last.

Grace started pacing again as I waited. Rod shivered and rubbed his hands to warm them. Trista stood, zipping and unzipping a pocket on her jacket.

It felt like hours later, but Officer Grady's voice finally came on the line, sleepy and gruff. "This had better be important," he grumbled.

Chapter Twenty-Five

Showdown at the (Not OK) Corral

Officer Grady cut short my crazy rambling, promised he'd take care of everything right away, and told us to get back to bed immediately. But his long, weary sigh as he hung up the phone made me uneasy. I pictured him rolling his eyes, fluffing his pillow, and settling right back to sleep. The Festival was tomorrow, after all. The biggest day for the Luna Vista police all year.

The phone beeped as I clicked it off. The three of them stared at me.

"So?" Grace asked.

I took a deep breath. "We've got to get over there. Now."

The Luna Vista Rancho and Stables were at least two miles away. No way we could sprint that far—and even if we walked like wild arm-and-hip swinging pro speed walkers, it'd take us at least a half hour. Right then, even the mansion glowing white above us on the hill seemed far off.

"I came on my bike," Rod offered uncertainly. "One of you could maybe balance on my handlebars?"

I couldn't tell for sure, but it seemed like he'd looked right at Grace when he asked the question. I felt something fizzle inside as if my heart had sprung a leak.

"Way too dangerous," Trista snapped, not even realizing she'd saved us from an awkward silence. "And not fast enough to be worth it."

"I have an idea," Rod said, straightening suddenly. He hopped onto his tiptoes and looked down the hill, then turned back to us, eyes gleaming. "Which one of you can drive?"

Minutes later Trista was gripping the steering wheel of Barb's golf cart with both hands, her eyes fixed on the mansion's side driveway like she was playing the final level of TrigForce Five. She'd only ever driven the hydraulic go-cart she'd made for the science fair that year, she'd admitted. "But I totally owned Formula One Fever, 1, 2, and 3," she'd said as she slammed her foot on the pedal and jolted us away from the float barn with a whiplashy lurch.

Rod and I clung to the back, side by side, the wind rushing in our ears and drowning out the cart's electric hum. He'd jumped on last like he was hopping a leaving train, and my heart had leaped a little as his shoulder touched mine.

Rod's idea had been a stroke of genius. Barb always parked her golf cart by the float barn in front of a big sign with her full name on it, key hanging from the ignition. Not that Trista wouldn't have been able to hot-wire it. As it was, we had to convince her it was better to quietly roll the cart out of its spot rather than ripping out wires to silence the cart's annoying beeping when it was in reverse.

"Hold on!" Trista warned as we hit a dip at the end of the driveway and turned sharply onto Luna Vista Drive. Trista didn't seem to have discovered the brake yet. Still, once we were cruising down the actual street at half the speed of a normal car, it felt like we were moving in slow motion. I was suddenly very aware of how long Mr. Zimball had already been at the overflow barn with Barb Lund. I looked at Rod, his face pinched, clutching the cart's roof, and knew he was thinking the same thing. I reached out and grabbed his free hand and squeezed it. He looked into my eyes and squeezed it back.

"Left at the light!" Grace called out, and Trista turned, following the route the van had taken us earlier. The Luna

Vista Rancho came into view. In the dim light outside the overflow barn I could make out two cars parked in front. One was definitely the Zimballs' minivan. I picked out one of the stars spread out like a canopy above us and wished on it, praying we were still in time.

Dust kicked up in a murky cloud as Trista skidded to a halt right next to one of the cars. We hopped out and dashed for the building, stopping short just outside. A horrible squeal of tires and rumble of an engine rang out from behind the half-open metal sliding door. We looked at each other in terror. Then Grace outstretched her shaking hand, palm down. I slapped mine on top. Trista added hers. Taking the cue, Rod joined. "Ready?" Grace said. "Break!" We flung our hands into the air and rushed forward.

We only took two steps inside before we froze. The beast of a forklift that Grace and I had seen sleeping in the corner was awake now. It roared toward us, headlight eyes gleaming even in the floodlit barn, two iron teeth pointed at us like daggers. At its wheel, barely visible over the tower of massive boxes piled on the front, was a wild-eyed Barb Lund.

"Go back! Run!" a panicked voice shouted at us. I turned to my right and spotted Mr. Zimball, face twisted in terror, trying to shield himself behind a giant wire frame in the shape of a rhino. The flimsy wire would be no match for the forklift's steely prongs. Barb cried out, and made a sharp zigzag directly toward him, toppling one of her boxes. Grace shrieked as it crashed to the ground in front of us.

"Stop!" Trista hollered at Ms. Lund. "The police are right behind us!" she lied.

Barb waved her hands and gunned the engine, shouting something we couldn't hear over its roar. She'd lost her mind entirely. Three witnesses, just kids—one of them her victim's son—and she still barreled ahead. Or, backward, actually. She threw the forklift into reverse, gearing up to come at Mr. Zimball again.

"Take cover, Dad!" Rod yelled, cupping his hands around his mouth.

Mr. Zimball made a dash for a tall stack of wooden pallets left over from flower deliveries, sawdust flying as his feet pounded across it. Then he stumbled and stopped short. Grace gasped.

"Quick! Go!" Rod screamed again, his voice cracking.

But Mr. Zimball couldn't go. He'd stepped right through the wooden slats of one of the pallets on the ground with such force that his entire foot up to his ankle was now firmly lodged in it. He stood helplessly, like a man sinking in quicksand, as Barb careened wildly around to come at him again.

Rod leaped forward to rush at the forklift, as if he thought he could wave a red cape at Lund like a bullfighter and distract her. I flung out my arm and pulled him back. "We need a plan of attack," I cried, furiously trying to map out paths through the maze of floats and frames and piles of rusty scaffolding.

Before I could figure one out, footsteps thundered behind us. Five uniformed officers burst in, their shouts echoing in the rafters and their nightsticks swinging. Behind them in a sweatshirt and jeans, hair rumpled, was Officer Grady.

I nearly fainted in relief.

Chapter Twenty-Six

Forked Over

As the officers charged forward to surround Barb and free Mr. Zimball, Officer Grady hustled us outside. It wasn't until I saw Grace's trembling hands that I realized how much I was shaking too.

Officer Grady put his arm on my elbow and guided me to the squad car. As I turned to thank him for coming, he held up a hand. "I know, I know," he said wearily. "'You're welcome,'" he sheepishly repeated what we'd said to him when we'd tipped him off about Deborah Bain.

"Actually, I wanted to say thanks," I said with a weak smile. "For believing us."

He cocked his head at me. "For believing you?" The red lights of the ambulance parked next to us flickered across his face as he rubbed his stubbly chin. "Sophie Young, at this point you could call and tell me that Martians had landed in your backyard and I'd believe you." He raised an eyebrow, thrust his finger toward the squad car, and added, "I just hope next time *you* believe *me*. Now stay put. All of you." He pivoted toward the barn.

We sat in silent shock as an officer came out, reassured us that Mr. Zimball was safe and everything was under control, then drove us directly to the Luna Vista police station. Lauren Sparrow, Rod's mom, Grace's and my parents, and Trista's dad rushed forward all at once, hovering around us so frantically that my heart raced faster. Our parents came with us into Grady's office as he took each of our statements separately. I felt as if I were in a hazy dream as I repeated our theories and told him where they could find the charred key chain on the Girl Scout float. I was too tired and nervous and barely made sense, but it was such a relief to be listened to, at last.

"Took pictures to show you didn't tamper with the evidence, huh?" Grady nodded, impressed. "That'll be a great help." However, he—and my parents—followed up with a sharp reminder that I should have come directly to them, or at least Ms. Sparrow. I started to explain that we'd tried that, then clapped my mouth shut. Sometimes adults only hear what they want to.

As I answered Grady's questions, I pictured Barb

careening back and forth around the broken down floats and shuddered. I guess we'd been wrong about Lily being mixed up in it all. Barb would surely have dragged her to help take out Mr. Zimball, too, if they'd been in it together. Lily was always at her side. Lund had clearly lost her mind. How else could she have let herself take everything so far? A grown woman in Winnie the Pooh overalls trying to run a man down with a forklift? Our crazy theories didn't seem crazy anymore—not after that. Especially when Mr. Zimball finally joined us in the waiting room and—after hugging Rod and Rod's mom very, very tightly—told us his side of the story.

"Barbara called me and was terribly upset," he said. "Stacks of boxes and some equipment were blocking the door, and she was convinced if we didn't take care of it, we'd be delayed getting the floats in position tomorrow. She begged me to come. It's always easier to help her and be done with it." He sighed. "My son here was listening to the call. He warned me—told me that he thought Lund might be behind Steptoe's death and be trying to take out the Royal Court judges."

Grace's mom drew in a sharp breath. Ms. Sparrow shifted on the waiting room bench. She looked more than a little rattled. If she hadn't already known she was a target, she sure did now.

"I thought our fine pages had put ideas in his head," Mr. Zimball continued, shooting us an apologetic look. He patted Rod on the knee as he added that the warnings didn't seem believable. "Things go haywire every Festival. I thought this year it was simply more cursed than most. I wanted to make sure things went right. What can I say? I got tunnel vision." He tossed up his hands and let them fall to his lap again. "And frankly? Barbara has always been a bit, well . . ." As he searched for the right word, his wife found one of her own a nanosecond earlier.

"Odd," she offered.

"Difficult," Mr. Zimball finished at the same time.

Rod's mom and dad exchanged a smile, and I finally saw where Rod got his pretty hazel eyes.

"Truth is always stranger than fiction, huh?" Trista's dad bellowed, shaking his head.

Mr. Zimball explained that when he'd arrived at the float barn, Barb was already in the forklift driver's seat. When she threw it into gear and roared full speed ahead at him, he saw his life flash before him, remembered the email we'd found, and realized he'd been wrong about Barb.

"She was completely unhinged," he said, talking faster as he remembered. "She kept screaming something about an accident as she came at me, and I realized she was probably trying to stage one. I dove for cover, but she kept coming for me. She was all over the place. I was actually trying to pull out my cell phone and call 911 when you came in." He shook his head and turned to us gravely. "I'm so lucky you four called the police. But next time—you keep yourselves safe. Let them do the work. Understood?"

We nodded. While Grace's dad gave her a scolding look, my mom chimed in too. "You could've gotten yourselves killed on that cart! Driving? In the middle of the night, no less. Does it even have headlights?" She frowned worriedly as she tucked a strand of hair behind my ear.

"Oh, definitely, Ms. Young. Pretty bright wattage too," Trista answered for me. "And, don't worry. They were in excellent hands," she added, tugging on the flaps of her jacket proudly. "I took first place in the Monaco, Portuguese, and Italian Grand Prix." She shrugged. "Only virtually. But still."

My mom gave Trista's lamb pajamas the once-over and hid a smile.

"Then I recommend you quit while you're ahead," Trista's dad chided.

"Or stick with remote-controlled driving only," Ms. Sparrow laughed.

We all laughed then, even Trista. We were still chuckling when Officer Grady came out of his office again. He looked puzzled and insecure, like a little kid who wasn't sure if adults were laughing at him. Then he cleared his throat. "Thank you for your help tonight, all. I have some news."

Chapter Twenty-Seven

Wonder Women

When Officer Grady announced that Barb Lund had been arrested for attempted assault and was being held for questioning regarding Mr. Steptoe's death, the tension slid out of me all at once, and I suddenly felt so exhausted I could barely sit up straight. Sighs of relief rippled through the station waiting room as Grady, looking even more tired than I felt, explained that the current evidence gave them "probable cause" to hold Lund for at least twenty-four hours while they investigated more. "With the Festival taking place tomorrow afternoon, we are especially mindful of the need for extra precautions," he added.

Trista, Grace, Rod and I looked at each other, dazed but beaming in victory.

Officer Grady patted the copy of Barb's email that Mr. Zimball had given him, mentioned they'd found the key chain and button undisturbed, and thanked us again. He would keep us updated about the investigation.

"Can you believe it?" Grace whispered, nudging me. "We did it!"

Ms. Sparrow and the adults leaned in to discuss whether perhaps, under the circumstances, it might be best for us to head home and consider our royal assignment completed. "It's only one more day, after all," Ms. Sparrow said. "And maybe you all can still ride on the float?"

Grace stood up suddenly. Her parents looked startled.

"Why not ask us?" she said quietly. Then she turned to Trista and me. "Because I think we might want to uphold the pledge we made as royal pages. Right, guys?"

I looked at my parents. It was hard to think of anything better than going home and falling into my own bed right then. I missed my mom and dad. I missed Grandpa. I even missed Jake. A lot, actually. And I certainly could do without slathering Kendra's shoulders with bronzer for the big day.

"It's up to you all," Mr. Zimball said. "We sure would miss you. But the Winter Sun always shines, no matter what." He smiled as he repeated Mr. Steptoe's favorite motto.

My eyes met Trista and Grace's. The thing was, the Festival kind of did feel like a family now. Sure, we all had our annoying habits. Jardine and her picky eating. Kendra and her exaggerated injuries. Danica and her Axe body-spray obsession. But just like I loved Jake even though he put his stinky feet all over everything, I cared about the Court, too. I cared about Mr. Steptoe—and about making the Festival the best it could be, considering.

"I'd like to go back to the mansion," I said, standing up next to Grace. My parents had already been whispering about the logistics of picking up my things in the meantime. Their eyes widened.

"Me too. We belong with them, right?" said Trista. Then, as if embarrassed by her feelings, she added, "Besides, I still have some work to do on the Root Beer float."

Our parents looked at each other uncertainly. Ms. Sparrow put a hand on Janice Yang's shoulder, who seemed shaken. Trista's dad gave a half-laugh and held up his hands. "At this point, they've been through it all! What else could happen? I say, might as well let 'em!"

That night, after our parents had driven us back to the mansion and we'd said our good-byes on the terrace steps, I felt uneasy. The parade was tomorrow. We'd literally saved the day. I should have felt like skidding through the mansion halls slapping high fives and throwing another dance party so Grace could be part of it too. Instead, as I crept into our room and crawled into bed, I had a nervous feeling in my stomach like the time I'd forgotten to do the back side of my math test. I was so tired that even Denise and Danica's snores didn't keep me from falling into a deep sleep.

The next morning, I jolted awake to the sound of Danica and Denise's squeals as they burst into the bedroom.

"Town heroes!" Denise cried out, bounding onto my bed. She sure wasn't faking enthusiasm this time.

"Again!" echoed Danica as I propped myself on one elbow and squinted in the light streaming in through the curtains. I heard paper crinkle as I smoothed my wild hair, looked down, and realized all the emails I'd been looking at were still in my bed. I hid them under the covers again, then looked up and smiled sheepishly as Danica swallowed me in a hug that amazingly didn't smell even a bit like Axe body spray. "You saved Mr. Zimball's life, roomie. You saved the Festival!" she said. Then she repeated, "You saved Rod's dad," as if realizing she might have made the Festival sound slightly more important.

Ms. Sparrow had let the three of us sleep in, but the tailor had already arrived for the final dress fitting. It was time to start getting ready for the big day. I pulled on sweats and my tai chi T-shirt Jardine had made at our craft night, then followed Danica and Denise into the hall. Two Brown

Suiters striding toward us immediately stopped and showered me with thanks and pats on the shoulder while Danica and Denise repeated their "town hero" chorus as proudly as if I were their own sister. The happy lightness in my chest I'd expected to feel last night surged through me. As I continued down the hall, I felt as if I were floating.

Grace and Trista, cheeks glowing, flew to me as soon as I came in the door of the Queen and Court sitting room, and we did our special team hand slap and finger wriggle. Grace threw her arms around me in a happy hug, and then reached toward Trista to do the same when she paused suddenly. "Oops," she said, biting back a smile. "Sorry. Your flair." She straightened Trista's jacket instead.

"Thank you," Trista grinned, truly pleased by Grace's thoughtfulness.

Grace linked arms with me. "Best. Day. Ever. Am I right?" Her eyes were shining.

"Best. Day. Ever," I repeated, pulling her arm closer to my side. It really was.

The tailor rustled in with our dresses so we could do our final fitting before heading to the Royal Court to help them with theirs. They'd taken our measurements the first day, and judging from the way Trista had grumbled through them, I expected her to refuse to put on whatever dress they brought for her. But after she inspected the bright-blue dress's fabric as if it were the subject of a science experiment—she carefully folded up her cargo jacket, laid it on her bed next to her stuffed tiger, then put the dress over her head and plunged into it like she was diving into uncharted seas. Of course, two seconds later we heard her muffled cries for help as she got lost somewhere in the satin waves and had to wriggle around headless until we rescued her. After we zipped up the back, she walked right over to the full-length mirror on the back of the door and stared. Grace and I looked at each other and held our breath. It felt like something was going to explode.

Something did explode. A laugh of pure joy. "I can't believe it. I look *amazing*," she said, staring in the mirror in disbelief. You'd have thought she was meeting a celebrity. Then she whooped and hooted, spinning around, her black curls twirling with her. The shiny folds of fabric rustled and rippled as she strutted her big self around the room, pursing her lips and pretending to be a supermodel on a catwalk while Grace and I cheered. She did look amazing. Really, really amazing.

She stopped abruptly and looked down at herself, frowning. "I don't think I even need my jacket," she said, dead serious. "Do you?"

As Grace screwed up her eyes and cocked her head, pretending to think about it, the tailor shot her a puzzled look. "Better without," Grace said at last. The tailor and I nodded exaggeratedly.

Butterflies fluttered through me as I slipped into my own dress. It was the same blue satin but tight around my legs and hips. I think I was supposed to look like a mermaid. I braced myself before looking in the mirror. I never felt like myself when I was wearing a dress, anyway—let alone one that transformed half of me into a fish. But when I saw my reflection, I felt the same surprise that Trista must have. The dress didn't look bad on me at all. It looked really good, actually. I stood up on my tiptoes. "Maybe I should see if Ms. Sparrow can dig up some wedges, to, you know, add height?"

Grace broke into a wide smile. "You look so pretty, Sophie," she said. "Pretty and perfect."

I smiled back and picked a stray piece of lint from her shoulder. "You look fantastic too, Agent Yang. Like a town hero."

"Who knew? Right, Sophie?" Trista was shaking her head. Then her face darkened. "Oh man," she said.

"What?" I looked down at my dress, worried she'd seen a stain.

"I just realized why we haven't been able to get the Luna Vista float cranking up to full speed. The pulse duration control's set wrong." Her dress wrinkled as she slouched and sighed. "I wonder if there's even time to fix it."

I had no idea what the heck a pulse duration control was. It didn't seem like it could possibly matter now. "It's all right, Trista," I said. "You've done your best. What more is there?"

Trista stared glumly into space, not even seeming to hear me. The tailor gave our dresses one final check, then we slipped back into our regular clothes and followed her to the official Royal Court sitting room to help the Court with their fitting. Trista took one look at the line-up of Coral Beauty rose bouquets, sneezed one of her roaring sneezes, and muttered something about needing to find her allergy meds.

"Woo-hoo!" Jardine cried out and sprang to her feet the instant she saw us. As the Court flocked around us, at first I thought they were just excited to try on their dresses. Then they swept us up in hugs as if we were long lost relatives and pressed us with a zillion questions about the night before.

We puffed up our chests proudly, answering every last one. Jardine laughed and high-fived Grace. I felt a surge of dread as I guessed what was coming next.

It was worse than I ever could have imagined. Jardine flung her arms up and crossed her wrists above her head, then twirled around, belting out the theme song from Wonder Woman at Trista-like volume. "Won-derrrrrr Womannnnnn!"

I froze, numb, as the rest of the Court chimed in, laughing and singing while Jardine continued her spinning. Pookums sprang forward with his own imitation, dizzily following Jardine's whirls. I felt Trista's eyes on me. My whole body felt like it was burning as I braced myself for Grace's reaction.

"Ha! Wonder Women." Grace chuckled, giving a bashful smile. "That's good. Aren't we, though?" She stretched her arms out and struck her own Wonder Woman pose.

Jardine laughed. "You mean, aren't *you*?" she slung her arm around Grace's shoulder. "Right, guys? She really is Wonder Woman!"

Grace looked at me and shrugged, as if embarrassed she was getting all the credit for Barb's big arrest. A sinkhole opened in my chest. Some small part of me hung onto the hope that she might not care. "Grace, I have to explain something—" I started.

"But I mean, like, get it?" Jardine interrupted, irritated

that Grace was missing the joke. She pointed to her backside. "Wonder Woman."

Grace's face crumpled in confusion. She nudged me. If Jardine weren't Queen Jardine, Grace would've definitely given her a full-on crazy look. Instead she fake-laughed, pretending it was absolutely normal that Jardine thought her butt had superpowers.

"Love it," Sienna chimed in. "Perfect way to own the embarrassment, you know? Worst moment and best moment: same great nickname!"

"Wait. What?" Grace asked. Jardine stopped singing. I watched in horror as a slow, awful wave of recognition spread across Grace's face. Within seconds, she turned a deep reddish-brown, like she'd been lying out in the desert sun for weeks.

She whipped around to me, her eyes dead inside. "Seriously?" Her bottom lip quivered. "Why would you tell them that, Sophie?"

Her question wasn't even a question, really. It fizzled into a sentence that came out as a rasp.

I stood, dumbstruck. The flowery drapes and wallpaper of the Queen and Court sitting room blurred around me as my insides throbbed with shame. I would've done anything to go back in time a day and do it all over. "I'm so sorry,

Grace. I didn't think—I mean—I wasn't thinking straight," I stammered. "And last night everyone was sharing stories, and if you'd been there I thought you might have . . ."

Grace spun on her heels and walked away.

"Wait!" I called after her. "Let me explain!"

Grace whirled back. "There's nothing to explain, Sophie," she hissed.

As she thundered out the door and down the hall, a lump the size of a fist formed in my throat.

The Court stared in shock.

"Uh-oh," Sienna said at last.

"Ouch," Jardine said, slowly letting her hand fall from her mouth.

Sienna patted my shoulder in sympathy. "Don't worry, Sophie. She'd have totally told us the story herself. She'll get over it. It's no big deal, right?"

Trista, who had quietly watched the whole scene, shook her head sadly.

I looked to where Grace had disappeared, tears stinging my eyes, then back to them again. "It is a big deal," I said, my voice more of a croak as I stared down at Grandpa Young's dog tags. "A really, really big deal."

"Uh, guys?" Kendra interrupted then. "I think this might be a really bad time, but . . ." She held out a crumpled pair of riding breeches and fanned her hand in front of her wrinkled nose. "Pookums just found these?"

Everyone turned to me, eyebrows raised.

At least that was one mess I'd be able to clean up.

Chapter Twenty-Eight

Pretty Perfect

Ms. Sparrow found me scrubbing the poo-stained riding pants in the bathroom off the sitting room. She'd changed already into her own outfit for the parade that—no surprise—matched the rose theme perfectly. She'd paired a lovely cream-colored silk blouse and coral cardigan with bright-coral pumps and the same rose-patterned skirt she'd worn the day she'd shared the horrible news about Mr. Steptoe. My mind reeled as I realized all that had happened since then. Five days was all it took to find a killer and lose a best friend.

"You doing all right, Soph?" Ms. Sparrow said gently. Tears sprang back into my eyes at her question. She quickly stepped in to help me rinse out the breeches. "There's a tissue on the vanity," she said, turning her attention to the pants in order to give me a moment of privacy. "The girls told me what happened," she said after I'd blown my nose. "I thought I'd check in."

I looked back at her red-rimmed eyes and for a minute I thought she was actually so sad for me that she was also tearing up. I almost passed the tissues to her before she complained that the Court's royal bouquets had made her allergies act up like Trista's. She looked tired too. Her Pretty Perfect make-up could maybe take ten years off, but it couldn't erase the dark circles under her eyes. It had been a late night for all of us.

"Yeah, I'm all right, I think," I said. My words came out sounding strangled.

"You've had quite a weekend." Ms. Sparrow nodded. "And we're all really, really proud of you girls." She hung up the breeches to dry and turned back to me. "Don't worry," she said gently. "Friends have their ups and downs, you know."

I laugh-sniffled and had to wipe my nose again. "Especially when they're trying to catch a killer, huh?"

Ms. Sparrow didn't laugh back. She just patted my shoulder. "Sometimes friends make mistakes they can't ever take back. But that's not what happened here. Grace will realize this mistake isn't worth losing a friend over."

"You think so?" I said, crumpling my tissue into a ball.

"I know so," Ms. Sparrow said. "I've had enough of my own friend trouble to know the difference. We made mistakes. And we fixed them. You'll be able to make this up to Grace. She'll forgive you. I know she will."

I looked down and took a deep breath. The roses on Ms. Sparrow's skirt blurred together, and I felt a sudden wave of sadness that Grace hadn't had a chance to make the tiny roses out of ribbon to decorate the buttons of Ms. Sparrow's shoes. They would have matched perfectly.

I realized it with a jolt. The roses. The morning she'd broken the news about Steptoe was also the day the Royal Court announcements *should* have taken place. The same Royal Court announcements where Mr. Steptoe would have proudly unveiled the Festival's secret flower theme. My hands trembled as I pictured Harrison Lee on the mansion terrace the next day, revealing Mr. Steptoe's "final gift to us all," as the tiara—with its beautifully shaped Coral Beauty rose—spiraled into view on the pedestal.

Only the people at Miyamoto's Jewelers knew that Mr. Steptoe had decided a Coral Beauty rose would grace the Sun Queen's tiara that year. And yet Ms. Sparrow just happens to slip on a rose-filled skirt that matches the theme almost perfectly? Sure, lots of people own flowery skirts—even *I* had the one my mom made me wear sometimes. But that was one lucky coincidence for a woman who loved to match. At that very moment even her shoes were the same pretty pink color as the roses.

I froze. The buttons. I blinked. Twice. Then I rubbed my eyes. A bright-pink round button blinked back at me. It was a shiny plastic one that looked just like a button from the sleeve of a sports jacket. And—if it had been navy blue—I would've have known exactly where to find its match. It was the same size as the one we'd discovered in the campfire. The same shape. It had the same wide ridge along the outside—even the same uneven crisscross stitches across the four tiny holes at the center.

I pretended to drop my balled-up tissue and leaned down to take a closer look. As I did, I remembered. The blue button couldn't have been Mr. Steptoe's—not if Grandpa Young was right. He'd been so touched that Mr. Steptoe had "died in the line of duty." I didn't recall his words exactly, but he'd said something about Mr. Steptoe being found in his Festival brown suit. As I lifted my head slowly back up, my body went numb.

I looked up at her puffy, watery eyes and felt sick as I realized they'd looked almost exactly the same when she told us about Steptoe. I'd assumed they were tears. As she sniffled and cursed her allergies, the clues suddenly came together like iron filings zooming toward a magnet in one of my science labs. If my hunch was right, we'd all just made a horrible, horrible mistake.

Barb Lund was no killer. The real one was standing right in front of me.

I took a deep breath and tried to slow my heartbeat. Then I looked up at Ms. Sparrow and gave a weak smile, praying she wouldn't realize it was fake. "Thanks," I said. "You don't realize how much you just helped me."

"Oh, it was nothing, Sophie," Ms. Sparrow smiled back. A chill ran through me. "Now what do you say you go talk to her, huh?"

"That's a really good idea," I said, breathlessly. I flung my tissue into the wastebasket, spun on my heels, and jetted out of the bathroom, past the flurry of the Court swishing around in their dresses and out to the hall, where I broke into a run.

I slid into my room, grabbed the pile of emails from under my bedcovers, then flew to Grace and Trista's. I pounded on the door hard, twice.

Grace cracked it open, saw me, and then moved to shut it again. I threw out my hand to stop it.

"Grace, please," I panted.

"Not now, Sophie," she said as I wriggled myself halfway

inside. She was in her blue dress again already and had started to put on a tiny bit of make-up.

"You've got to listen to me. Just one minute. We have a lot to talk about. A lot. And I don't even know where to begin except to say I'm so, so sorry." I looked up at her, pleading.

Grace shook her head and pointed to the door. "Go get dressed and help the Court with hair and make-up, Sophie. I'll be there in a second," she said flatly.

"The thing is, Grace, I think we're making a big mistake. A really, really big mistake." My voice sounded high and strangled.

Grace stiffened. Her eyes glinted with rage. "We're making a big mistake? *We?* No. Not we, Sophie. *You.*" She flicked her hair behind her like a whip, then pointed her finger at my chest. "*You've* made a big mistake! "Newsflash: You're not the only one on the planet with feelings. I have them too. And guess what? They can get hurt." The lacy curtains at the window twitched as she whirled away from me. Her shoulders slumped. Then, in a quiet voice, she added, "You can't just expect to brush them away that easily."

"Grace, I'm not trying to brush them away. Not at all! It's just, I think we need to focus on something else right now and we can maybe—"

Grace's mouth dropped open as she pivoted back to me. "Focus on something else? Listen to you! You're brushing them away, right now, Sophie! I may be 'Wonder Woman' and all"—she said with air quotes—"but I'm not superhuman." She jabbed her finger to the door. "Now leave me alone."

I didn't move. Sadness swelled through my body like a stinging wave.

"I know that, Grace," I said quietly. My eyes were filling with tears, and hers were too. I looked around the room. Just two nights ago we'd been sitting on those same beds, laughing about Danica and Denise's silly "name that tune" wall-knocking and sorting through our suspects. Now I wasn't sure we'd ever laugh together again. "I don't know why I told it, Grace. I told this dumb babyish story, and the way they looked at me . . . I just . . . I guess I wanted them to think I was cooler."

She folded her arms and stared at me for several long beats.

"You are cool, Sophie," she burst out, her chin jutting forward. "It's so weird you can't see that! The only time you aren't cool? When you're trying too hard to be something you're not."

I shrank back. Her words felt too true. "Listen, Grace,

I don't expect you to accept my apology. You shouldn't. I know I never, ever, ever in a million years should have told that story."

"Well, maybe just never in a hundred thousand years, but yeah." She pointed to Grandpa Young's dog tags. "Whatever happened to 'Always Loyal,' huh? What else have you told everybody? Some things are supposed to stay between us, Sophie." Grace's mouth tightened into a hard line.

I raised my eyebrow. "You're right. They are. And they will, *always*," I said firmly. "I wish I could take the whole night back somehow," I said.

"Well, not the whole night." She arched her eyebrow. "We did catch a killer. Again."

My face fell. "Grace. When I said we made a mistake? I meant it. We made a mistake. I think it's a big one." I shut the door behind me and sat on her bed.

Chapter Twenty-Nine

Sealing the Deal

When I'd finished running down all my theories, the blood drained from Grace's face. She reached for her radio headset and spoke into it more cheerfully and calmly than even Ms. Sparrow herself. "Page Bottoms! Page Young and I need some help with the emergency make-up kits. Can you please report to our room ASAP?" She then made fake static noises with her mouth in a very clear rhythm. Four short bursts, three short bursts. *S*. Three short bursts, four short bursts. *O*. Then again, *S*.

Her dress rustled as she slowly sank onto her bed. "This all sounds crazy, Soph. The question is: Why would she do it?"

I jumped as the door banged open and Trista charged in, frowning. Her hands were smudged with make-up. "Got your SOS, people. But I think I might have just taken out

Kendra Pritchard's right eye. What were they thinking putting me on mascara duty?" She looked sideways at Grace and me. "So, you two, uh . . ."

Grace smiled and sniffled. "We're good. I mean, we're a work in progress. But that's not important now."

"Phew," Trista said. "I thought the SOS might have something to do with that whole business and, uh, that's not my specialty, you know." She scratched the back of her neck and looked at the carpet.

"No, we'll deal with that SOS ourselves. This one, though . . ." Grace turned to me. "Tell her what you told me, Sophie."

I handed Lauren Sparrow's email over to Trista. "Remember how we didn't focus on Ms. Sparrow because she didn't have a motive? I think we missed something. And if I'm right? Barb Lund did not kill Mr. Steptoe."

Trista squinted one eye and cocked her head. "We're talking about Barb Lund, the one who almost turned Rod's dad into a pancake? That Barb Lund?"

"Yep. Get this," I began, lowering my voice as I launched into everything I suspected. I told her about Ms. Sparrow's shoe buttons and how they looked exactly like the blue button we'd found in the campfire. I pointed out the rose-patterned skirt she'd worn the day she shared the news about Mr. Steptoe, and what a ridiculous coincidence it would have been if she just so happened to match the top-secret rose theme Mr. Steptoe had chosen. "The tiara delivery receipt was time-stamped at quarter to eleven that night." My words rushed out so fast they tripped over my tongue. "Steptoe should have been alone in the mansion. But I think Sparrow was there that night, and I think she saw the rose tiara." I took a breath. "You know her and her matching. I mean, even the tint of her sunglass lenses matched her shirt yesterday." Then I reminded Grace how red Ms. Sparrow's eyes had been the morning Kendra had found Mr. Steptoe. "And right after she rescued us, she told Trista she can't set foot in the float barn without her allergies going nuts. Remember?"

Through it all Trista shook her head, her messy curls making her look even more baffled than she was. She stared down at the email. Then she sat down on her bed, wriggling around to get comfortable in her dress. "That all might be true, Sophie," she said, finally. "But wearing a matching skirt? It's a flower festival. She'd match as long as she wore flowers, basically. And having red eyes when someone you know just died?" She shrugged. "That seems pretty normal to me."

I sank back on Trista's bed. Maybe I had let my

imagination run wild. The thing was—one or two coinci-
dences I could have brushed off. But that many?

"What about the navy button?" Grace asked. "How does
a button exactly like the ones on Ms. Sparrow's shoes end
up next to the body, huh?"

Trista admitted that was strange.

"And a *rose*-patterned skirt?" I added. "I mean, owning
a skirt with pink roses on it is pretty normal. Lots of skirts
have flower patterns. But for a woman who basically has
raised color coordination to an art form to wear it on the
exact day that the rose theme is supposed to be announced?"

Trista scrunched up her face. "That's what gets me. Isn't
that pretty stupid? To place yourself at the crime scene? I
mean, even she doesn't love matching *that* much."

I looked down at the floor and bit my lip. She had a
point. "Maybe she slipped up."

"Every criminal does," Grace added softly. "And she
caught her mistake. She didn't wear it on the actual day of
the announcements."

"Okay, for argument's sake, let's say she's the killer,"
Trista said. "Why'd she vote us in as royal pages?" Trista
folded her arms. "She should have kept us out."

"I think she tried to. At the auditions I overheard her
suggest that we ride in the lead car with Harrison Lee

instead of being pages," I said. "Then she backed off."

I felt the same hollow pang as I described her pity and worries about our "fitting in," even though I now suspected she hadn't really meant it at all. As I repeated what she'd said about me, Grace rolled her eyes at Ms. Sparrow's ridiculousness. "It makes me so mad she ever made you feel that way, Soph," Grace said. "'Diamonds in the rough.' Pssh. She's the rough! We're the diamonds!"

Trista nodded slowly and smoothed down the folds of her dress as if she'd just noticed she was still wearing it. Sitting on her bed near her army duffel bag and folded cargo jacket, she looked like she might have wandered into the room by accident. "Guess she realized she couldn't be too obvious about shutting us out. Town heroes and all that." She sighed. "So the next best thing was for her to keep close watch over us."

I nodded, not sure if I was relieved we were slowly convincing Trista, or if I was more scared than ever. "She was probably thinking 'They're twelve. I got this,'" I added.

"Adults always do, don't they?" Trista snorted.

"She didn't know who she was dealing with," Grace said. Then she paused and looked toward the window. We could hear the bleating of trucks backing up and the rattle of snare drummers practicing. The smell of fresh-cut grass and salty ocean air rippled into the room with the breeze.

"Also pretty weird that the day she figures out we suspect Barb Lund murdered Steptoe, a burned-up Winnie the Pooh key chain is lying in the campfire of the float she practically brought us right to!" Grace added.

"The day after a fire in her office," I said, raising an eyebrow.

"That would explain why the smoke detector didn't have batteries. She took them out for her little project," Trista said. "Something caught fire when she charred the key chain."

"And by the way, Grandpa Young told me Mr. Steptoe was found in his brown suit. So that navy button couldn't have been his. But it sure could have been Sparrow's."

"There's only one big problem with all of these theories," Grace chimed in. "We saw Barb Lund go after Rod's dad with our own eyes."

Trista shook her head. "Did we though? All I could think that night was this is a lady who needs driving lessons. Or at least to log some serious screen time with Formula One Fever." As Trista continued, an image of Barb Lund waving her arms over the towering boxes on her forklift flashed in my head. Could she have been asking for help?

"She was monkeying with the controls. Waving her

hands off the wheel," Trista continued. "She should have been able to flatten him like that." She made a crashing sound effect as she brought her hand down on the bed. "Sorry," she added, realizing she'd gotten a little carried away.

"I always thought it was weird for Barb to pick driving as the best way to kill Mr. Zimball," Grace said with a sly half smile.

"Uh, true. Very true." I couldn't help but laugh. It all was just so crazy! And yet—like a piece of a puzzle that you'd never imagined could belong where it does—it all clicked into place. "Mr. Zimball did say she'd screamed something about an accident at him," I said with a shrug. "She could have just been warning him."

"All right, people," Trista said. "Let's think through a scenario. Lauren Sparrow was at the mansion late that night—late enough to see the tiara being delivered. But how does Steptoe end up in that float?

A cluster of voices rang out from behind the door as people passed by in the hall. Panicked, Grace locked the door and shoved Trista's desk chair in front of it.

"We don't have much time," I whispered, realizing Ms. Sparrow knew exactly where to find us. "If she overhears us . . ."

"You're right, Sophie," Grace said, her jaw clenching. "We have to hurry."

"Take a look at the email," I pointed to the paper I'd handed Trista. "I think there's something there, but I can't figure out what."

Grace and I huddled over Trista's shoulder and we all read together:

To: Jim Steptoe <jimsteptoe@wintersunfestival.org>

From: Lauren Sparrow <msprettyp@prettyperfectfaces.com>

Subject: SUPPLIES

Just a note to say thanks again. I can't believe you all managed to get a double order delivered on time! No wonder they've put you in charge. I know how tough it is for you to keep everything on track this season, as it is. I really do hope that alternative sourcing routes come through soon. Last breeding season already produced a far smaller crop—and, obviously, the harvesting is hardly environmentally friendly. Of course, beauty has its price. And no one can argue with gorgeous results! Still.

Please do alert me if you anticipate any slowdowns.

You're a dear. Feeling lucky to have you in my corner—

All my best,

LLS

"Look at the wording," I said. "*Breeding season. Harvesting. Hardly environmentally friendly.* I mean, I guess you could use those words for flowers. But *breeding* reminds me more of . . ."

"Animals." Grace and Trista's voices echoed with mine. Their faces clouded over.

I nodded. "And we know how much Mr. Steptoe cares about animals. So much he's willing to make sure Lily wasn't Sun Queen." I stood up and began pacing, feeling like Grace. "Remember how he had all those jars of Pretty Perfect? Maybe he was looking into something."

"Something so bad it was worth killing him?" Grace asked.

"People have murdered for far less. If it has something to do with her business . . . ," Trista said.

"The Pretty Perfect video Jardine was going nuts over,"

I said, stopping midpace. "Remember?"

"Oh, yeah. I remember," Trista said, rolling her eyes. "Jardi-J."

"The seals!" Grace whispered.

"Exactly. Jardine asked me to paint them all over her T-shirt." A thought came to me. "Hey, Mr. Steptoe had those YouTube videos in his search history, too. Maybe he was researching something?"

Trista nodded. "The secret ingredient?"

"Maybe she was messing with the environment. Hurting the seals somehow." Grace looked pained. "Or worse."

The printout crackled as Trista held it up. "But why does she send him this?"

Grace and Trista slumped back on the bed. My head was throbbing. I knew we were on the verge of something. But my thoughts were too slow to catch up. Workmen's gruff shouts rose up along with the crowd murmurs from outside, and the Court's voices rang out from the sitting room and floated down the hall to us. We really didn't have much time.

I took the email from Trista and looked it at again. "Jardi-J," I said, feeling a hazy thought push its way past the muddle in my head. I pictured Jardine as she told her story about texting Lucas by accident. "J-squared. J-JIM! Thank you, Jardine!" I gasped.

Trista and Grace looked at me strangely as I turned back to them. "She never meant to send that email to Mr. Steptoe," I said. "She sent it to a different Jim. Sort of. *Jiménez.* Think about it! They start with the same letters."

Trista's face lit up. "Autofill. Email autofill."

"Bingo," I said. "We've all done it before. You want to email something quickly, start to type, the name pops up—you don't look twice, and whoosh, you've sent it off to someone else."

"Like when you sent me that question about math homework and it went to Tristan Bowers instead," Trista said to me. "Nice of him to try to factor that polynomial, but, whoa, so off base." She rolled her eyes.

Grace jumped up suddenly, her dress rustling as it straightened. "I get it. So Mr. Steptoe—Jim—saw this, started checking into things. And then . . ."

"And then." I nodded, swallowing hard.

We flinched as our radio headsets crackled.

"Royal pages?" Ms. Sparrow's crisp voice floated to us tinnily. "Where are you? Please report to the Queen and Court sitting room for final preparations!"

We stared at each other, wide-eyed. Grace bit her lip. "On our way!" she barked into her headset. "Just changing!"

Grace leaned in, eyes darting to the door. "Okay, quickly:

 326

she's got celebrities talking up Pretty Perfect moisturizer like it's the Second Coming. She can't have anything threatening that business. Something big was riding on her keeping this secret."

"Something so big she was willing to kill for it," I said, not believing the words coming out of my mouth.

"It's a lot less crazy than Barb Lund, when you think about it. Taking out everyone in town who kept your daughter from becoming fake royalty?" Trista made a face.

"You guys," I said glumly. "If any of this is right, Barb is missing her favorite day of the year. While sitting behind bars." I pictured Ms. Lund's overstuffed office spilling over with all its Royal Court headshots and souvenirs, and felt a stab of guilt. Barb Lund was "odd," as Rod's mom had said, but it had started to sink in that we really might have misunderstood her. All her commands and barking at everyone with her megaphone—it could be because she cared just a little too much. I could see why Rod's dad had taken one look at her threatening email and gone to her to ask about it. It was crazy . . . but it was also very her.

Grace shook her head, and sighed. "Listen, we still have some time."

"Her office is shut tight, but if we get a chance to sneak in . . . ," I said.

Trista smiled. "I never met a lock I couldn't pick," she said.

We made a quick plan. Grace and I were going to see if we could get back to Steptoe's office and check his search history for those Pretty Perfect videos. Trista was going to find a chance to sweep Sparrow's office either on her way to or from trying to fix the Root Beer float so it could hit its full speed. When Grace and I shot each other a hesitant look, she scolded us in a perfect whisper. "I got this spying thing down, I swear! Though . . ." Her satiny dress rustled as she wriggled around. "It's hard to go stealth in this."

Grace and I stifled our laughs. "Speaking of which, Soph—you have to get ready!"

Trista, Grace, and I reached for each other's hands. "We've got this, Wonder Women," Grace said. "I know we do."

"All right. Off I go," Trista said. She reached for her cargo jacket on her bed, then changed her mind. She spun back to us and outstretched her arms. "Better without?"

"Better without," Grace and I replied, grinning.

Trista nodded and smiled at herself in the mirror one more time before disappearing through the door.

Chapter Thirty

Winter Clouds

"There you are, pages!" Ms. Sparrow greeted us as we walked into the Queen and Court sitting room. Grace had hurriedly helped me change back into my dress. It clung so tightly to my legs I had to take tiny steps and shuffle along like a penguin. Behind Ms. Sparrow hairstylists buzzed around the Court folding beautiful hair into all kinds of impossible updos, braids, twists, and flowing curls. The tiaras sat in a row on plush velvet holders in front of the make-up stations we'd set up the day before, sparkling in the light that streamed in through the blinds. My heart thudded against my chest. It was a miracle everyone in the room couldn't hear it, even with all the swishing of dresses and chattering.

Ms. Sparrow frowned. "Where's Trista?"

"She had to do a final check on the Root Beer float.

She'll be here in a minute," I said with a shrug.

"Ah, of course." Ms. Sparrow nodded. Then she smiled at us, eyebrows raised questioningly. "Everything . . . a little better?"

Grace and I looked at each other and nodded, flashing her our own fake smiles. "We all make mistakes," Grace said. She gripped my hand so tightly that it throbbed. "Right, Soph?"

"Right," I said, squeezing her hand back. We might have been acting for Ms. Sparrow, but her words felt true. I hoped they were.

Kendra and Sienna nudged each other and mouthed an *awww*. Ms. Sparrow held her smile as she pointed to Grandpa Young's dog tags around my neck. "Those don't match so well, do they?" she said, as if I'd simply forgotten to take them off. She leaned forward to help me slip them over my head.

"Oh, no," I cut in, stepping back. "They're for luck," I explained.

Ms. Sparrow's eyes twinkled with amusement. "Ah, I see," she said, then waved us over to help the stylists.

Grace and I set to work, trying to appear as normal and cheerful as possible as we handed over brushes and compacts, brought herbal tea to the princesses, and checked their dresses for stains and loose threads. I didn't even flinch when Sienna asked me to rub sparkly bronzer over her shoulders. Meanwhile, Grace dabbed concealer over Kendra's tiara injury. Danica and Denise tended to Her Majesty Jardine, who spouted a constant stream of regal orders. Ms. Sparrow breezed in and out so unpredictably we couldn't find a chance to slip away, but we darted glances to the door, expecting Trista any minute.

She never came.

⚜ ⚜ ⚜

By our 11:30 a.m. float-boarding time Grace and I were fighting to hide our panic that Trista was still missing as the Brown Suiters ushered us all down the grand staircase. We swished across the wide lawn and through the tall wrought-iron mansion gates to the Luna Vista Boulevard staging area where the floats were parked in order. The bleachers that Jake and other high-school volunteers had set up weeks ago lined the sidewalk just ahead. Families crowded in front of them with folding chairs. Brown Suiters rushed around in a flurry, fresh Coral Beauty roses pinned to their lapels next to round buttons printed with Mr. Steptoe's favorite motto: THE WINTER SUN ALWAYS SHINES. My throat tightened as I realized that Grace and I had to make sure that it really did.

Music blared from speakers, filling my chest with a bass thump and making my heart race even faster as we approached the Royal Court float. The dolphins Grace and I had hidden behind as we eavesdropped on the police now leaped gracefully over waves made of irises and Queen Anne's lace. A figure of Neptune jutted out from the front of the float, his grassy white beard flowing into the "waves." He pointed the way down the parade route with his trident made of silverleaf toward the real ocean, blue and sparkling below the bluffs. Grace reached for my arm. I clutched it as if she'd thrown me a lifesaver.

Rod's dad buzzed by on a white scooter, then circled back to check on us. "Look at you two! The best ambassadors the Festival could hope for," he said with a smile. "I just saw your families sitting in the main bandstand. They couldn't be prouder of you all. And I couldn't be more grateful," he added. Then his face clouded over. "Where's Page Bottoms?"

"Oh, she'll be here any minute," Grace said, trying to sound casual.

"I was worried she'd had second thoughts!" he said. "Rod says hello, by the way," He pointed to the huddle of white jumpsuits behind the prancing team of Palominos we'd seen at the barn. "But, as my dear old friend Jim would have said, 'Doody calls.'" He winked and zipped off on his scooter again.

Grace and I traded a look. A drip of sweat trickled down my back. "Maybe she's using the parade as a distraction?" I whispered hopefully. "While we're all out here, she went in there." I jerked my head to the mansion.

"And miss seeing her Root Beer float in action?" Grace looked skeptical. "I hope you're right." She glanced toward Ms. Sparrow, who was striding past Neptune, her eyes flitting around frantically. I felt the air squeezing out of my lungs, and it wasn't just because my mermaid dress was so tight. I craned my neck to look for Grandpa Young among the VFW vets in their military uniforms lining up several floats behind ours, but I couldn't make him out.

Around us trumpets and tubas blared warm-up scales. Horse hooves clip-clopped on the pavement. At the corner where the parade route officially began, the crowd shuffled and murmured and laughed as they settled into the bleachers, looking like a rippling colorful patchwork quilt. The noon sun made everything feel sharp and too bright.

"Okay, my princesses and Queen," Ms. Sparrow called out, "Group hug!" She waved us all around, her coppery hair tousled from the breeze and her cheeks flushed. The Court's faces glowed with excitement, and their eyes glistened. Their perfume mixed with the sickly sweet smell of the flowers, making me feel a little ill.

"Places, everyone!" Ms. Sparrow called out. One of the Brown Suiters handed each of us a tiny radio earpiece so we'd be able to follow the parade announcer's feed throughout the route. Two others began to help us board the float.

Jardine stiffened. "Where's Trista?" she asked, refusing to take another step. "We can't board without Trista!" She crossed her white-gloved arms over her chest. "My whole Court needs to be together."

Kendra nodded. "We're Festival family. We can't just leave her!"

"I'm sorry, ladies. There's no time," Ms. Sparrow said, waving us toward the giant half clamshell we were supposed to stand in front of. "I've sent some folks to look for her. She'll be along any second, I'm sure." She cringed and lifted her shoulders apologetically. "But you know as well as I do how Trista felt about being paraded through the whole town in a dress today. We have to stay on schedule, no matter what. It's our big day. *Your* big day."

My insides turned to ice. Grace pressed her arm against mine. The image of Trista whirling, twirling, pouting, and strutting around the room in her blue dress had to be tumbling through her head too. I wasn't sure if my heart was still beating at all. I definitely wasn't breathing. Trista was in trouble.

Reluctantly, the Court let the Brown Suiters help them up to the float. The noise of the crowds and music faded behind the roar of panic filling my head. I looked down the gently sloping parade route, past the ragged bluffs, and fixed my eyes on the solid still blues of the water and sky, hoping the sight would calm me. My heart only beat faster.

Near the line of TV cameras under the announcer's booth I spotted Mr. Zimball taking his place next to Harrison Lee in the parade's lead car, an old Model T. They sat with one of Grandpa Young's friends from the VFW, the oldest war veteran in town. Dressed in his full Navy uniform, he saluted the waiting crowd. I felt for the dog tags hanging around my neck and said a little prayer for Trista.

"Up you go!" a Brown Suiter took my hand as she helped me up the portable boarding stairs. My legs felt shaky. Grace reached out from the float to steady me, then led me forward into our positions. Jardine took her throne under the giant clamshell and closed her eyes as if she were meditating. Danica and Denise looked at each other worriedly. But when the herald trumpeters blasted their horns to signal the parade's start, Jardine's eyes blinked open like someone had turned on a switch, and her lips spread in a dazzling white smile.

It was Festival time.

"This is it, Royal Court!" Ms. Sparrow called, beaming from the street as she gave us the "washing the window" parade wave we'd been practicing all weekend. "Now remember. No need to worry, just—"

"Be ourselves!" the Court echoed back, giggling.

"Only better," Sienna added with a smile.

I squeezed Grace's hand and smiled too. For a moment, I even wondered if everything might turn out okay after all.

Mr. Zimball and Mr. Lee's Model T backfired as it rattled forward, startling the crowd. The Royal Court thrust their shoulders back and exchanged secret looks, smiles blazing. I pasted on my own smile and met their eyes, desperately wishing the adrenaline bolting through me was because I was excited too. I kept twisting my neck, looking for Trista to come rushing down the street, dress flying behind her like a superhero's cape.

"What do we do, Grace?" I muttered like a ventriloquist through my clenched smile. In a minute we'd be pulling out of the line-up and passing the first set of bleachers.

"I have no idea, Sophie. Get through this?" She turned

and blew a kiss to a little girl along the sidewalk jerking a balloon up and down to get our attention. Behind her a clown on stilts teetered around twirling fire batons as several onlookers oohed and ahhed.

The speakers suddenly blared with marching-band horns, and the floats in front of us lurched forward.

In the announcer's booth at the top of the grandstand, the longtime "Voices of the Festival," Mr. Diaz and our local Channel 5 newscaster, Elise Hoffman, kept up a stream of goofy narration when they could get a word in edgewise above the bands. It crackled over our radio earpieces.

"Now how great is that?" Mr. Diaz boomed, and I worried he might dive into a long history of the Palominos again. "Kicking off our 'We Are Family' theme in style is the It's All Relative! float, one of the several entries sponsored by AmStar this year. This one commemorates the hundred-year anniversary of Albert Einstein's theory of relativity. As I understand it, creating ol' Albert's wild mane of hair required half a truckload of white pampas grass! Now that's some circumstantial pampas . . . or should I say . . . pampas circumstance?"

Elise Hoffman chuckled along with the adults in the crowd at what I guessed must be some kind of pun. "Speaking of pomp and circumstance, Fred, here comes everyone's favorite, the Route Integrity Team, otherwise known as our beloved Pooper Scoopers! Look at this fine crew of young men and women, ably led by Mr. Joshua Katz."

"You know, Elise, I'm not sure white is the best choice of color for those jumpsuits. Talk about dirty work!" Mr. Diaz guffawed.

Huge outdoor TV screens across from the main grandstand flashed images of the Palomino riders in full Western gear. Small monitors hidden in the mini seaweed-covered treasure chests on the float in front of us displayed the same feed. I squinted at one of the screens and spotted Rod in the crew behind the horses, his shovel glinting as he twirled it. The crowd roared and laughed as one of the crew scraped up something from the road and dumped it in the gray trash barrel that Rod tugged along with his free hand. The Pooper Scooper team took bows as the marching band behind them raised their horns and burst into Kool and the Gang's "Celebration." Rod joined in the team's funny little dance as he grinned at the crowd. At least one of us could enjoy the moment.

"This is some parade route, isn't it, Fred?" Ms. Hoffman continued cheerily. "These bands will be marching two miles in the sunshine today, but it'll be worth it. This first half-mile stretch ends at right at Luna Vista's stunning bluffs, then they'll turn south onto Vista del Mar and continue with a gorgeous ocean view the rest of the way."

The marching band in front of us lifted their horns and high-stepped ahead, knees bobbing. Our float jerked forward to fill the empty space. I sucked in a breath. It was happening. It wouldn't be long before Mr. Diaz announced our float.

"Here she comes, Elise," Mr. Diaz called out as Luna Vista's 125th anniversary Root Beer float wheeled past them, its giant frosty white "mug" puffing out soapy bubbles as Ridley root beer advertising jingles through the ages blared from its hidden speakers. "If you don't drink Ridley, you don't know diddly!" went one cheesy tune. "Bring good cheer, buy Ridley root beer!" ordered another.

"The first-ever remote-controlled Festival float," Mr. Diaz sang out. I recognized the AmStar employee beside him, who grinned and held up a black remote control box he was steering the float with. "Thanks to AmStar's team of top engineers and the help of techno-whiz Royal Page Trista Bottoms, there's one less driver sweating away in one of those tiny compartments today," Mr. Diaz declared. "Now what would our founder Willard Ridley make of that?"

Grace turned to me with a wince. If Trista were safe, she'd have been with us—or at least watching.

"He'd be pleased as punch, if his twin is anything to go by," Elise chimed in as the outdoor screens filled with the towering animatronic figure of Willard Ridley atop the float, sporting a root beer mug in one hand and waving with the other. He looked a little *too* jolly, like my Grandpa Young after a night of playing cards at the VFW.

As our float rolled to a stop in front of the first set of bleachers, the Court began their 'wiping the window' waves to the crowd. Grace nudged me, and I pulled my lips back into the best smile I could manage. I squinted as I waved, scanning the crowd ahead for Trista.

"Now, the engineers say anyone can drive this float. It's that easy," Mr. Diaz exclaimed.

"So we've pulled someone from the crowd to launch this beauty in style," Ms. Hoffman asked. "And *style* is the key word here. Please welcome the most stylish lady of them all, our own special adviser to the Queen and her Court, Ms. Lauren Sparrow!"

The Court hooted and hollered behind us as Ms. Sparrow's face splashed across the screens. The engineer standing near Mr. Diaz handed her the remote control.

Grace and I traded a look. My stomach heaved. Lauren Sparrow was last person who should have the honor of launching Trista's brilliant invention.

"Now, given what I've heard about some of the driving around the Festival lately, we were worried about handing this task off," Mr. Diaz joked. The crowd murmured and looked horrified by his tasteless joke. "But you seem to be doing a great job, Lauren."

Ms. Sparrow grinned bashfully. Her eyes were redder and puffier than I'd ever seen them. Allergy medicine was no match for the pollen of five jillion fresh flowers, clearly.

The marching band in front of us burst into "Under the Sea" and my heart leaped to my throat. Our float rolled into action again. The Court stood at attention.

"The Royal Court, Ladies and Gentleman!" Mr. Diaz exclaimed when we reached the main grandstand. The audience roared. The band blasted. We all waved. I tried to spot my family in the stands but couldn't find them among the endless blur of pink and brown faces in the stands. Danica, Denise, Grace, and I picked up the giant palm leaves on the float and turned to fan the Court with them, pretending to be their real servants. Their royal eyes glistened with tears as they waved, faces tilted to the crowd in amazement.

"Serving the Court this year are royal pages, Danica and Denise Delgado, and Luna Vista's town heroes, Sophie Young, Grace Yang, and Trista Bottoms," Mr. Diaz continued. "The Winter Sun would not be shining today if it weren't for the work of these girls and Luna Vista's finest. Let's hear it for them!"

The crowd applauded, but a murmur rippled through the bleachers as people lifted their heads, looking for Trista.

I shot Grace a helpless look. *Wave,* she mouthed as she dropped her palm leaf and did just that, her elbow hinging back and forth like a pendulum as her hand swept daintily through the air. No sooner did our marching band finish their version of "Under the Sea" than the speakers ahead of us squealed with feedback. The crowd cringed and reached for their ears.

"Uh-oh, there seems to be some technical trouble with the music on the Luna Vista Root Beer float," Mr. Diaz's voice floated through our earpieces. "Can you do something about it with that whosie-whatsit, Lauren?" The camera zoomed in on her as she shrugged. Grace flashed me a puzzled look.

"What's that?" Ms. Hoffman cupped her ear. "You're in the clear, Lauren," she joked. "The engineer tells me the music can't be operated from the remote control."

"But who's going to stop that racket?" Mr. Diaz asked.

The crowd groaned as the ad jingles stuttered from the float in deafening bursts. When feedback shrieked a second time, and the halting spurts of music restarted, it hit me.

The music was blaring in a pattern. I waited for a pause, then counted. Four blasts, three blasts. *Silence.* Three blasts, four blasts. *Silence.* Then, again: four blasts, three blasts.

It was a Polybius code.

I didn't have to decipher it to know it spelled disaster.

Chapter Thirty-One

Trista at Sea Bottoms

My fake smile fell. I counted the blasts again as the music erupted once more into the same, clear halting pattern. There was no doubt about it. It was an SOS.

"She's in there!" I screamed to Grace. "Trista's inside the Root Beer float!"

Grace's face twisted in shock, then she whirled toward the small TV monitor in front of us. Lauren Sparrow's image filled the tiny screen as she gripped the remote control and waved it at the camera playfully.

"Better keep your eyes on the road, Lauren!" Mr. Diaz yukked it up. "You've got a whole marching band ahead of you."

I squinted down the sloping hill of the parade route. The paved road curved gently to the left at the bottom, not far from the jagged cliffs jutting above the ocean. Panic bolted through me as I realized what Lauren Sparrow might have in store.

"The bluffs!" I shrieked. "The floats have to turn before the bluffs, Grace! What if . . ." I pictured the Root Beer float rolling straight past the turn, plowing through the dusty lookout point, and tumbling right over the cliff's edge.

Grace grimaced. "I know!" she shouted back as The Royal Court shot us nasty looks between their waving and smiling. The crowd beamed and cheered cluelessly as a skywriter dotted the perfect blue sky above them with a HAPPY WINTER SUN FESTIVAL! greeting.

Lauren Sparrow couldn't be that crazy. Could she?

I looked toward the bluffs again. They looked red in the noon sun. Crazy or not, we couldn't risk it. I whirled around to Grace and reached out my hand, palm down. "On three. Ready?" She nodded and slapped hers on top of mine. "Break!" I shouted. We flung up our arms and dashed to opposite sides of the float, dodging Danica and Denise as they stared at us in horror.

I grabbed one of the dolphin's fins and leaned over the side of the float. The asphalt below rolled by in a blur. We weren't moving fast. Just a few miles an hour. But the cut of my dress made it impossible to jump.

The float rocked, and I turned to see Grace leap over the side, her dress billowing behind her like a parachute. I glanced back at the announcer's booth and my heart stopped.

Lauren Sparrow was gone.

Mr. Diaz and Ms. Hoffman were grinning, flipping through their notes to comment on the next entry.

Did she still have the remote?

I wasn't about to wait to find out. I leaned over, hiked up my dress, and stuffed its ends into my pantyhose, Grace-style. At least I wasn't wearing Wonder Woman underwear. The top folds of the dress bloused back around me like a puffy miniskirt, thankfully. I sucked in a deep breath, then sprang off the float through one of the ocean "waves" of white flowers, bending my knees to cushion the short drop.

Then, I ran. I ran past Neptune's silvery trident pointing ahead. I ran past the marching band, the saxophone players looking at me out of the corner of their eyes as their cheeks puffed like fish. I know I must have run past my family in the bleachers, too. I cringed thinking about how I must've looked—dress half shoved in my stockings, ruining the whole Festival.

In my earpiece, I heard Mr. Diaz and Ms. Hoffman,

papers rustling, *uh*ing and *ahem*ing as they scrambled to say something. "Was this planned?" Mr. Diaz asked, his voice muffled, obviously thinking that he'd safely covered his microphone.

My lungs bursting, I strained to pick up my pace. Ahead of me the blue-and-white-striped uniform of the band's leader marching was a hazy blur through my wind-stung eyes. His baton thrust upward as he kept time. I thought of the staffs we'd been practicing with in tai chi class, and a plan sprang into my muddled head. The baton was only half the length of our staffs. Still, my idea could work. If only I could get my hands on it in time . . .

Just then something soft caught my legs and sent me sprawling to the asphalt with a sharp sting. I winced and pushed myself onto all fours, only to find myself staring into a wild-eyed grin. Pookums. He panted back at me, thrilled, his tiny tiara off-kilter.

"Go back! Back to Kendra!" I stood up and pointed, but he just danced around in his sparkly blue vest and yipped. The Root Beer float barreled on ahead of us, the wide blue ocean looming in the background behind it. I spotted Grace on the other side of the marching band, sprinting, chin high as she held her dress at her waist.

We didn't have time for games. I faked out Pookums

and made a break for the bandleader. The little puffball followed, barking and weaving his way through a line of bewildered trumpet players. They tried to step clear, their legs tangling. Seconds later, I heard a jumble of drooping trumpet notes and a crash of cymbals on pavement. I didn't dare look back again. The crowd's puzzled shouts joined the uproar as I zigzagged through the flute section and dashed behind the bandleader. I hesitated only a moment, then hopped onto my tiptoes and snatched his baton midthrust before charging onward like a football player headed for the end zone. The root beer mug towered ahead, right next to the red cherry that I'd nearly fallen off scaffolding to decorate. My skinned knees burned and I could barely breathe, but I was almost there.

"Folks, it looks like we have a little situation to clear up. Not to worry. Everything's under control!" Mr. Diaz practically yelped. Then, in the background, he rasped to someone: "Where'd she go? She didn't take the remote, did she?"

A piercing shriek rang out behind me. I glanced over one shoulder and saw Kendra tearing after Pookums, strands of blond hair from her former updo flapping around her face like wet party streamers. Her cries seemed to only push Pookums faster and farther away, like a leaf cartwheeling away in a gust of wind.

"Look at these Royals showing off their athletic talents," Ms. Hoffman chimed in for cover. "An unusual choice for the anniversary year, but it sure is a memorable one."

The spectators murmured skeptically. A stabbing pain split my side, but I pumped my arms harder and jetted past an acrobat doing handsprings and the fire-twirling clown on stilts. Finally, I approached the float. It was rocking from side to side as someone—it had to be Trista—pounded against the driver compartment hidden behind the cascading scoops of white cotton fake whipped cream on a sundae. The float's Willard Ridley figure toward the back of the float swayed a little with each of the blows, his white grassy beard rattling like maracas.

"Hang on, Trista! We've got this!" I yelled, jogging to keep up with the black seaweed-covered wheels of the float thundering down the route. I hoped she could hear me even if I couldn't see her.

"Next we have the Sheep Family Thrills float?" Ms. Hoffman's hesitant soprano piped up. "Look at the fun those sheep are having on that Ferris wheel! Made of polyurethane foam and covered with onion seed, those cuties took twenty volunteers a solid week to decorate. . . . Er, is someone going to stop those girls?"

349

My plan was a long shot. I'd have to time my move just right. It was the best hope we had, though. I tightened my grip on the bandleader's baton, made a wish on Grandpa Young's dog tags, then sank low into Needle at Sea Bottom, thrusting the baton into the front right wheel's spokes as smoothly as if it were a tai chi practice staff. A painful jolt ran down my funny bone as the baton twisted. Metal scraped and sparks flew—but the float squealed to a halt. Trista cheered just as Grace joined me, panting, her hair a wind-whipped mess.

The marching band behind us had melted into blue-and-white chaos. A wail of sirens kicked up, followed by the far-off roar of motorcycles. The float's electric engine still whirred, begging to push forward. One slip of the baton and we would. I scanned the route ahead. The lead car and first float had already hung the left onto Vista del Mar, the Palominos clip-clopping after them. Rod and his crew strutted cluelessly onward in their white jumpsuits.

Trista's wide eyes peered out at us through the fluffy carpet of white flowers that camouflaged the driver compartment just above the front wheel. "She bolted me in!" she shouted. "The door's completely jammed."

"We're coming!" Grace hollered back, then turned to me. "You first," she said, boosting me up over the wheel hub and onto the float. She hauled herself up after me, sending clumps of carnations flying. As Trista's eyes bulged even wider, we both madly tore away the flowers hiding her compartment until we'd exposed the metal-grate door underneath. A wrench had been wedged—possibly even hammered—tightly through the steel loop of the door latch.

Grace and I looked at each other. If Lauren Sparrow was unhinged enough to lock Trista inside a parade float, who knew what else she'd be willing to do.

"Don't worry. We've got this," I called to Trista, hoping she didn't hear the doubt lurking in my voice. Grace clutched the end of the wrench with both hands and tugged, the cords of her neck straining. It didn't budge.

I should've known it wouldn't be easy. If Trista couldn't get herself out, we didn't have much hope. I wrapped my hands over Grace's, braced my foot against the float, and on the count of three, we both heaved as hard as we could. There was a bone-jarring screech of metal on metal, but the wrench only gave way a tiny bit.

"You need more leverage!" Trista called out.

We reached out to try again when suddenly something clanged and squealed beneath us. Grace toppled into me with a shriek as the float gave a single horrible lurch forward. We grasped at the metal grill of the compartment door as the float jolted again. Apparently, a baton was no match for a gajillion pounds of flowers, plastic, and chicken wire determined to barrel ahead.

Trista was breathing as heavily as we were.

"You got your inhaler, right?" I called in.

"It's in my cargo jacket," she answered calmly. "But as long as I don't panic, I'm fine," she added in a singsong, as if she'd been repeating the words to herself nonstop for the past half-hour. She probably had. "As long as I don't think of these flowers, I'm"—she closed her eyes—"fine," she finished.

I remembered her telling herself to take her allergy meds that morning, and I prayed she had. An image of her panicking in the refrigerated flower shed flashed before me. We had to get her out. Fast.

Grace and I eyed each other, then both hurried to yank the wrench again. Nothing. The float shuddered under us. Grace's eyes went wide. It wasn't until I heard the crowd gasp behind us that I realized that she wasn't worried about the float rolling ahead. She was staring at something behind my right shoulder. I spun around to look.

I froze. The fire-twirling clown tottered on his stilts alongside the Root Beer float by the rear wheel. High above the road, concentrating on his spinning wheels of flame, he hadn't noticed that Pookums Pritchard had just darted directly into his path.

Kendra ran close behind. In the meantime her up-do had fully unraveled. Her hair streamed behind her and her dress was torn. "Watch out!" she shrieked to the stilt walker, arms waving.

Startled, the man looked down to find Pookums running crazed circles in front of him, yipping up at his spinning fire sticks. He staggered to avoid the dog, flinging out one arm to regain his balance. Everything would have been fine, were it not for one small detail. His hand had grazed the side of the Root Beer float.

And in that hand was a flaming ring of fire.

There was a *whoosh* and crackle as flames leaped up from the cottony white foam of Willard Ridley's root beer mug. My legs went numb.

Trista cocked her head at us. "Something wrong?" she asked.

In a minute she'd smell the smoke herself. In a minute it might be too late, anyway.

"Not yet," I said, tugging at the wrench again. Grace looked back at the fire then back to me in panic. The flames had already raced up Willard Ridley's arm and caught his grass beard. Black smoke spiraled up from his head, clouding the blue sky.

Another grating screech of metal split the air. Grace and I shrieked as this time the float rolled forward and kept rolling, careening around like a bad shopping cart as it slowly gained speed down the hill.

Trista locked eyes with us as we clung to the door. "I should have never fixed the pulse duration," she said quietly. I had no idea what she meant until I remembered with horror why she'd worked on the Root Beer float that morning in the first place: it hadn't been reaching its full speed. Who knew how fast it could go now.

The sirens wailed louder, closer. They had to reach us soon. Time had slowed down so much it felt like they never would. The rest of the parade dimmed around me, though I knew Brown Suiters had to be rushing toward us to help. The voices of Mr. Diaz and Ms. Hoffman in my ear had fallen silent.

I looked ahead. The last of the "Celebration"-blaring marching band was marching onto Vista del Mar. Nothing was in front of us. Just the road, the bluffs, and the wide, wide blue of the ocean waiting to swallow us.

"The police are coming any second, Trista!" Grace

shouted, her voice hoarse. "Everything'll be fine!"

Trista turned to us, her panicked eyes tearing up. She smelled the smoke. She had to have by now.

"Jump!" she shouted, her voice cracking. "You've got to jump off!"

My throat felt like it was closing. I knew she was right, but I tightened my fingers around the metal grate and leaned closer. Grace clutched my arm.

Trista frowned, trying to look stern despite tears running down her cheeks. "Keep your heads! Leave me! Now!"

Grace let out a sob. She looked toward the fast approaching bluffs and back to the fire. The sirens' wails were finally closer. I prayed there was still some chance they could save her. Maybe a fire truck would zip right in front at the last second, blocking the way. Maybe the Brown Suiters could jam the wheels like I had. I could hear shouts and footsteps thundering toward us. People were trying to help. Maybe they really could.

I fumbled for the dog tags around my neck. I wanted Trista to have them. I needed Trista to have them. I reached them out. "*Semper fidelis*, friend," I said, choking on the words. But just as I was about to shove them through the slats of the door, an idea came to me as bright and clear as the glint of the sun that caught in them.

"Help me, Grace!" I shouted as I looped the dog-tag chain around the wrench. Trista was right: we needed more leverage. Grandpa's dog tags might be able to give it to us—and if Trista said they were indestructible, they were. I grasped the chain and leaned back with all of my weight. Grace wrapped her arms around my middle and leaned with me. The chain vibrated as it went taut. We rejoiced as the wrench slid back another good inch. Meanwhile, the float rocked as it bounced from the pavement onto the dusty lookout point.

"You don't have time!" Trista shouted. Tears stained her cheeks as she pleaded with us to jump off.

"One more try," Grace cried out as if she hadn't heard Trista. We were so close—but the bluffs were too. We leaned back again, grunting as the chain cut into our fingers. A clang echoed out and I spilled backward into Grace. I looked down. The wrench was swinging from the end of the dog-tag chain I still clutched in my hands. We'd done it. We'd really done it.

The door crashed open and Trista burst out.

"What the heck are you waiting for?" she shouted, sweeping over us in a giant satiny-blue wave. She grabbed our hands and sprang from the float, tugging us overboard with her. I tumbled hard to the dirt and rolled. Clouds of dust billowed as the wheels of the float thundered by, fire streaming from its back end like flames from one of AmStar's test rockets.

A second later it sailed over the jagged red bluff. We watched, breathless, as it seemed to hover in the air a moment—a flaming dragon against the bright-blue sky—before plummeting out of sight. A sickening crush of metal and rocks echoed up from below.

We stared at each other, dazed. Trista started to cry for real. Grace shakily rose to her feet and helped us up. Sobbing, Trista wrapped us in a hug so tight I wasn't sure we'd ever come out of it again. I wasn't sure I wanted to. My tears came then, too, fast and hot. Trista finally pulled back.

"You know, you're still rocking that dress," Grace said, smiling through her own tears.

"Thanks," Trista said, sniffling. She wiped her cheeks. "Should've worn it with the jacket, though."

I couldn't tell if we laughed or sobbed then. The strange sound that came out of us was a cross of both. Seconds later, we heard the shouts of police and their boots crunching in the dust. Hordes of faces gathered around us. Red lights spun.

I don't really know what happened next. All I remember is seeing Rod standing next to me like an angel in a white jumpsuit, carrying a kids' skateboard that he must've used to race back to us. His face was creased with worry as he gazed at me. I can't even imagine what I looked like, covered in dirt, dress hiked up, my hair a wild mess. I didn't even care.

A police officer started toward him to clear him away, but Rod grabbed both my hands. "Are you all right, Sophie?" he said, his voice cracking.

I squeezed his hands and nodded back. I wished I could just stay there for a minute, staring into his eyes. "Listen," I rasped, craning my neck to look back at the stands. Crowds had poured into the streets. "Barb Lund didn't kill Steptoe." My words poured out in a rush. "Sparrow did. And she locked Trista in that float."

Rod's eyes bulged. "I just saw her!" he cried out excitedly. He wheeled around and pointed up the hill past the throngs of people. "She was by those bleachers."

Just then Officer Grady pushed his way through the crowd of midnight blue uniforms and over to us.

"You have to find Ms. Sparrow!" Grace shouted at him.

Officer Grady's brow wrinkled in confusion. He patted Grace on the shoulder. "Listen now," he said, gently. "You've had a shock. Ms. Sparrow is going to be just fine. *You* are going to be just fine." He eyed our cuts and bruises then turned to call over some of the paramedics who'd already swarmed around Trista.

I looked at Grace. We didn't have time to help Grady understand. "Quick," I cried, grabbing Rod's arm as I started up the hill. "Let's go!"

We tore toward the bleachers, ducking through the surprised crowd. Scuffles and shouts rang out behind us as the police and paramedics chased after. My head throbbed as my feet pounded on the pavement. If we could just stay ahead of the police long enough to find Sparrow, we could lead them right to her.

I saw a flash of red in the stands and called out to Grace and Rod, only to realize it was a little boy clutching a stuffed animal. Out of the corner of my eye I spotted Mr. Katz, his brown blazer tossed over one shoulder and his sleeves rolled up as he jogged toward us. I ran faster.

"There! On the sidewalk!" Rod hollered, pointing to a figure pushing upstream in the rubbernecking crowd, her coppery hair shining in the sun. It was Lauren Sparrow. It had to be.

She wasn't gliding with pride. Not even close. Her body jerked and her hair flounced as she pushed past a dad pushing a stroller. She was headed directly for a gap between the stands.

"Split up and surround her!" Grace shouted, waving me to the left. I obeyed, dodging an elderly man with a cane and a middle-aged woman wearing a purple visor.

Lauren Sparrow must have heard Grace. She whirled around, her green eyes bulging as they met ours. Heavy boots pounded and radios blared behind us as we closed in. Sparrow darted panicked glances left and right, then tried to duck past several families clustered on the sidewalk. A kid waving a balloon animal stepped into her path, then a salesman pushed an ice cream cart past, unknowingly blocking her in. She stopped short and slumped in surrender.

She turned to us. Her hair fell over her face as she heaved a sob. The crowd backed away, bewildered as police officers skidded to a stop around us. They followed our eyes to Ms. Sparrow, then shot each other strange looks.

"Is someone going to tell me what's going on here?" Officer Grady panted, hands on his hips.

"It's all my fault. All of it," Ms. Sparrow cried out suddenly, trembling. "I never meant to hurt anyone, ever. You have to believe me!" She held up her hands and stepped forward. Tears streamed down her swollen face and smeared her make-up. I hardly recognized the woman in front of me. She looked as if the winter sun were melting her down like a candle. Rod reached out and grabbed my hand, squeezing it tightly.

The police officers turned questioningly to Grady, who seemed as baffled as they did. He looked at us, then back to the officers. "Take her in," he said with a nod.

Chapter Thirty-Two

Just Right

"**N**obody goes anywhere until I say they do," Officer Grady barked as his radio blared static. "Including you." He pointed at a puzzled Mr. Katz, who'd finally caught up to us, red-faced and panting. "Find the AmStar engineer who was in the booth," he muttered to Officer Carter, the lanky rookie cop we'd overheard in the float barn. "Hoffman and Diaz as well. I need statements from everyone. Royal Court included. Bring 'em all to the mansion, stat."

Minutes later Grace and I had been hustled into a squad car headed there too. Mr. Zimball had taken Rod ahead of us. I pressed my face against the window and stared out at the ruined parade route. Members of the marching bands had grabbed their instruments and found their families in the crowd. Floats that hadn't even rolled past the first set of bleachers waited at the top of the hill, their flowers ruffling in the breeze. As I looked back at Grace, her hair plastered to her head with sweat, a dark smudge across her forehead, it hit me how lucky we were to still be alive.

She looped her arm through mine. "Nothing feels that important anymore, does it?"

"Some things do." I squeezed her arm. "I'm really sorry about telling everyone that dumb story, Grace. I don't even know what I was thinking. It's not even that funny."

"It's okay, Soph. I'll get over it. And at least it was inspiring?" Grace smiled as her eyes fell to my dress, which I'd finally tugged back down.

Relief flooded me as the squad car rolled through the tall mansion gates and I spotted our parents waiting for us on the terrace steps. As soon as the officer opened the car door, they rushed forward and almost suffocated us in hugs. The Yangs looked like they'd never let Grace leave their sides again. I buried my face in my dad's shirt as he ruffled my hair, not even caring that I probably looked like I was six. My mom rummaged in her purse for Band-Aids for my skinned knees. If someone had told me a whole year had passed since I'd said good-bye to them on those same steps, I would have believed it. Three days had never felt longer.

The police ushered us into the packed Ridley Mansion

living room. Maybe it was the stiff way everyone sat on the antique furniture, but I felt as though I was walking into a living version of a museum oil painting. The velvet drapes had been pulled back, but the room was dark and stuffy. Everyone was there. The Royal Court, their parents, Rod and both of his parents, Mr. Katz and his wife, Harrison Lee—and a bunch of Brown Suiters and other people from the crowd who I didn't even recognize. Mr. Diaz and Ms. Hoffman sat in armchairs opposite each other, still in their thick make-up for the news cameras. Up close, they both looked orange.

The Royal Court and the twins huddled around us worriedly. They'd changed into their sweats and orientation T-shirts, and it felt good to see them looking real again. Jardine wrapped me in a tight hug that caught me off guard. "We were so scared for you. So, so scared," she whispered in my ear.

Trista came in with her mom, who looked rattled. "They say I'm fine," Trista reported with a shrug as she joined our huddle. "My blood pressure's just a little elevated."

"No kidding." Grace giggled. I was pretty sure that my own blood pressure wouldn't be back to normal until New Year's Day.

It spiked even higher when I caught sight of Lauren

Sparrow sitting hunched in an armchair by the front window. Two police officers, Officer Carter and a woman I didn't recognize, stood guard on either side of her, their expressions as solemn as the Ridley ancestors' in the portraits glaring down from the wall.

Officer Grady paced in front of the fireplace and waited for everyone to settle in. Then he cleared his throat and explained that he'd gathered us all to get the facts. "And I plan on getting every last one of them straight," he said, his narrowed eyes darting around the room. "Ms. Sparrow has been advised of her rights. She has opted to speak publicly about her role in this afternoon's incident . . . and in the death of Jim Steptoe."

A hush fell over us. Someone's chair creaked as they shifted in surprise. Lauren Sparrow stared into her lap and picked imaginary lint from her skirt. It almost looked as if she were trying to pluck the telltale pink roses right off.

"First things first," Grady continued, his deep voice rumbling through the room. "Ms. Bottoms, could you tell us how you ended up stuck in that float?"

All eyes turned to Trista. Clutching her mom's hand, she began describing our entire morning in her loud, clear voice. Lauren Sparrow flinched as Trista detailed everything that had tipped us off to Sparrow, from her strange email to the button we'd found on the Beary Happy Family float. "When I had a chance to slip into Ms. Sparrow's office while she was busy with the Court, I took it," Trista explained, adding that a locked file cabinet got her attention. "Took three of my hairpins, but I had it open fast," she said with a hint of pride. "That's when I saw them. Right in the bottom drawer." She shook her head in disbelief.

"Saw what, Ms. Bottoms?" Officer Grady's brow creased. Everyone in the room seemed to shift forward in their seats as they waited for the answer.

"Winnie the Pooh key chains," Trista declared loudly. "Eight of them, at least. All charred different amounts. Like they'd been barbecued."

Someone snorted. For a second, I thought it was me. The thought of Ms. Sparrow toasting mini stuffed Winnie the Poohs was ridiculous. The corners of Trista's mouth turned up as she described the various burned states of the Winnie the Poohs—as if she were only now realizing how crazy it all was. Meanwhile, Ms. Sparrow's cheeks turned redder than the background of the living room rug.

"Grace, Sophie, and I had a theory that Ms. Sparrow started the fire by accident," Trista continued, her curls spilling over her shoulders as she leaned forward and talked faster. "There hadn't been a breeze that night, so how could a curtain blow into her candle? When I saw those Winnie the Poohs, I knew we were right."

Sienna squinted. "So, she burned a key chain and put it in the Beary Happy Family's campfire to pin this all on Ms. Lund?"

"She burned *eight* of them?" Jardine's eyebrows practically leaped to her hairline.

"Guess she had to singe it *juuust* right," Mr. Diaz piped in. Ms. Hoffman shot him a glare. She was so over the puns.

A heavy feeling was spreading through my chest. I thought it was anger—but there was sadness, there, too. I'd trusted Lauren Sparrow—liked her, even. How could my instincts have been so wrong? Even as she sat in the chair in front of me, ready to admit all of it, I couldn't imagine her as a killer.

"That was the same day we got in trouble for spying," I said, realizing Sparrow must've been panicking about our snooping around.

"Exactly," Trista said. "We thought maybe someone was targeting *her*. But that wasn't it at all. She was busy barbecuing dolls to send us on a wild goose chase." She pointed to her head and twirled her finger at the craziness of it. "She knew you all would be at the stables the next day—and it wasn't much of a leap to guess you'd go poking around."

Trista looked straight at Lauren Sparrow, who was twisting her hands nervously and still staring into her lap. Her pink fingernail polish gleamed. It was the only thing that still looked perfect about her.

"I wasn't trying to *frame* Barbara!" Lauren Sparrow blurted out. "I knew the police could never arrest her just because some kids found a key chain." Her voice was hoarse, as if it had broken along with the rest of her somewhere along the way. "I needed to throw you girls off somehow, that's all," Sparrow added quietly.

Next to us, Rod straightened in his chair. "So you're the one who shut them in the refrigerated flower shed!" he exclaimed. "Then you pretended to come looking for them."

Lauren Sparrow nodded. "I didn't want anyone to get hurt. I swear. I was just trying to scare them a little. You all were so . . . persistent." She rubbed her temples. "It never occurred to me that Trista—"

"Enough." Officer Grady held up a hand. "We'll hear from you in a minute," he said gruffly.

"You scared us all right," Grace said, leveling her gaze at Ms. Sparrow. Rod looked over at me, eyes filled with concern as if he were remembering the moment.

My parents and the Yangs sat next to each other on the sofa, mouths half open, their heads swiveling between us all as if they were watching a tennis match.

"For everyone's information, Barbara Ridley-Lund was released earlier this morning due to insufficient evidence," Grady announced a little defensively. He explained that by matching the pictures we'd taken with our disposable cameras with the ones they took at the crime scene, they'd realized the key chain had not been there the day Steptoe was found and therefore didn't link her to the scene. Lund's story about the forklift misunderstanding seemed plausible, so they didn't have solid enough evidence to detain her any longer. "Ms. Lund claimed she'd become impatient waiting for Mr. Zimball to help clear some equipment and attempted to operate the vehicle herself." His mouth twitched as he held back a smile. "As we know, that didn't go so well."

Grace, Trista, and I looked at each other. We'd made an honest mistake—no one could say we hadn't. Still, it was hard not to feel guilty that Barb Lund had spent a night in jail.

Trista tensed up as she told the next part of her story. "I put one of the Winnie the Poohs in the Ziploc bag Grace had given me for evidence and shut the cabinet," she said. "But just then Ms. Sparrow walked in the door." She described how she shoved the plastic bag down her dress, made something up about looking for a hair tie, then booked it out of there—heading straight for the Root Beer float to see if she could fix the speed issue they'd had. "I remember hearing something clanging outside, but I was crouched under the dash working. I didn't think much of it." Her eyes darkened. "Not until I tried to leave."

Trista said she saw the wrench jammed through the latch and knew Sparrow had to have done it. "I tried hard not to panic," she explained. "My inhaler and refills were in my cargo jacket that I'd left in the mansion." Her breaths quickened as she thought back to the moment. "It didn't really go with the outfit, you know?" She outstretched her arms and looked down at her dress. "At least I'd taken my allergy meds." Trista described how she shouted for help but couldn't make herself heard above the marching bands warming up. "I had to take it easy. If I worked myself up . . ." She trailed off, leaving us to remember what had happened in the refrigerated shed.

"And the float team had already left to get good seats along the route," the AmStar engineer said, running his hand through his thick gray hair.

"So you cranked up the music and sent the Polybius SOS," Grace said.

"The Polly-be-what?" Mr. Diaz asked, his smooth announcer voice sounding especially out of place.

"Okay, that's kind of genius," Jardine said after Trista explained how she blared the music to signal us.

"So that's why you guys were always knocking and making weird noises with your mouths on the radio," Danica exclaimed. "Everyone knew that wasn't static, FYI," she added, raising an eyebrow. Grace and I looked at each other sheepishly.

Trista tossed up her hands as she wrapped up her story. "And . . . I guess you all know the rest. . . ." As she looked out at the faces in the silent room, I could see the memory of the fiery float flickering in her eyes. I felt like I could still hear the thundering wheels and see the flames blazing behind like a comet as Willard Ridley and the float disappeared over the cliff. I swallowed hard. It really had been too close a call.

Lauren Sparrow kept shaking her head, over and over. Trista's mom narrowed her eyes at her in a death-stare that seemed like it could have actually killed Sparrow. "So you thought you'd get away with sending my daughter over the bluffs? You were going to kill a child? *My* child?" she shouted through clenched teeth.

Trista flinched. "Mom . . . ," she pleaded quietly.

"That was the last thing I was thinking!" Ms. Sparrow cried out. Everyone shot each other puzzled looks. If locking a kid in a parade float and then trying to zoom it over a cliff wasn't attempted murder, what was? "I—I was buying time—to—to get away," she stuttered, wiping her nose with a tissue. "That's all."

The AmStar engineer cleared his throat and spoke up. "But then we ran into you by the bleachers."

Lauren Sparrow nodded and explained that she'd rushed back to the Royal Court float to help us, knowing that she'd raise suspicion if she disappeared before the Festival was off and running. However, before the floats rolled into action, the AmStar engineers and Mr. Diaz and Ms. Hoffman had pulled her up into the booth to do the honors of steering the float.

"We thought she'd be the perfect person," Mr. Diaz said. "What did we know?"

The AmStar engineer explained that Sparrow had handed the remote back and slipped away, but that he couldn't control the float. "Something must've happened when Ms. Young jammed the float wheel," he said, then turned to me apologetically. "Though you did the right thing. Don't get me wrong."

"You jumped to conclusions," Lauren Sparrow said, looking pleadingly at me, Grace and Trista. "I wasn't trying to do anything to Trista's float at all. I'd never do that. That's nuts!"

Harrison Lee sputtered in disbelief. "And charring Winnie the Pooh and planting them for kids to find isn't nuts?"

Officer Grady frowned at Ms. Sparrow. "It seems they didn't jump to any crazy conclusions when they suspected you killed a man, did they?" He asked Ms. Sparrow if she was ready to tell her story, and once again reminded her she did not have to confess publicly. She waved her hand.

"I want everyone to hear the truth—straight from me. I'm not a murderer!" she cried, her bulging eyes making her look pretty much exactly like a murderer. The officers next to her stiffened, as if worried she might do something rash. But she just told her story in a quiet voice that only occasionally broke as she wiped away tears. It felt strange to see any adult be such a mess, let alone smooth Ms. Sparrow.

"You have to believe me. Mr. Steptoe was alive when I left him on Tuesday night before the Royal Court announcements," she began. "At least, I thought he was." She bit her lip and exclaimed that it had all started a few days earlier when she sent a thank-you email to her chief chemist for rushing an important order.

"Raúl Jiménez," Grace interrupted. The Court whipped their gazes to Jardine. So much for those marriage plans.

Sparrow nodded. Her cheeks flushed like they had the

night we'd been gathering around the TV. It was funny to think how much I had misread her blushing that night.

"I didn't think anything of it until I ran into Jim the day before the Royal Court announcements," Sparrow continued. "He wanted to talk about Pretty Perfect's ingredients."

Grace and I nudged each other as she described exactly what we'd figured out: thanks to her email autofill, her message had gone to *Jim* instead of *Jiménez*. "I panicked," Sparrow said, her voice cracking. "It's hard for me to admit this, but Pretty Perfect's famous 'secret ingredient' is actually a special protein that Mr. Jiménez discovered in harp seal pups. Extracting it from them was highly illegal, and I knew it—but they assured me the seals weren't hurt in the process." She ran her hands through her hair nervously. "All I knew is that it worked miracles for people's skin."

She studied the rug for a beat too long. "Then I learned the truth." In a halting voice, she went on. "The protein is found in harp seals while they're still white, a few weeks after they're born. Pretty Perfect could only stockpile enough to make our product just after birthing season." Her voice went higher as she looked up at the room. "I promise, if I'd have been aware of this from the get-go, I never would have gone along with it. It was such a shock to find out."

Jardine gasped, breaking the silence. "So—so—when

they get the protein—the seals—*die*?" she stuttered.

Ms. Sparrow closed her eyes and nodded slowly.

"Beauty has its price," Grace muttered the line from Sparrow's email to herself as a murmur rippled through the room. Jardine covered her mouth with her hand, looking as if she might be ill. I looked at the seals I'd painted on the T-shirt she was wearing, remembered the seals in the video, and felt sick too.

"You have to believe me," Ms. Sparrow pleaded frantically. "As soon as I found out, I was horrified. I begged Mr. Jiménez to find alternative sourcing options." Her face grew blotchy and red. Her hands trembled. "I wanted to put a stop to all of it right away."

"Then the celebrities started endorsing Pretty Perfect," Trista said, folding her arms.

Sparrow nodded. Her glassy eyes swept across the room. The air felt stuffy—almost humid.

"Demand skyrocketed," she said. "We couldn't keep up. I was sick about it. I really was. But if we didn't continue, the secret would get out. Everything I'd worked for—the whole business. It'd die."

"Better your business than the seals!" Jardine cried out, jutting her chin angrily. "And you say you're not a murderer?"

Officer Grady shot Jardine a sharp look and pressed his finger to his lips. One of the cops next to Sparrow nudged his voice recorder closer to her as she continued her confession.

"I was going to make sure it all stopped," Ms. Sparrow said. "That was what I was trying to tell Jim that night, but he wouldn't listen. My mention of 'breeding seasons' in my email tipped him off that we might be harming animals, and he'd started to look into it. He threatened to go public as soon as he had more evidence," Ms. Sparrow said. "I—I just couldn't face it."

"So you killed him to keep him quiet," Grace said.

"No! It was an accident!" she practically shouted. Her messy hair shook around her shoulders, and a vein popped out in her neck. I thought they might need to cart her off, but she collected herself again. "That night, we met in his office. Our discussion got very heated. I admitted to him that there were some irregularities in Pretty Perfect's ingredients, but that I was clearing them up. We were interrupted when you came, Josh." She turned to Mr. Katz.

"It makes sense now," Mr. Katz said, nodding. "I felt the tension. I was also still angry. I just chalked up the awkwardness to your roles in my, er, transfer to Route Integrity. I took my pictures from the wall and scrammed. I was embarrassed. Figured I'd come back for the rest the next day." He looked at us and smiled. "But I was embarrassed then, too. I'm proud of my Pooper Scooper team now, but it took a little getting used to," he added.

Lauren Sparrow continued. "I went back to reason with him just as the delivery person from Miyamoto's came with the tiara. Jim told me our discussion was over, as far as he was concerned, then he went to lock the tiara in the pedestal for its unveiling at the Court announcements. When he went to the float barn to do his nightly float check, I followed him, pleading, but he ignored me." Her voice quavered with emotion, and she wiped tears from her eyes. "I was angry. I wanted him to hear me out, but he wouldn't. He was leaning over the campfire of the Girl Scout float when . . ." She closed her eyes and drew in a deep breath. "I stomped my foot in frustration. It hit something—I don't know what. It happened before I knew it. The s'more feature—it swung down hard and knocked Jim over." Her eyes pooled with tears.

"The manual override on the hydraulics," Trista said, mostly to the AmStar engineer, who nodded. "I knew it had to have been triggered by someone."

"I didn't know that Jim had died until the next morning," Sparrow said. "I ran out of there. I thought the marshmallow was made of foam. I didn't think it could be a serious injury. When I left that night, I was upset. All I wanted to do was make things right, so I emailed Raúl and told him to stop production immediately. I thought there had to be a way to make it all okay. I knew Jim would tell everyone— that he'd ruin me. I came to terms with that. But I never . . . I never expected . . ." She couldn't finish her sentence. "I was devastated when I heard the news."

Lauren Sparrow slumped in her chair, looking out at the faces in the crowd. I could barely believe that a few days earlier she'd been standing by the same fireplace in the same rose-print skirt, answering our questions. I knew she was telling the truth. If she'd knowingly killed Mr. Steptoe, she never would have placed herself at the crime scene by wearing a skirt that so perfectly matched the secret rose-theme.

"I was going to come forward then," Sparrow explained. "But when the police declared it an accident, it felt like I'd been given a second chance, you know? And it *was* an accident. Confessing wasn't going to bring Jim back. Nothing was going to bring Jim back." Her throat bobbed as she swallowed back tears.

"Then we got on the case," Grace said, her chest puffing up with pride.

"Then you got on the case," Sparrow repeated quietly. "I overheard you talking at the Beach Ball, and I thought it was a good idea to keep close tabs on you. If you were going to be royal pages, I could. At least, I thought so. It's crazy how much you can lose sight of right and wrong when you're busy trying to be perfect."

Grace, Trista, Rod, and I all shared a look. Rod smiled at me. We knew a thing or two about that.

"That's the truth, Ms. Sparrow," Officer Grady said, a twinge of regret in his voice. "The force is guilty of that, too. We rushed this. We were way too focused on the Festival." He turned back to Officer Carter. "Sometimes you got to stop and listen to the rookies, right, Officer?"

Officer Carter turned even pinker. "That's right, sir." He winked at us.

"We all make mistakes." Officer Grady fixed Ms. Sparrow with a steely gaze. "But some of them are unforgivable."

Chapter Thirty-Three

We Are Family

The next afternoon we all gathered for a town picnic on the lawn in front of the Ridley Mansion terrace. The white catering tents fluttered in the breeze under the bright-blue sky, the "125th Anniversary" brown bunting still hung from the mansion balconies, but the mood felt casual—like the Winter Sun Festival had changed out of its frilly dress and slipped on a comfy pair of jeans. Just like I had.

Rod had too. He waved and came over as soon as he spotted me by the buffet table with my family.

"No blazer this time?" I asked.

His ears turned red as he shook his head. "Nope. No skirt for you?"

"Maybe another day."

"We look nice, though, right?" He grinned.

"Gorgeous," I smiled back. We were both quiet a

moment, taking in the scene around us. A small brass band was playing oldies on the terrace. A bunch of adults drifted over to dance near them. Trista's sister, Tatiana, was running around on the lawn with a bunch of other little kids. Grandpa Young and his VFW buddies were chatting under the white tents, trying not to turn up their noses at the all-vegan menu Harrison Lee had arranged in honor of Mr. Steptoe.

The Luna Vista police officers who had guarded Lauren Sparrow in the mansion living room were hanging out not far from them. It seemed like years ago, not just the day before, that they'd shuttled her off after her confession and Officer Grady had stayed behind to explain to us and our parents that she would be undergoing a full psychiatric evaluation before they did anything else. "Pretty Perfect is pretty far from it," he'd muttered.

Rod and I headed over to the buffet line, and I nodded to the spread on the table. "Mr. Steptoe would've liked this picnic, don't you think?" I asked.

He laughed. "No doubt about it."

Grace and Trista grabbed paper plates and joined us, looking rested and happy. Maybe they'd gone to bed while it was still light out, like I had.

"You didn't stay up late playing TrigForce Five for eight

hours or something?" I teased Trista. She shook her head. "I was going to. But it seemed kinda boring, actually!" She jerked her head toward her little sister, who was now running around with Pookums on the mansion lawn. "I hung out with Tati," she said. Then, lowering her voice to a real, actual whisper. "I let her put make-up on me."

"Seriously?" My voice pitched up an octave.

Trista laughed. "Wasn't the first time." She made a face. "She likes to play beauty salon."

Harrison Lee walked past us with a plate of food towered so high, I was worried it'd spill over. He beamed when he saw us, and told us to be ready for a casual ceremony after the cutting of the Luna Vista anniversary cake. "We'd like to honor you four," he said. "I mean, as long as I was never one of your suspects." He winked.

"Well, we did see this one email . . . ," Grace said sheepishly. Harrison Lee's eyebrows shot up in surprise as she told him about our suspicions that he was dipping into the festival accounts.

"Cash gets low when all the flower deliveries pour in at once," he said, chuckling. "But I better be on my best behavior around you ladies, huh?" He took a big bite out of his garden burger. "Mm-mm-mm," he murmured, closing his eyes. "Food tastes so much better now. Glad the doctors ordered me off those energy drinks that did me in."

"Energy drinks?" I asked, realizing I hadn't seen Lee carrying around his purple thermos since he got back from the hospital. I laughed. "We were worried you'd been poisoned!"

"Pretty much *was* poison," he muttered. "Serves me right for trying to get a little extra energy boost to juggle everything."

"We all can push things a bit too far, can't we?" a voice rang out behind us. It was Barb Lund. Lily stood next to her in jeans and a red cardigan. Her hair hung loosely around her shoulders, and she wasn't wearing any make-up for once. As they both waved, my stomach twisted. Officer Grady and our parents had assured us she didn't hold anything against us, but it still felt like Ms. Lund must've etched our names in stone on some central Watch List nationwide after what she'd gone through.

After an awkward silence, Grace, Trista, Rod, and I started blubbering apologies all at once. She waved them away. "Please," she said. "It was a wake-up call. I was cray-cray enough for you to think I was a murderer? Maybe something's finally sunk through this noggin." She tapped her head with one finger. "My darling daughter's told me a thousand times and I was too busy shouting in my own megaphone to hear it, but you know what? Not everything's under my control."

Lily tossed her arm around her mom. "Especially forklifts," she said, eyes dancing.

Barb laughed. "And golf carts." She turned back to us. "Yep. Festival Schmestival, I think it's time for me to take a step back. I'm officially retiring. No more Grand Pooh-Bear. Sayonara, Floatator. Adios—"

"We got it, Mom," Lily said, her cheeks turning the same shade as her red cardigan.

"I guess what I'm trying to say is I can go overboard." Barb let her arms slap to her sides.

"The Festival will do that to you, I guess," Jardine Thomas chimed in as she, Sienna, and Kendra joined us with their own full plates. Jardine looked at us apologetically. "I was a royal pain, wasn't I? When I saw you guys headed for that cliff, all I could think was that my last words were commanding you to get me some herbal tea." She shook her head. "Kinda looking forward to being a commoner."

"It's a pretty good life," Lily said quietly, shooting her mom a knowing look. "People were talking about a Willard Ridley curse on the Festival. Maybe it was a blessing."

"In serious disguise," Trista added.

Barb laughed, then turned to Rod. "Now where's that

 384

cutie-patootie dad of yours off to?" she asked Rod. She didn't wait for him to answer. "You see, I'm thinking he did a bang-up job getting those floats in order without me. I'm going to try to rope him in to take over."

Rod ducked away quickly, pretending to go off looking for his dad. Meanwhile I was pretty sure he was going to give him a heads-up. I had a feeling that was one warning about Barb Lund that Mr. Zimball would listen to.

As Jardine and rest of the Court gathered around Ms. Lund to welcome her back, Marissa lingered behind Kendra, laughing with Danica and Denise. She flicked her blue eyes up and down my outfit, as usual. This time, though, she gave me a little wave after, even adding a half-smile. "That was really awesome yesterday," she said. "For real."

"Wasn't it, though?" Sienna said. "What's it called again? Tai chi? I've got to get my coach to look into working that into the Riptides' practices."

Danica and Denise ran over to put in a request for the band to lead us all in a game of "name that tune" that I prayed would be rejected. The Court spread out, mingling, accepting compliments politely—just like Ms. Sparrow had taught them. I suppose she'd passed along some good lessons, too. I even saw Jardine listening patiently to Anna Sayers, who I swear was still talking about her idea for a sea-creature backpack as a beauty accessory.

Behind us we heard a happy burst of yipping. Pookums was prancing in circles with Tatiana on the lawn near the band.

"You know, Pookums really seems to have turned a page," Grace said, not recognizing the double meaning.

I broke into a grin. "I hear that can be the path to a new you," I said.

"I thought that was horse poo," Grace replied.

"Both are, I guess." I shrugged. Pookums raced from Tatiana to Kendra, as if she wanted Kendra to join the twirling game.

Grace laughed. "I guess there are lots of ways to be yourself," she said.

Just then the band kicked up into a blaring, upbeat version of "We Are Family." I looked to the dance floor and spotted the Yangs and my parents laughing and raising their hands in the air. If it were any other day, Grace and I would have probably denied knowing them, let alone admit they were related to us. Right behind them Grandpa Young was seriously busting a move with Barb Lund. She was bumping her hips around like she was grooving to that conga song and clapping her hands above her head.

"Young! Yang! Bottoms! Zimball!" she yelled, motioning

us over. "On the dance floor. Let's see you shake those tail feathers!"

Grace raised her eyebrow at me. "Should we?"

I smiled mischievously. "Looks pretty 'awesome possum,' if you ask me."

"Heck, yeah," Trista exclaimed from behind us, strutting past. Grace and I followed, and as we all rushed by Rod, he laughed and linked arms with me. Pretty soon we were bouncing and spinning and Trista was doing her wild shaking dance. Grace and I did our jumping jack can-can move from the dance party that she and I'd had in my room. Grace looked right at Jake and waved goofily, not even caring how silly we looked.

As Grandpa Young and Ms. Lund twirled toward us, I held up his dog tags and asked if I could keep them longer. He nodded yes to the beat of the music as everyone around us sang out the song's bouncy "We are fam-i-lee!" chorus. Then he cupped his hand to his mouth and shouted: "Did they come in handy?"

Grace and I looked at each other.

"Definitely!" we chorused back, and he saluted us. Grace laughed and tugged me off the dance floor to get another brownie. As we stood off to the side, brushing brownie crumbs from our chins, we looked out over the picnic. Half the crowd was on the dance floor by then, faces beaming as they shimmied and hopped around. Laughter rang out everywhere.

Grace slung her arm over my shoulder.

"I guess it wasn't the best Festival yet," she said.

"Not even close." I squeezed her shoulder. "But it sure ended well."

A plane rumbled high above us. We watched as it stretched its white trail in the sky over the flat, blue Luna Vista Bay in the distance.

"You know, I've been meaning to tell you all day . . ." Grace smiled at me. "Last night I was reading about the coolest code."

"Yeah?" I said, as her smile grew wider. "I can't wait to hear all about it."

Acknowledgments

Arousing Winter Sun Festival cheer for the parade of people who helped me bring this story to the page: Annie Berger, who warmly welcomed Young & Yang and lent such patience, enthusiasm, and insight as we shaped their story; Rosemary Brosnan, whose confidence in me bolsters my own; Andrea Martin, my sleuths' original champion, who made sure their second adventure was the best it could be; and—of course—the excellent team at HarperCollins Children's who labor with love to bring my stories to young readers. The Royal Court queen of agents, Jennifer Laughran, deserves a diamond tiara for making it all possible in the first place.

A Coral Beauty rose for McCormick Templeman—genius, guru, dear friend—who ensured I finished this book sometime within the twenty-first century, and who reminds me daily about what really matters.

I'd like to raise my glass to the James Thurber House for their generous support. If living in a Victorian mansion for a summer weren't already inspiring enough, the always-effervescent Pampleton-Thurbers and the ghost made it twice so. Thank you.

A special Royal Court wave to my fan Ali Flynn, who wisely suggested this story needed a little dog—and to Penny Cummins Dorfman, Pomeranian extraordinaire, in memoriam, for inspiring me with her unparalleled joie de vivre.

I wish I could host a Beach Ball for all who offered me their expertise as I was writing: many thanks to Marc Fiedler for police procedure tips, to Andrew Koenig for his "pretty perfect" cosmetics know-how, to my students at Westridge School—especially Hannah Kim—for coining some classic awkward slang, and to Emily Pipes, Bridget McDonald, and Maureen Sprunger for enriching the Winter Sun Festival with their fond Tournament of Roses memories.

I'm showering my friends and fellow writers with buckets of confetti and gratitude. Thanks to Melanie Abed, Tania Casselle, Cecil Castellucci, Alison Cherry, Brandy Colbert, Hilary Hattenbach, Kara LaReau, Cindy Mines, Elizabeth Ross, Sarah Skilton, and Claire Wright-Coleman for their tireless encouragement and guidance, not to mention to

Melle Amade, Ingrid Sundberg, and Hayley Finn for early inspiration.

The booksellers, librarians, and teachers who connect kids to books deserve their very own parade of appreciation.

Lastly, a standing ovation for my mom—eagle-eyed proofreader, patient listener, and confidante—and to my husband, Kai: a marching band serenade, fireworks display, jet flyover, full-stadium *Ola*, and chorus of vuvuzelas still wouldn't be enough fanfare to express my gratitude. Ich liebe dich, mein Schatz. Danke.

CLEVER, COMPELLING MYSTERIES

ABOUT TWEEN SLEUTHS SOPHIE & GRACE